ESCAPE FROM ASYLUM

MADELEINE ROUX

HARPER

An Imprint of HarperCollinsPublishers

For the entire Asylum team at HarperCollins
and for fans of the series, old and new.

Library of Congress Control Number: 2016936053
ISBN 978-0-06-242442-6 — ISBN 978-0-06-249015-5 (int.)

Typography by Faceout Studio

16 17 18 19 20 CG/RRDC 10 9 8 7 6 5 4 3 2 1

❖

First Edition

"I am not an angel," I asserted; "and I will not be one till I die: I will be myself."

—CHARLOTTE BRONTË, *Jane Eyre*

I am not made like any of those I have seen. I venture to believe that I am not made like any of those who are in existence. If I am not better, at least I am different.

—JEAN-JACQUES ROUSSEAU

PROLOGUE

*H*e hadn't wanted to be the first. Even the silence of this room sounded like screaming, the scrape of a footstep or the shrill cry of his own doubts in his head, magnifying until he was deafened. It was a good thing to be the first, the warden had assured him. It was an honor. After all, the warden had been waiting for him—for the right person—for such a very long time. Wouldn't Ricky just be a good boy and cooperate? This was special. To be the first, to be Patient Zero, was a privilege.

But, still, he didn't want to be the first. This room was cold and lonely, and somehow he knew in his marrow, in the wellspring of his humanity, that to be Patient Zero was bad. Very bad.

To be Patient Zero meant losing himself, not to death, but to something much worse.

CHAPTER

№ 1

Brookline, 1968
Three weeks previous

They brought him silently into the little room. Ricky had been down this road before, only the last time it was at Victorwood in the Hamptons, and he had gone willingly. This was "retreat" number three. It was starting to get annoying.

He hung his head, staring at the floor, putting on the performance of a lifetime. Did he feel remorseful? Not even a little bit, but he wanted out of this place. Brookline Hospital. It might have been a loony bin, but it sounded as pompous and stupid as the retreat centers. He didn't want anything to do with it.

"I need to see my parents," he said. Talking made them grip his arms more tightly. One of the orderlies pulled a restraining mask into view, and Ricky didn't need to put on an act to look shocked. "Whoa, hey, there's no need for that. I just want to talk to my mom. You gotta understand, there's been some kind of mistake. If I could just talk to her—"

"Okay, kid. Sure. A mistake." The orderly chuckled. He was taller and stronger than Ricky, and bucking against him was futile. "We don't want to hurt you, Rick. We're trying to help you."

"But my mother—"

"We've heard that one before. A thousand times."

He had a nice voice, this orderly. Gentle. Kind. It was always like that—sweet voices saying sweet things, covering up dark, mean intentions. Those voices wanted to change him. Sometimes he was even tempted to let them.

"I need to see my parents," he repeated calmly. It was hard to sound anything but terrified when he was being hauled into a cell in a place he didn't know. A cell in an *asylum*. "Please, just let me talk to them. I know it sounds ridiculous, but I think I really can make them understand."

"That's all over now," the orderly said. "Now we're going to take care of you. Your parents will come get you when you're feeling better."

"Warden Crawford is the best," the other man said. His voice was just as warm, but his gaze was cold as he stared at—*through*—Ricky. Like Ricky wasn't there at all, or if he was, he was just a speck of dirt.

"He really is the best," the taller orderly added mechanically.

Ricky fought them at that. He had heard those words before, about other doctors, other "specialists." It was code. It was all code, everything these people in "resorts" and hospitals said. They never said what they really had in mind, which was that he would never get out, never be free, until he became a different person altogether. The taller, stronger orderly on his right swore under his breath, struggling to hold on to Ricky's arm and reach for something out of Ricky's view.

The room was cold, chilled from the spring rain outside, and the lights were too bright, bleached and pale like the rest of the

room. The outdoors had never felt farther away. Maybe it was just a few feet to the wall, and then a few inches of brick, but the free air may as well have been on the other side of a mile of concrete.

"This is your choice," the orderly said with a grunting sigh. "You make the choices here on how we treat you, Rick."

Ricky knew that wasn't true, so he fought harder, tossing his weight from side to side, trying to smash his forehead into one of them and break their grip. Their voices became far-off almost the second the needle slid into his arm, pricking harder than usual, biting deep into the vein.

"I just want to see them," Ricky was saying, crumpling slowly to the linoleum. "I can make them understand."

"Of course you can. But you should rest now. Your parents will be back to see you before you know it."

Soothing words. Nonsense. The details of the room blurred. The bed and the window and the desk all became similar blobs of milky gray. Ricky let himself go fully into the dark, the oncoming numbness almost a relief from the knot of fear and betrayal winding tight in his gut.

Mom and Butch must be already on the road back to Boston. Long gone, long gone. He'd always talked his way out before, and he knew he could do it again if he just had a minute alone with his mother.

"He'll be all right here, won't he?" his mother had asked. The Cadillac rolled smoothly up the hill to the hospital, rain beating relentlessly, rhythmically, like tiny toy soldier drums on the windows. "It doesn't look anything like Victorwood . . . Maybe this is too extreme."

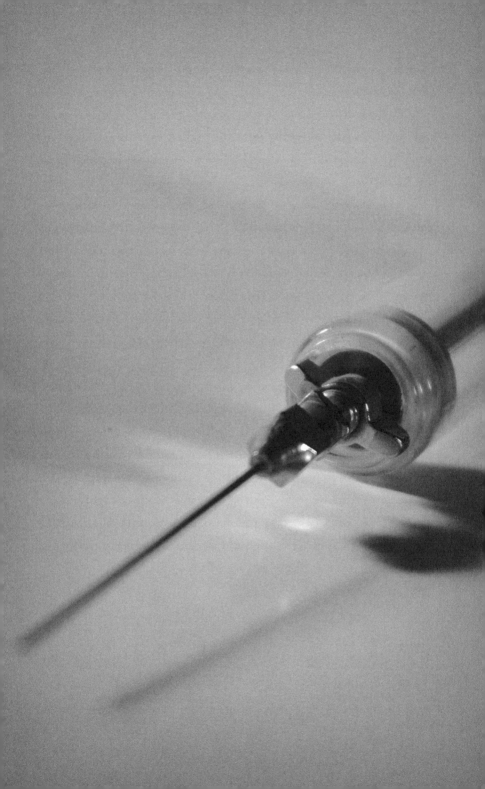

"How many more times, Kathy? He's a freak. Violent. He's a goddamn—"

"Don't say it."

It had felt like a dream then, but it felt even more like one now. At first he'd been so sure they were just taking him back to Victorwood, a home for "wayward" boys like him. The staff there were chumps, pushovers, and as soon as he'd had enough of the place, it had taken only a few tearful calls to get his mother racing up the manicured drive, her own eyes filled with tears as she welcomed him into a hug. But they hadn't been taking him to Victorwood this time. Somewhere along the way they had turned off, changed course. That *Next Time Will Mean Real Consequences* moment that Butch liked to reference was finally upon them.

Damn. He shouldn't have let himself get caught with Martin like that. Butch had finally made good on his threats. The long, angry car ride to the hospital, to Brookline, had been punishment enough, and the whole time Ricky was thinking they wouldn't really do it. They wouldn't really commit him.

And now here he was, slipping into unconsciousness far away from home, with two strangers hauling him onto a thin mattress and his last clear thoughts: *They did it. This time they really did it. They're locking me up and they're not coming back.*

CHAPTER
№ 2

*H*e stared at the ceiling for hours and hours, his hands folded tightly over his stomach. His voice felt scratchy from yelling at the orderlies and then, when that hadn't worked, from humming to himself to try to stave off some of the anxiety. Now he was quiet. The tips of his fingers were so cold, he worried they might just freeze and grow brittle and break off.

That cold had set in the second they came through the doors of the hospital, and it had been his first warning. The yard surrounding Brookline was pretty and well-kept, a sturdy black fence the only indication that the freedom to come and go depended on your status as patient or parent. Brown brick buildings chased along in a U shape next to the hospital. They stood out because they were of a totally different construction than the hospital, dark and old and collegiate. Disheveled young men in sweater vests and corduroys ambled from one building to the next—students preparing to leave for their summer vacations, Ricky would later learn.

Next to those old buildings, Brookline was pure white. Clean. Even the grass had been clipped to a perfectly even height. It had felt fake under his shoes, he remembered that. And there were patients outside in the garden, backs bent, meticulously deadheading the flowers and pruning the hedges while orderlies in crisp uniforms looked on.

It was all pristine and picture-perfect, until you stepped inside, and that cold hit you like a jolt of electricity.

Drowsy as he was, Ricky was certain that he would never get a wink of real rest in this place, not even if they gave him another one of those sedative shots. He kept nodding off and snapping awake again, sure that someone was on the other side of his door, listening in. And his uneasy sleep was broken by a sudden scream in the night. (He assumed it was night—it was difficult to tell in the shuttered cell.)

His limbs were leaden as he pushed into a sitting position. The scream came again, and then again, forcing him fully awake. He drew up and shuffled to the door, pressing himself against the frigid surface. Ricky's hand slipped lower, coming to rest on the handle; he was shocked when it gave under that little bit of pressure. This couldn't be. He wouldn't be allowed to wander the halls of Brookline alone. He could tell from his strong-armed welcome that this wasn't that kind of place. Had the orderlies screwed up and forgotten to lock him in? It was dark and still in the hallway, with no nurses or orderlies in sight, no other patients, no signs of life whatsoever except a thrum like a heartbeat that drummed low and slow from beneath his feet. Maybe it was the pipes or an old-timey furnace, grumbling below like an ancient, slumbering beast. The root of the building. Its core. The living, beating heart of the asylum.

Ricky wandered down the corridor to the staircase, his bare feet as icy-cold as the floor. A milky light filled the whole place, illuminating the steps as he padded down to the first-floor landing. The beating heart called to him, steady, and he followed. He didn't feel safe, exactly. More like reckless. What could they do, kick him out? It wasn't his fault those idiots had left his door unbolted.

Also—and he knew this was weird—the deep *bum-bah-bum* of the asylum's heartbeat gave him courage. It almost felt comforting.

It wasn't until he reached the lobby that his anxiety returned. He had sat here just hours earlier watching Butch fill out the paperwork while his mother wept.

"Won't you miss me?" he had murmured, giving his mom huge, childlike eyes.

"Honey . . ." She'd almost gone for it, her lip quivering as she stared at him.

"No, not this again." Butch had finalized it, broken the spell. And Ricky hated him for it.

Now he could feel the dread and the disbelief of that moment rise up harder and stronger, blasting over him like a wave intent on drowning him. He hurried over to the doors that led outside, thinking for a wild second that he'd be better off making a break for it than trying to get ahold of his mom on the phone, but his luck from before ran out—these were definitely locked.

The heart—or the furnace, whatever the hell was making that noise—called more insistently, and he followed once more, but reluctantly this time. "Nowhere to Run" came to mind: the song, the idea. The sound that was emanating from the basement was like the baseline of that song, climbing, driving, dark, and infectious.

Nowhere to run . . .

He was in a part of the asylum he didn't recognize. That wasn't exactly a surprise. He hadn't even been here a full day. The

lobby was behind him, and ahead, offices and storage rooms lined a narrow hall that disappeared into a yawning mouth of darkness. An arch. An arch that led down.

So down he went, into the colder and colder depths, feeling the rough stones on the walls, smelling the wormy, wet-earth scent that permeated the basement. The stairs seemed to go on forever, and that steady *bum-bah-bum* roared louder, reverberating until it was part of him, interwoven with his dread, interwoven with the brick and mortar itself. The pipes rattled, creaked, sudden taps inside of them making him wonder if they were about to burst open any second.

Searching. He was searching now, he realized, desperate to find not a phone or an exit but the source of the heartbeat.

Ricky followed the drumming all the way to a long, tall corridor, the ceiling so high above him it may as well have been empty sky. Something scratched at his back, but when he turned to look, there was nothing there. That's when he realized he must be dreaming—when what felt like sharp human nails scored through his shirt and burned against his skin, and still nothing was there. He was alone in the hall.

He gritted his teeth against the pain and pressed on toward the heartbeat, passing windowless doors on either side of him that were shut and locked. In the nightmare he knew they would be, but he tried each one anyway. He was suddenly sure that the screaming he'd heard earlier had been coming from this hallway. That someone behind the far door on the right had been crying out so loudly that he could hear it all the way in his room, and the heartbeat had been guiding him straight to the source.

And when he reached the final door on the right? It was open like his. More negligence, surely. He had to go inside, escape the claws scraping at his back and find the heartbeat thundering in his ears. It was his own heartbeat now, his own pulsing fear.

He stopped outside the door and peered in, the scratching nails inside him now, tearing up his stomach and crawling up his throat. There was no scream and no heartbeat, just silence. Then he saw her. A little girl stood in the empty room, her nightgown tattered and soiled. She turned a slow circle, around and around, but every angle Ricky caught was just long, dirty hair.

There was no face beneath the hair but somehow he felt her eyes. Her eyes were there, watching, measuring . . . He was part of this place now. He had been seen.

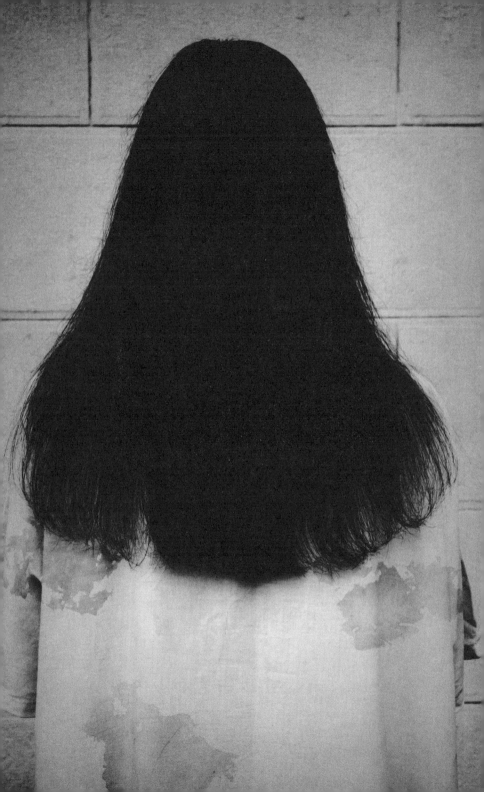

CHAPTER

№ 3

He was feeling more like himself by morning, rising with "Nowhere to Run" stuck in his head. It was all just an anxiety dream, he decided. There was no way he had actually left his room in the middle of the night.

Just to make sure, he checked the bottoms of his feet. Clean. That was a bigger relief than he wanted to admit.

It was back to plan A: finding a telephone. His parents—or at least his mother—would return for him and soon. She couldn't live without her sweet little Baby Bear. She would come back for him, with or without Butch, because she was too weak and fragile not to. That wasn't an insult, it was just the truth. She couldn't handle her life without him, not daily decisions, not major responsibilities, not any of it.

And damn. He had almost gotten her, there in the lobby, but Butch had had to ruin it. It was why she had remarried so soon after his real father disappeared. After a year, the courts granted her a divorce based on "abandonment" and Butch was already in their lives by then, like he was just chomping at the bit, waiting to take his dad's place. She couldn't be on her own. She couldn't be accountable for *anything*. Ricky didn't know if he hated his mother, but he certainly didn't like her.

Still. Blood might be thinner than water, in his opinion, but it would win him his freedom in the end.

Soon he would be back in Boston, back in his room, surrounded by his posters of Paul and John, surrounded by his clothes and his things, his books and his baseball cards. He'd probably even get the Biscayne back—his real ticket to freedom, which he'd barely had time to take advantage of before this string of glorified time-outs.

Ricky could already picture it: windows down, music up, the spring wind carrying the glorious scent of hamburgers and hot dogs sizzling on dozens of suburban grills. . . . Mom at least had let him have one last hamburger yesterday before they made it here, but Butch had refused to turn the radio to anything but baseball results.

A short, shy knock came at the door. Ricky sat up in bed and then swung his legs over the edge, running both hands through his rumpled hair as the door opened and a kind-faced, red-haired nurse stepped inside.

"Hello? I'm not interrupting anything, am I?"

Ricky snorted, standing and leaning against the bed. "Is that what passes for a joke around here?"

She wasn't pretty, necessarily. More like harmless. Clean. And about as sharp in the corners as an origami crane. She stared at him, obviously bewildered.

"Oh. No. I wasn't making a joke." She held her clipboard tight to her chest. "I'm Nurse Ash, and I'll be overseeing your care here at Brookline."

"*Ash*. Nurse Ash. Huh. That's a fittingly macabre name for this charming little dungeon."

Her expression went blank and she shrugged, looking down at her notes.

"I won't fuss if it helps you to have a sense of humor about all this," she said, almost breezily. "We're going to have to get to know each other, and I prefer my patients cheerful, if at all possible. Cooperative, at the very least."

"Aye, aye," he said with a salute. Usually he was dealing with buttoned-up counselors glaring at him behind spectacles, but maybe he could have a bit of fun with this one. She was closer to his age, surprisingly young for a nurse. If he played his cards right, she might be his friend, and a friend might be able to help him place a phone call to his mother. "And how do you run the Good Ship Loony Bin. Is it a *tight* ship or a loose one?"

It never hurt to use a little flirtation when making friends, even if that approach had fallen flat with the dusty old psychologists he was normally assigned.

"I know this must be difficult for you, seeing as how you . . ." Nurse Ash scrutinized her notes, which included the paperwork from Butch. Her sentence trailed off, and he could just about pinpoint the instant she located the exact reasons for his being there. After his name (Carrick Andrew Desmond, although nobody but his grandmother and Butch when he was angry called him Carrick), his age, his weight, and his date of birth, there would have been whatever euphemism Butch had picked for his *problem* this time.

The last two times, he'd also cited "violent outbursts" on these applications. But that was just the one time, and really, Butch deserved the fork that got flung at his head for the things he was calling Ricky.

"Seeing as how I got caught in bed with the neighbor boy. Or I should say, young man. I'm not *that* much of a pervert."

"You're not a pervert at all, Mr. Desmond," Nurse Ash said flatly. Huh. That was new. "I don't like words like that. They don't do anything but shame. Treatment is not about shame."

Maybe she really was different. He doubted it, but anything was possible.

"You shock me, Nurse Ash. But in the very best of ways."

She smiled then and it almost made her pretty. "Please let me know if you have any trouble settling in. Accommodating to life here can be"—the nurse bit down on her lip, hesitating—"perplexing."

"Oh, trust me, nothing I can't handle. I was born to jailers." Possibly an overstatement.

As she moved to go, she frowned, shaking her head. "I'm afraid life must have been very unfair for you so far." But *that* was an understatement.

"I'm afraid it's very unfair for everyone."

"I'll check in with you again shortly," she said, trotting to the door. She seemed to turn away from him quickly, perhaps to hide the blush creeping down her neck.

He was feeling even better, downright smug, when a familiar girl's scream cut through the silence. The door shut hard and locked with a click, and Ricky's smile vanished. That wasn't just the scream of someone gripped by madness. It was a shriek of pain.

CHAPTER

№ 4

*B*reakfast occurred at seven. Lunch at noon. Predictable. Regimented. When Ricky asked the sharp-faced nurse escorting him to lunch what he could expect to eat, she shook her head and said with a humorless chuckle, "Soup and bread, Mr. Desmond, soup and bread. You'll learn."

She wasn't as nice or as quick to blush as Nurse Ash.

Breakfast had been soft porridge and eggs (not quite scrambled, and not quite real, he suspected, but powdered). Nothing one could possibly choke on. He guessed that was the reason behind the soup and bread, too.

He ate his lunch in observant silence, his eyes scanning the "cafeteria," which seemed to be a large, multipurpose room with a gated corridor to the kitchens and an arched doorway to the main hospital hall that also could be shut up and locked if necessary. White. Everything was white and blisteringly clean. It was clean enough to eat off the floors in here, but luckily they hadn't made him do that.

Rain drummed against the walls; he could hear it distantly, a reminder that life continued on while his stalled inside Brookline.

The soup draining off his spoon was the color of diluted blood. At one point it had probably resembled a hardy

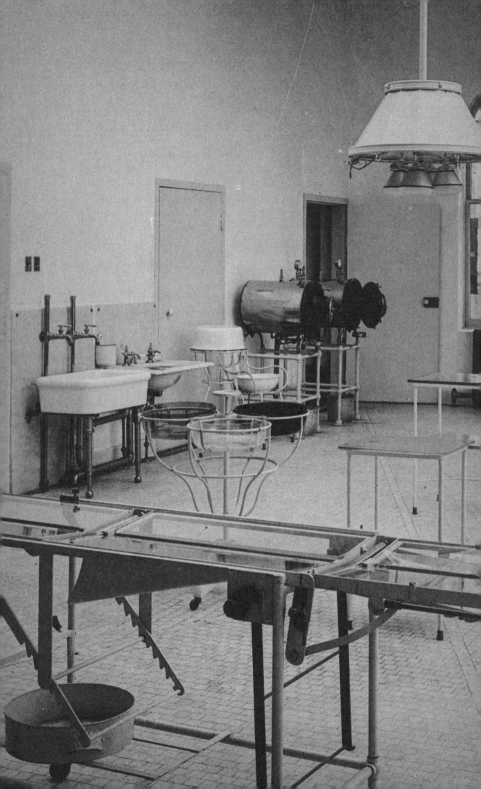

vegetable soup, but it had been watered down and reconstituted to a tepid, tomato-flavored water with the occasional chunk of celery. Setting down his spoon, Ricky watched a few other patients file into the room. They were brought in shifts; his table was already full, and now the bench directly behind him was filling up.

It was like high school, only these weren't cliques choosing their own little spheres. They weren't even talking. The other patients were eating so quickly they might have been having their last meal, and Ricky hurried to finish his soup, figuring they knew something he didn't. Nurses stood at opposite ends of the long, white tables wearing identical expressions as their eyes roamed the room.

At the table in front of him, an elderly woman sat elbow to elbow with a short-haired girl who looked like she wanted to glance over her shoulder, maybe to catch his eye. But each time she started to turn, she glanced first at the nurses and thought better of it.

Ricky scraped the last of the soup out of the bowl and crammed half of the stale roll in his mouth. The nurses began walking down the bench behind them, tapping each patient on the shoulder, their signal to leave. A big, broad-shouldered hulk down the bench from Ricky hesitated, taking an extra second to eat some soup.

"Dennis."

She clapped, once, and Ricky watched wide-eyed as the giant man scrambled up off the bench, hanging his head as if he were a kid caught with his hand in a candy jar. Whatever the nurses did here to keep their patients in line, it was clearly working.

When the rain stopped they were marched outside for "work hour."

Ricky stood in the grass and stared up at the dull sky, letting records play in his head. Otis, Stevie, Smokey . . . All the records he could only play when he was home alone. His parents hated his taste in music, especially Butch.

Ricky wrinkled his nose as Nurse Ash appeared in the yard, carrying a basket filled with gardening gloves. Yeah, this felt about right. Chore duty usually landed heaviest on his shoulders when Butch came home early from work and caught him playing Smokey Robinson's latest on full blast. On Butch's hi-fi, no less.

I won't have any of that goddamn noise in my house, a man wants peace and quiet when he gets home.

Oh, Butch, I really don't think my mother would appreciate that kind of language in this house—

Outside, Carrick. Now!

Nurse Ash didn't scream at him as she handed him a pair of gloves. She was still as neat and tidy as the other nurses, but now Ricky noticed her hair looked wilder under her hat, not clipped or curled or rolled into a perfect bun.

"What am I supposed to do with these?" he asked wryly.

"Put them on your hands, I imagine," Nurse Ash responded, equally dry.

He smirked. "I figured out that much, but . . ." He nodded to the other patients, who had grabbed pairs of gloves and immediately peeled off to predetermined locations to begin work.

"Every day after lunch we have supervised gardening. We can't

let you have anything too sharp, obviously, but Warden Crawford thinks this kind of exercise is good for you. Why don't you
join Kay? She's going to deadhead the azaleas."

"Groovy," he muttered. Before Nurse Ash could move down
to the next patient, he said, "Look, do you think . . . Is there a
way you could maybe put in a good word for me with that warden guy? I really need to talk to my mother. If I could just make
a phone call, it would mean the world to me."

Instead of rejecting his request outright, she calmly handed a
pair of gloves to the patient after him.

Right when he'd resigned himself to being ignored, she
asked, "Is something the matter?"

Ricky's guffaw was so loud it startled everyone in the yard.
All eyes were on him as he cleared his throat and lowered his
head, trying to shake off their attention. "I don't belong here,"
he said, softer. "Look at me. Can't you tell? I'm not . . . one of
these people. A crazy."

She sighed. "Order, routine, discipline, and—yes, occasionally—
correct medication. That's what we do here. That's what keeps our
patients healthy. That's what keeps them from harming themselves." She paused and then said significantly, "Or others."

Right. So maybe that incident was what had really landed him
in Brookline. Maybe this had nothing—or little—to do with
him and Martin.

"It was one time," he whispered.

"Your stepfather had a fractured wrist," she pointed out. "Try to
get along here, Ricky. It's for your own good. Order, discipline—"

"Yeah, I got it."

Ricky yanked on the gloves and turned slightly, facing the

driveway beyond the wrought-iron fence. A row of bushes, aza-leas apparently, grew along the fence, outlining the borders of his prison in green and pink. A serious-looking and seriously strong male orderly guarded the gate itself while the girl Nurse Ash had pointed out knelt next to one of the azalea bushes. The morn-ing mist that should have dissipated by now hung like a wreath of smoke around the fence, a ghost spread across the entire yard.

He made his way toward the girl but kept his eyes on the gate. Ricky briefly considered rushing the guard, but between the sedative, the eggs, and the watery tomato soup, he didn't exactly have much energy for tackling.

"You can stop looking at the road," the girl said when he reached her. He hadn't noticed her watching him. Her eyes were still on the azaleas. "Nobody's coming for us."

"Not yet, anyway." The yard sloped down toward her and the bushes. As he knelt beside her, recognition dawned—she was the girl who had tried to scope him out during lunch. She was black and her hair was cut short, unevenly, but even the bald patches couldn't take away the fact that she was a looker. Tall, slender, managing to look poised even in the baggy, sack-like shirt and trousers they'd given her to wear.

He rested his knees in the mud and started picking at the flowers, even though there weren't any that were obviously dead. "What happened to your hair?"

"They make me cut it short, so I tear it out sometimes instead." She said it softly, sadly. Her voice was gentle and low, as if some-one were sleeping nearby. Ricky had met a few New Yorkers at Victorwood and Hillcrest, and he could hear a similar influ-ence in her accent, though he couldn't be sure. "Order and discipline aren't really my style. Never seen you here before."

"I'm new," Ricky replied. He stopped his picking, turning fully toward her. "My name's Rick, or Ricky. Carrick, actually, but only when I'm in trouble."

That made her smile. "Kay. I guess we both like to keep it short and sweet."

"And you're here for what? Tearing your hair out?"

"No, that's just my one little rebellion. I try not to draw too much attention to myself," she said, pausing and wiping the back of her hand across her forehead. When she rested back on her thighs Ricky could tell she was even taller than him, by a few inches. "You might've noticed, but anybody gets caught talking too much or out of turn and they're disciplined. Still, we find our ways." She pointed to his right, where Nurse Ash was supervising an old patient who didn't seem to be working so much as admiring the tulip beds. He had grave scarring along one half of his neck. It was well healed but still gnarled and pink. "That's Sloane. He's convinced he can fly. Tried jumping off a few roofs until his kids got tired of scraping him off the pavement. Far as I can tell he's been in here for forever. And that's Angela," Kay said, indicating a middle-aged woman tending to daffodils at the top of the hill. She didn't look insane to Ricky, just bored. "Took her husband apart and tried to serve him to his stepmama."

Ricky gave Angela another look, wide-eyed this time. "Really?"

Kay nodded. "He was beating her up for years. Cops wouldn't do anything to help because he was one of them. Makes you sick to think about."

"God, that's awful. Shouldn't she be in prison?"

"Maybe a judge went easy on her. I don't know her whole life story," Kay explained nonchalantly.

"That still leaves you . . ."

"And *you*," Kay replied.

"Uh-huh, but I asked first," Ricky said, enjoying this little game.

"I didn't have to give you all that information. It's hard to get answers around here, you know. Hard to even talk without getting in trouble. Took me a month just to get a word out of Angela during work hour."

Then he was lucky she was talking to him at all, and in an almost friendly way. Looking away, he shrugged and said, "That's fair. I like other boys. Well, I like girls, too. I don't really have a preference, and that's the problem, I guess."

"According to your parents," Kay said in her soft voice.

"According to pretty much everyone." He studied her for a moment before saying slowly, "But not you."

"No. Not me." She clenched her jaw, and together they watched Nurse Ash finally tug Sloane off the gate and urge him back up the shallow hill toward Brookline's entrance. He still couldn't make out her exact accent. It sounded like she had polished the rough edges off whatever it was. "Is that it? You do something else?"

"Not really," Ricky lied. She didn't need to know about the one bad time he'd lost his temper. About his stepfather's fractured wrist.

"They tried to put my auntie in some hospital in California for that. I almost ended up there, too. Thank God we moved back to New York before they could get that idea in their heads. Some terrible things went on in that place. They wouldn't even tell me all of it, said it was too much for a child's mind. Shame they didn't think putting me in here would be *too much*. I guess no horror stories get told about this place."

Ricky shivered. The previous "resorts" his parents had tried were horrible in their own way. Even so, he had occasionally enjoyed tricking the staff there and finding ways to get around. It was like a game. He still thought Brookline could be a game, too, once he got the hang of it.

"So you're like me?" he asked, trying not to think too hard about how long he might be at the hospital. He didn't think he could stand being here for a month.

Kay laughed at that, glancing at him sideways. "I'm not sure I would put it like that."

"So what then? Do you want me to guess?"

"I wouldn't make you do that." Kay chewed her lip. It was rough and worn, as if she resorted to chewing it quite a lot. "And I should take pity on you, seeing as how you've been talking to me like I'm a lady."

Ricky blinked. "Because . . . you are one."

She chuckled, rolling her eyes. "You really think so?"

"Is this some kind of trick question?" he asked, his face suddenly warm. "I mean, you are," Ricky insisted.

"I wasn't always that way."

That was something to think over, but not now. He didn't like to be on the back foot in a conversation, didn't like feeling foolish. He took what he hoped passed for a casual glance at her. "Well, you've looked like a girl as long as I've known you." That got a short laugh. "You sort of have that Diana Ross look going on, it's nice."

"Diana Ross . . . ," Kay whispered it, staring past Ricky, her eyes becoming slightly unfocused. "That would be nice, wouldn't it? Only she wasn't born Daniel Ross, was she?"

"Miss Ross and I aren't exactly on a first-name basis," Ricky said lightly.

"Kay is short for Keith."

Kay waited, watching, smiling wider the longer the silence went on, like she was used to this. After a moment Ricky nodded. He just nodded. What else was there to do? He understood and it seemed like she had more to say.

"My parents are both beanpoles, and my pops couldn't grow a beard if his life depended on it, all that's lucky for me." She laughed, wistfully, shaking her head. "My brother found out I was hopping a train to Baltimore. Ratted me out. I heard about a doctor there that helps out girls like me. Guess that was for nothing now."

"That's why they keep cutting your hair here?" he asked.

Kay nodded, smoothing her long fingers over her patchy hair. "Before they put me in here it was so nice and long. Wish you could have seen it."

"What's in Baltimore?"

"An open mind or two," she murmured. "I was afraid, you know, and I didn't really want to leave home, but what else can you do? You have to grow up, I guess, or try to."

"I'm not sure I could've gotten as far as the train station," Ricky said honestly. "That takes a lot of guts."

"I didn't get on it," she said a little shyly. "Who knows if I would've made it all the way."

"Hey, you two, work hour is over."

Nurse Ash hurried up to them, her white skirt and jacket streaked with mud from helping Sloane. The yard had emptied except for the three of them and an older man with spectacles and a long white coat who stood watching from the doors. Ricky hadn't noticed him before, but now he could feel the weight of the older man's eyes on him and it left him unsettled. Was he in trouble? Kay said they weren't supposed to talk so much. Maybe this was what she meant.

"It's rude to interrupt," he said half-jokingly, cocking his head to the side.

"That's cute, Mr. Desmond, but it's time to go inside."

Kay started back up the hill obediently. "Just do what they say, Ricky. Take it from me—it's much easier that way."

CHAPTER

№ 5

"*W*ho is he?"

Kay looked up from her pad of paper. With a soft blue crayon she had doodled a sailboat nestled into a cloud. Her gaze strayed from the paper just for a second. "Warden Crawford."

"He's got a staring problem," Ricky said, watching the man at the door. It was the same person he'd seen watching them two days earlier during their supervised gardening. Just like then, the man watched Ricky steadily, conferring in whispers with Nurse Ash. She shrank in his presence, hunched, her eyes darting away from him constantly.

In fact, all of the employees of Brookline acted strangely when the warden was in the room. They became quiet, motionless, as precisely still as toy soldiers.

"Wouldn't you love to look at what they're scribbling on those clipboards all day long?"

"I'm not convinced I want to know," Kay said. "You stop noticing it, and the less attention he pays us the better."

"Day three," he said in the most stuck-up, nasal voice he could manage, "patients still here and still completely nuts." Ricky dropped the voice. "Does he really think he can change you?" *Or me.*

She shrugged, adding a few trees under her sailboat and

cloud. "He keeps me here as a favor to my pop. I hope the money is enough to make him happy. If he's happy, he might just leave me alone."

Ricky smirked at that, but his smile dimmed quickly. He hated being studied like this. The warden and Nurse Ash weren't even being subtle about it. They were obviously discussing him, treating him like some kind of specimen under glass. He stared back, daring them to do something about it.

Next to the warden and the nurse, on the wall, hung pictures Ricky had seen several times now as he came and went from the large common area. He tried not to look whenever he passed the pictures. They didn't seem like the kind of thing that ought to be freely displayed. Images of patients—patients like them—some sitting quietly in their rooms, others strapped to tables in the center of a full lecture hall. Somehow those photos were even more morbid with the warden standing next to them, utterly unaware or bothered by them, as if they were watercolors or family portraits.

"Those pictures . . . ," he said. They were supposed to be working in their little yellow pads with their sad, stumpy crayons, the only writing implements they were trusted with. Ricky had no interest in suicide, but it was true that at this point he might put a pencil through his eyeball just to get a frantic visit from his mother.

"I hate them," Kay murmured with a shudder. "I never look at them."

"Doesn't it seem odd that they're out in the open like that?" Ricky asked under his breath. "Creeps me out."

"I think that's the point," she said. "I think they're supposed

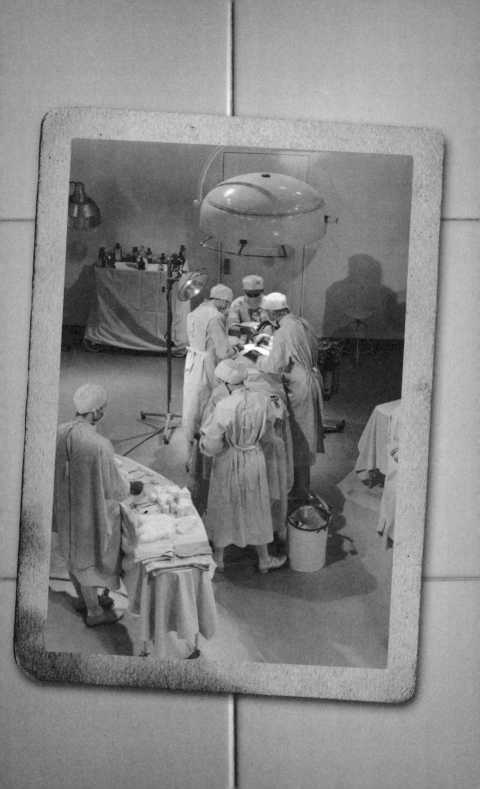

to be like a threat. A warning."

"They *are* a warning."

Ricky glanced away from Kay, turning to the young man who had spoken up. Ricky hadn't really paid him much attention before, since like the other patients he worked in almost total silence. Obedience. He looked to be a little older than Ricky, but it was hard to be sure. He had a handsome, ageless look, with sleepy blue eyes and a friendly mouth.

"You two talk a lot," the boy added. "I should know, I was—well, I just *know* that the nurses don't like chatter. Our whole table could be disciplined. They're watching."

"Relax, Tanner," Kay replied. She wasn't testy, just gentle. "We'll keep our voices low, okay?"

That didn't appease Tanner. He wore a haunted expression, like he had seen some serious, bad things in his time.

"Oh, great, he's coming over."

It was too late for lowered voices, apparently. As the warden approached, Ricky didn't break eye contact. He couldn't have even if he'd wanted to. Most adults didn't intimidate him much, but there was something different about this warden guy. He didn't look mad or even concerned, just blank, like his skin was a mask for another face behind.

"Am I getting us in trouble, Kay?" Ricky whispered.

"I told you," Tanner muttered, head bowed over his journal.

"Don't panic, either of you," Kay said. "He probably just wants to say hello. You're the new kid, remember?"

"I never forget, thanks to you."

Kay flipped the pages of both their journals back to the half-hearted paragraphs they had started for their daily entries. The warden crossed the room at a leisurely pace, and Ricky started to see spots in the corner of his eyes. Blindingly intense bulbs lit the all-purpose room. You could never forget in this room that you were in a hospital—a place where surgery was conducted.

The thought made his throat tighten. Kay had told him more about the hospital in California where they sent her aunt. They did all kinds of brutal experiments on the patients there. Because they were "undesirable" and "perverted" the doctors could do whatever they wanted. At least, Ricky reassured himself, Brookline wasn't that kind of place.

"Hello, Mr. Desmond."

The warden's voice was as calm and blank as his demeanor. He raked his eyes over Kay, a flash of memory in his eyes before he fixed his attention back on Ricky.

"Afternoon," Ricky said. He finally broke eye contact and looked down at his nonsensical journaling. His stomach tightened in a knot. Most adults hated when he stared back at them, defiant, challenging, but the warden hadn't seemed to mind. He'd seemed to *welcome* it, smiling that unwavering half smile, a ventriloquist dummy's smile.

"I'm Warden Crawford, but I'm sure you knew that. Nurse Ash informs me that Keith is just full of information," he said. Even then he didn't take his eyes off Ricky.

Kay flinched, the pointier end of her crayon digging into the paper, making a tiny wax divot.

"Here we encourage our patients to write in their journals. Dreams. Thoughts. Your own point of view of your time here, whether it's successful or otherwise . . . I find it useful to reflect on such things. I trust you're both embracing the exercise with the full effort it deserves." His smile flared, but not in a friendly way. Ricky shifted his hand, covering his paragraph of random song lyrics. Half of "Sittin' on the Dock of the Bay" smudged under his wrist.

"Yup. We definitely are," Ricky mumbled.

"Definitely," Kay corroborated.

"As our newest patient, did you have any questions for me?" the warden asked, leaning in closer as if to try to get a peek at what Ricky had scribbled.

Just one question sprang to mind.

"Do you know when my parents might visit?" Ricky asked, trying to take the heat off his new friend. That, and he was honestly curious. There had to be some kind of visitation schedule set up eventually. At Hillcrest, parents were supposed to visit every weekend. Just like with the eye contact, asking blunt questions tended to throw off adults, but he was beginning to realize he'd have to get trickier, smarter, to deal with this man.

If you were such a genius, you wouldn't have ended up here. You would've kept your stupid temper.

"Soon, I'm sure," the warden replied gently. "Nurse Ash assures me you're settling in nicely, which tells me it's high time we began your treatment in earnest, mm?"

"My treatment?" His eyes flew to Kay, but she was trying to disappear into the table. "And what will that be like?"

The warden chuckled, craning back and tucking his hands into his coat pockets. He pulled out a tiny metal tin and opened it, popping a mint into his mouth. "I'll be seeing to you myself, Mr. Desmond, so don't worry. Your curiosity will be satisfied soon enough."

CHAPTER

№ 6

"*F*riday work hour is different for everyone," Nurse Ash explained. Her red hair bounced under her hat as she led him through the main lobby. A new family was being welcomed by the front door, though Ricky couldn't tell from looking at them which one was the patient. He almost called out to them—caused a scene—but then a rank of nurses appeared from the far corridor where Nurse Ash was leading him, clipboards in hand, deployed to check on patients in their individual rooms. They nodded each in turn to Nurse Ash, then stared at Ricky like they knew what he'd been thinking. He shivered.

Continuing through the hall, Nurse Ash and Ricky passed a rickety old elevator—the kind with the metal gate in front of the doors. It was coming to a stop as they walked by, but it was coming from below. So there *was* a basement, just like in his dream.

Nurse Ash led Ricky through a heavy door to a kind of reception area. This must be the administration wing. At Victorwood, he would often hear the nurses laughing and chatting at the drug dispensary stations, the sounds of their excited gossip drifting through the halls. Here it was utterly silent.

Across the expansive room, Ricky saw a glass-paned door labeled "Warden Crawford." For a heart-fluttering moment, he thought Nurse Ash was taking him in there, but she moved instead to unlock a nondescript wooden door to the side, and he breathed a sigh of relief.

"What's in here?" he asked.

"Brookline has operated for decades," she explained. "And, frankly, we can't always keep up with the amount of paperwork there is when you're dealing with as many patients and families as we have. We try to stay on top of it now, but things weren't always so smoothly run here."

"Filing," Ricky muttered. "Wonderful."

"Was that a complaint?" She stopped, the door halfway open, and gave him a cold look.

He had forgotten that she was one of them. That there was always the threat of "discipline," even if he didn't know what that looked like yet. He wasn't spoiling to find out.

"I just prefer the outdoors, that's all," he amended.

Her expression softened. "Of course. I think we all do. Here, let me show you what you'll be doing today."

Beyond the door was a small, cramped room, lined with shelves. It wasn't like the halls and rooms and cells of Brookline, not perfectly scrubbed and tidied, but much more haphazard. Dusty. Accordingly, Nurse Ash handed him a small rag from the pocket of her coat.

"Clean as best you can," she said. "Start here, with the old patient intake and outtake cards. Just remove the files, alphabetize them, and replace them in the storage box. Get as many done as you can, please. I know it's a bit tedious, but maybe it will give you a chance to think about your reasons for being here."

Ricky nodded, but he wasn't fully listening. A box on the shelf

directly across from the door was spilling open, old black-and-white photographs and tintypes visible above the bulging edges. He drifted toward the box, tugging out one of the photos and studying it. A young girl stared at the photographer, her expression lifeless, her small face overshadowed by the giant doctors crowded around her. The only impulse he felt was to help her, save her . . .

"These photos," he said softly. "They're like the ones in the hall. In the cafeteria."

"Yes," Nurse Ash replied. She joined him at the shelf and gently took the photo out of his hands, sliding it back into the box and out of view. "I find them troubling, to be honest. But the warden thinks it's important to be upfront about the work we do here. To be proud of it."

"Proud of hurting little girls," Ricky spat.

"We've come a long way," Nurse Ash said, maybe a little defensive. "We can't help what happened in the past, we can only try to do better." She paused. "We *have* to do better."

She sounded sad. Resigned.

"I'd still really like to talk to my mother," Ricky reminded her, sensing a moment of weakness, of vulnerability.

But Nurse Ash straightened up, correcting the sad slant to her lips as she brushed off her hands and swept to the door. "I can't help you, Ricky. Not like that. You know, it's a privilege to get this assignment, not every patient is allowed in here. I can only suggest you be on your best behavior. Order and discipline, remember? That's what we reward here."

"Yeah," he said. "I remember. And hey, I promise I'm one of the good ones. I'm gonna get that phone call out of you

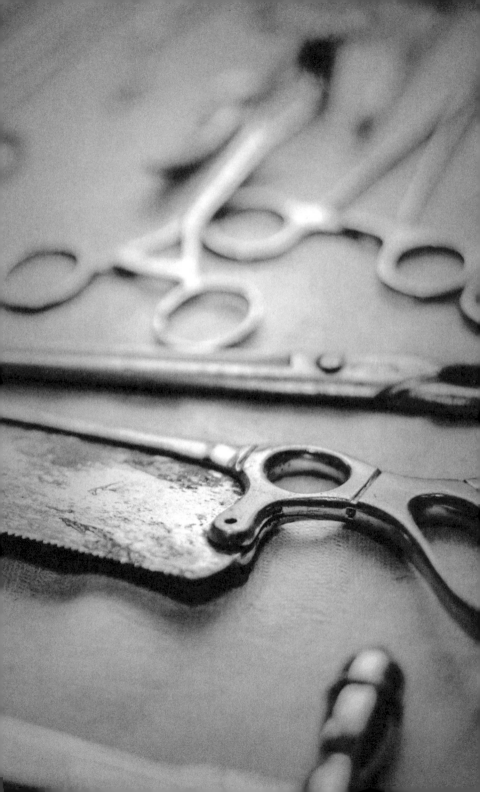

eventually." He winked.

"You'll have to do better than that."

And she was gone. He heard the key turn in the lock. There wasn't all that much light to see by in here, and for a moment he was overcome by the claustrophobia of it all. Dust choked his lungs. He heard the pipes creaking and settling in the walls, and it reminded him of that strange, dark heartbeat he had followed in his dream. A dream . . . a vision . . . As the week had gone on, and his sleep had been interrupted again and again by that terrible screaming, he'd been increasingly less sure what had really happened that first night.

"What a privilege," he said to himself.

He was drawn back to the box of photographs, and he decided to start his sorting there. A small act of defiance. He found the little girl again. She looked so terrified. Maybe terrified enough to be the one he heard screaming. But this was an old image, and he didn't recognize any of the orderlies huddled around her. There were images of equipment, surgical equipment, and doctors conferring over what must have been the latest and greatest. Saws. Drills. Syringes that looked big enough to be for elephants.

He recoiled and shoved the pictures away. If he were anywhere else, it might be fascinating, if morbid, but he was in a sanitarium now. These pictures were from Brookline, he reminded himself. Those tools had been used on patients just like him.

It was too real.

Chilled, he forced himself to sit down with the box of files Nurse Ash had pointed out. The whole thing was a mess. Half of the brown folders had spilled open, the cards and notes piling at the bottom of the musty box. The rag didn't seem like nearly enough to clean a square foot of the room, so instead he tied it around his nose and mouth to keep out the irritating dust. Some of the papers were water damaged, others simply blank.

He dumped out the box and began organizing. Nurse Ash was right about it being a tedious job, although really that didn't begin to describe it. Hunting down the stray scraps of paper all belonging to a single patient proved almost impossible, since the names were frequently smudged or altogether absent. After a while he decided to hunt and match by symptom or treatment.

Instantly the task became a lot less boring.

"God," he whispered. Some of the treatments made his week of gardening and writing in his journal feel like a vacation by comparison. Just like he was using guesswork to gather the files back together, these doctors had been using guesswork on people. New cocktails of drugs. Isolation therapy. Shock treatment.

Someone called Maurice Abeline had undergone such intense, prolonged shock treatment that he became unresponsive. There were no more notes about him after that.

"They killed him," Ricky murmured, slamming his fist into a filing cabinet. It didn't seem right for him, a patient, to see these things. It was like the pictures, so blatant, so unashamed. He dug back into Maurice's folder and pulled out the last description of treatment. He set aside that notecard and hunted through the next file and the next, collecting the latest note he could find on each patient as he went.

When that box was more or less organized, he sat cross-legged on the cold, cement floor and flipped through the final cards.

Unresponsive. Deceased. Complications from F.L. Unknown.

Deceased. Unknown. Unknown.

The unknowns alarmed him the most. Was it unknown what their ultimate fate was or unknown what had *killed* them? He looked through the cards again, trying to find patterns or some kind of explanation for so many sad endings. Most, he discovered, were males, and the frequency of deceased or unknown declarations accelerated after the year 1964. None of the cards were more recent than 1966.

Ricky had no idea what he was looking at. A slew of male patients died at Brookline in a two-year period. Why the short time frame? And why were the female patients more fortunate?

He shoved the papers into the back of the box, still grouped together. They were out of sight, but if he ever came back here he would be able to find them quickly. Standing, he adjusted the rag around his face. It didn't do much to keep out the damp paper smell of the room and it only made him feel more claustrophobic. There was still so much left to do. Sure, he had tackled one box, but there were dozens upon dozens in here.

So many . . . There might be just as many dead patients waiting to be found in the other containers. He sighed and hefted the organized box of files back onto the shelf, then gave himself a little pep talk to start on the next. Bending to grab it, he stopped, frozen, feeling a sudden gust of air on the back of his neck. It was a groan, a sigh, but chilled like no human breath could be.

His spine went rigid and he stood, turning, tracking the sensation. There was no one behind him and no vents that he could see, either. It was his imagination then. Paranoia. Like the screaming girl, the heartbeat. He whirled back around to face the box and almost let out a scream of his own. His throat closed up around the sound. A man, or perhaps a boy, stood right there in front of him.

Ghostly. Pale. A thin stream of dark blood trickled from his eye. He was wearing the same hospital pajamas as Ricky. And it—the thing, it couldn't be human—reached for him. Ricky jerked back, instinctively, no longer able to breathe in the tiny, dirty closet with its cold, ghostly breaths. With its *actual ghosts.*

He overbalanced, stumbling backward into the shelving unit to the right of the door. The figure was already gone, just a flash, there just long enough to reach for him and then vanish. Ricky tried to steady himself on the shelves but the unit was already teetering. Gritting his teeth, he pushed back against it, barely managing to keep the whole thing from toppling down on him. One of the boxes shook loose, too close to the edge, and it and all of its contents crashed onto the floor, dozens of pictures scattering across the cement.

Footsteps approached from the hall. Someone had heard the racket. On hands and knees, he frantically scooped the pictures back into the box. Knuckles rapped quietly on the door.

"Mr. Desmond? Ricky? Is everything all right in there?"

Nurse Ash. Had she been standing out there the whole time?

"Fine," he called through the rag, moving it aside to unmuffle his voice. "Just bumped a box, nothing to worry about."

Her footsteps didn't retreat. He worked faster, righting the box and reaching for the last few stray photos. There was something strange about the last picture on the ground . . . It looked familiar. Eerily familiar. *Painfully* familiar.

The key clicked in the door and he panicked, shoving the

photo back in the box and standing. Ricky could barely string two thoughts together as the door opened and Nurse Ash's smiling face appeared. The young man in the photograph resembled him—Ricky—in a way that made him think they could be long-lost cousins. Even brothers.

There was a vague family resemblance, of that much he was certain.

"That rag wasn't for your face," she said, exasperated.

"I need to call my mother. Now."

She held the door open for him, a worry line creasing between her eyes. "You know I can't do that for you," she said. "I really wish you would stop asking."

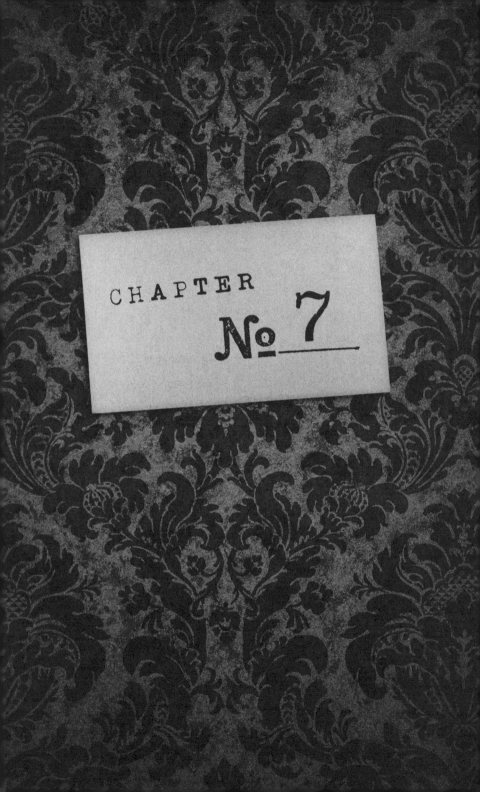

CHAPTER
№ 7

Journal of Ricky Desmond—June

They should really get better about checking under my mattress. Hiding this junk is almost too easy. No, it is too easy. Kay says they search her room every single night, hunting for the smallest infraction. Me? Nurse Ash hasn't so much as turned out my pockets since I was admitted. Not that I'm complaining, but it's weird. I guess Mom could be paying for preferential treatment, like Kay's dad did, but I don't think she would, not after what I did to Butch.

Fine. I take it back. If you can sense this, Mom, I'm sorry for going after your dumb husband, and I'll even apologize to his face if you just come and get me out of this place. Sticking it out didn't seem so bad for those first few days but now the dreams are coming every night. It's always that same girl. Is she even here? Is she even real?

I don't know what I saw in that room. That person in the photograph looked like me. I'm sure he did. Even if it's just a coincidence, I saw it, and I hate that I saw it. That I can't stop thinking about it. I tried asking Nurse Ash about it in a roundabout way. Do I seem familiar to you? That sort of thing. It just made her really uncomfortable. The other nurses won't even talk to me. It's like they don't really see us patients, or couldn't respond even if they wanted to.

The warden said he would start my "treatment" soon but he hasn't talked to me at all since then. I see him watching me. He's always watching me. What is he waiting for?

Yesterday Kay glanced at Nurse Ash's schedule when she was handing out a midday snack. They're going to give her shock treatment. Those stupid bastards. I don't know how they can look at her and not see what I see: just a nice girl. She's so quiet. Does what she's told. She's not hurting anyone and she knows basically every Barbara Randolph song in existence by heart. That makes her more than special and they want to shock her like they did to me at Hillcrest.

I told her it wouldn't work, that it wouldn't change her, but I don't know if she believed me.

I have to remember these things. I have to remember all of it. If Mom comes back for me, I don't want to forget, and maybe . . . Damn. I don't know. Maybe I could help get Kay out of here somehow. She doesn't deserve to be in this hellhole. None of us do. Fine, maybe Angela, but everyone else is just so quiet. It's like they're already dead.

But not me. Not Kay.

CHAPTER

№ 8

"*I* found something strange."

As soon as Ricky said it, it sounded stupid. They were in an asylum. Everything there was to be found in here was strange in one light or another. But Kay humored him with a look of real interest, and that was all he really wanted anyway. She'd been understandably withdrawn since her shock treatment had started, and Ricky had been feeling guilty, as if he were the cause of it somehow. Now they were on hands and knees next to each other, working with other patients to clean the common room. The floor was cold, as always, and the white, spotless gleam that came with their scrubbing only made it feel colder.

Kay had overheard two orderlies discussing some big event coming up, for which the warden wanted the whole place looking perfect. (Shouldn't they have a cleaning staff for this?)

"What kind of strange?" Kay asked.

"Have they ever made you clean the storage rooms?"

"Only once," she whispered, shrugging. He could barely hear her over the soft sound of a dozen rags swishing across the tiled floor. "It was nasty in there. Couldn't breathe right for a week after that."

"I know," he said. "But did you look at what you were cleaning?"

"I didn't want to, Ricky. I'm just doing my work until I get out of here."

"Maybe you should peek next time." Ricky stopped, checking to see that their nurse chaperones were still standing off near the doors. They were, and now they were conveniently distracted by the warden, who appeared to have stopped by to check on their progress. Like an unlucky penny, he just turned up everywhere.

"No, Ricky, you don't get it," she said with a sigh. She was indulging him again, but not in a good way this time. "Head down. Quiet. I'm not going to make a fuss. I want less discipline, not more."

He paled. Ten days in, and his own treatment remained easy—really borderline neglectful. He wasn't sure what Kay had done to deserve her more severe treatment, but she was right—if order and discipline were the obsession here, then blending in with the crowd was probably the best survival strategy. Still . . . He had felt that cold and ghostly breath on his neck. He had seen the odd patient cards with so many violent deaths. And he had seen the photograph that lingered in his mind. Trouble was finding him, whether he was looking for it or not.

"Well, lucky for you, I looked for both of us."

Kay cocked her head to the side, resting her weight on her palms as she studied him. Her eyes were gentle, searching, but she couldn't conceal the intense curiosity sparkling in her gaze. "Don't leave me in suspense, dummy. What did you see?"

"I don't think this place was always so polished," he murmured. "Patients were dropping like flies as late as a couple years ago. And the pictures . . ."

"As bad as those?" she asked, nodding to the ones on the wall.

"Worse. And I felt this weird presence. I mean, look, I don't believe in ghosts, okay? Let's get that one out of the way first. But I see all these cards talking about dead people, and then a minute later there's a person breathing down my neck and, I don't know, Kay, it's the kind of coincidence that comes back up when you try to swallow it."

"Or," Kay said slowly, gently, and Ricky knew he might need to hold his temper through whatever she said next, "you're making leaps. It doesn't surprise me that you would read about dead people and then see one."

"I considered that," he said honestly. "But that's not even the strange thing. See, in this one picture—and yes, I know how ridiculous this sounds—well, one of the men in the photos looked like me. And I mean *just* like me."

"*That's* a little stranger," Kay admitted with a grimace. "That wouldn't sit right with me either."

"Thanks. And thank you for believing me. About the picture anyway."

"I've cleaned this room from top to bottom with Sloane and Angela before," Kay said. "You should hear some of the stuff that comes out of his mouth in particular. He thinks everyone here is trying to kill him. Constantly. All the time. Even the mice in the walls. This conversation is reasonable if you ask me."

Their discussion came to an abrupt halt, cut off by sharp voices in the corner of the room. Near the tall double doors, two nurses were trying to block the patients from gawking at the warden, who had begun arguing with a man his own height.

They weren't just the same height, either; they resembled each other in the face, with pale, smooth skin, even though both men were middle-aged, and had long, dignified noses. The second man didn't wear spectacles, but the family resemblance was unmistakable even at this distance.

"If I've told you once, I've told you a thousand times. Do *not* barge in on me here," the warden was saying, heedless of his audience. Ricky glanced around the room. Most of the other patients were pretending to work, but their rags were circling on the tiles very slowly indeed. Everyone had an ear turned toward the outburst.

"I'm *working*," the warden finished.

"This doesn't look much like work," the other man said. "What do you expect me to do? You refuse to return my calls. Mother's estate must be settled and it won't be settled the way you want it done."

"*That* is a topic for another day and another location," the warden replied. "This is extremely irregular, not to mention unprofessional."

Two orderlies had appeared, and, together with the warden, they were trying to herd the man out the door, closing in around him in a tight circle. "Okay. Kick me out all you want, brother. I won't let this go."

The warden's sigh was audible across the all-purpose room. "You never do."

Something about the conversation had upset Sloane. The old man hopped to his feet, surprisingly spry for his age, and began to scream. "Brother!" he was crying. "Brother, brother! You were like my brother! Stop, stop! How *could* you?"

The nurses flew to him, pulling his arms down to his sides and holding them there. The orderlies surrounding the warden's brother heard the commotion, and without a moment's hesitation, they sprinted into the room to help. They muzzled the old man with the mask they'd threatened Ricky with on his first day, and the word *Brother!* died away behind the restraints.

"Whoa," Kay whispered, watching as the warden's brother stormed away and Sloane was carried out of the common room.

"I take it that kind of thing doesn't happen around here often?"

"Extremely irregular," Kay replied. "Like the warden said."

CHAPTER

№ 9

"*W*here's Nurse Ash?"

Ricky glanced around the reception area where Nurse Ash had brought him last Friday. An orderly he didn't recognize had brought him here, pulling him out of his room for what Ricky had assumed was lunchtime. Instead, he'd found a surly nurse waiting for him in the main lobby, tapping her foot as if they were running late for something.

"You will go inside," that nurse said now, pointing to the door that had "Warden Crawford" painted on the glass.

So he was finally going to see where the Big Boss spent his days. It was time to slow his steps, drag this out, because—finally, a week after the threat had been made—his treatment was about to begin. He couldn't tell if this was in reaction to something he had done earlier or what. Yeah, he'd been chatting with Kay while they worked, but surely that had been nothing next to all the other commotion in the room.

God, he hated the word "treatment." It had that nice, cute word at the beginning—treat. A treat! A treat was skipping school to go with Martin to Pier 6 and getting covered head to foot in crabmeat, butter, and Old Bay. A treat was a candy watch in your Christmas stocking or the way a new copy of *Rolling Stone* smelled.

Treat*ment* was getting shocked with a hundred volts of electricity at Hillcrest. Treat*ment* was sitting in a circle of guys at Victorwood and talking about what it had felt like to grow up in a home without a father. What would treatment mean at Brookline?

The warden's door was already slightly ajar, and Ricky put his hand on it to push it open farther. It was hot to the touch. Ricky yanked his hand back, his palm aching as if it had been scalded. For a moment he felt the warmth of a blaze on his face and heard a woman screaming. Footsteps raced by on either side of him. He leaned against the doorframe, catching his breath, blinking and finding that the heat and the noise had vanished.

"Inside," the nurse said, right behind him.

Pulling himself together, Ricky ducked into the office, where he was relieved to find that the warden wasn't here, not yet. He leveled his voice, not wanting the nurse to know what he had just felt. Escaping Brookline would be a lot harder if he was having visible episodes in front of the staff.

"I like Nurse Ash better, if my opinion counts for anything," he said with a forced smile. The nurse's dark, small eyes fixed on him and then rolled. It was the most emotion he had gotten out of any nurse besides Ash.

"It doesn't. Sit."

Ricky fell into the chair hard enough to knock the air out of his lungs. The nurse waited at the door, probably hovering in case he tried to take one of the warden's fountain pens and commit mass murder with it. He wondered if anyone stopped to realize that the patients here were all perfectly docile already—Sloane's performance in the common room yesterday notwithstanding.

Ricky and the nurse waited for what felt like hours. Was this all part of it, too? A strange nurse he didn't recognize barking at him; a long, uncomfortable wait in the warden's freezing office when he was starving, and while he could do nothing but replay the strange heat that he'd felt on the door . . . Maybe his treatment had already begun without him knowing it.

You're just out of sorts, he reminded himself. *And you're tired. Underfed. Homesick.*

Finally, the warden appeared, but not from the door behind him as Ricky had assumed he would. He came instead through a door on the far wall that Ricky had taken for a coat closet. Ricky caught a brief glimpse inside at what looked like stairs that led down. If the heartbeat of Brookline was in its basement, it seemed the asylum had many arteries and veins.

"Ah. Here you are, Mr. Desmond. Excellent, it's time we made introductions and got started. I'm very eager to work with you."

Ricky's back straightened into a rod. He listened as the warden dismissed the nurse, and then he heard the door shut and lock behind him. His eyes swept the room in a panic—there were no visible surgical implements the warden could use on him, but maybe this was just some kind of brief consultation or therapy session before the real torture began in the basement.

Just don't forget who you are, Ricky reminded himself. *You can get through this. You've gotten through it before. You can pretend if you have to, but don't really forget. Martin's crooked smile. The gap in his teeth. The lights on Boylston Street at midnight, that feeling of sneaking out and being free, happy, and alive.*

"Can we get this over with?" Ricky asked, folding his hands in his lap and staring straight ahead.

Warden Crawford took his time pacing a circle around his desk before returning to his chair and taking a seat. He sighed quietly as he regarded Ricky, like a disappointed grandfather saddled with chiding a bad child.

"This doesn't need to be an antagonistic relationship, Mr. Desmond. Have you not been treated well since you arrived?"

Ricky glared. "That's not the point."

"Isn't it?" The warden's eyes widened in mock-surprise. "Then what is 'the point'?"

"This is an asylum. I'm not here of my own free will. And you're hurting my friend, aren't you? You're using shock therapy on Kay, and she's done nothing wrong."

"Keith Waterston's aberrant behavior has nothing to do with you, nor does the treatment deemed appropriate by his overseeing physician."

Ricky had felt his fear and anger bubbling up distantly, but he didn't expect it to explode out at that precise moment. He never did. He slammed his fist on the desk, making the porcelain head statue on it bounce. "You're doing it to her and you'll do it to me, too! I knew it was just a matter of time. All those cutting-edge treatments your doctors told my parents about are a sham."

The warden fell silent, staring at him again. That was almost worse. He should be restrained for that outburst. Punished. Sedated. He wasn't being very orderly or disciplined. Whenever he lost his temper like that he felt so cold afterward. Ashamed.

"I understand your frustration, Mr. Desmond, but there is no need to raise your voice."

"I'm not—look, I just want to talk to my parents. My mother.

I don't know why you've basically been ignoring me so far and I really don't care. This whole stupid thing is a misunderstanding."

Leaning forward, the warden rested his elbows on the desk and adjusted his wire-rim spectacles. The lenses didn't exaggerate his eyes. If anything, they did the opposite, making his pupils smaller, more focused, like needles aimed at Ricky. "Every patient here is an individual. Accordingly, every patient is evaluated and treated based on their specific needs. We try to maintain a baseline level of routine. Especially at the beginning, the consistency is important. Your family entrusted you to my care, and I have no intention of betraying that trust. You and I can trust each other, too, Ricky, but not if you regard me with suspicion. Or worse, open hostility."

Ricky crossed his arms stubbornly over his chest, glaring. "Why would I trust you when all you want to do is change me? I know why I'm here, and it's not going to work."

For the first time, he saw real emotion flicker across Warden Crawford's face. The pale, smooth surface of his facade rippled, the ugly facsimile of a smile distorting his cheeks. He leaned further forward, nearly halfway across the desk.

"Why do you think you are here?" the warden asked.

Ricky stared back at him, refusing to answer.

"I see. It makes you uncomfortable to say it. That's not uncommon."

The door opened, startling them both. Nurse Ash strode inside, her neutral expression twisting to one of fear when she noticed the two of them together. "Oh!" she said, beginning to back out. She had a small tray with a lump of tuna fish and some crackers on it balanced on her right arm. "Excuse me, sir, I had no idea you were with someone."

"You should examine the daily schedule more closely," he barked at her. "It is subject to change, which you know but have somehow forgotten. And as is polite here and in general society, one should knock."

"I really do apologize. It's just usually you take your lunch at—"

"The *schedule*, Nurse Ash. Do not make me repeat myself."

He didn't know why he was so surprised. Of course this man was a bully. Nurse Ash practically sobbed another apology mixed with an excuse as she backed out of the office, closing the door so carefully and lightly Ricky hardly heard the door click.

"You treat everyone like that, don't you?" Ricky asked. "Your employees, your brother . . ."

That didn't get the reaction he wanted. The warden chuckled lightly, his demeanor once again calm and cool. "I imagine that bold attitude of yours unsettled previous physicians, yes? You will find that method is useless here."

"Is that so?" He knew it was stupid to back-talk, but sometimes he simply couldn't help it. He was supposed to be coasting. Blending in. But that hadn't been enough so far, and he certainly didn't think it was ever going to get him on the line with his mother and out of here. He just needed to figure out what would instead.

"It is. I welcome your observations. I find them amusing. You see, I have no intention of changing you, Mr. Desmond. I accept you almost exactly as you are. No, I want to *perfect* you."

CHAPTER

№ 10

*T*he words rang over and over again in his head.

I accept you almost exactly as you are.

He stumbled over the "almost" each time, but the rest of that phrase made him feel weird—exposed. No adult had said anything like that to him in . . . ever. He blinked back at the warden, waiting for the other shoe to drop, waiting for him to put a pin on that "almost" so he could wipe away the fleeting sense of belonging that urged Ricky to drop his guard.

"Come, I want to show you something." The warden stood, taking out his little metal tin of mints and having one before offering the open tin to Ricky. He flashed his teeth. "I know, I know—rules. Order and discipline. Go on. I won't tell. After all, they are *my* rules."

Ricky took one, his mouth puckering at once from the strong burst of wintergreen. He hadn't tasted anything but bland porridge, fake eggs, and watery soup in days. The warden stood and returned to the far door. Like the rest of the asylum, the office was incredibly neat. Folders and papers were stacked in rectangular towers. A shelving unit beside the far door displayed diplomas, awards, and trophies. There were no photos of the brother Ricky had seen that afternoon, just a small picture of the warden himself and more framed pictures of patients.

These were more medically leaning than those in the multipurpose room. Some had been taken so close up to an eye or to a specific part of the body that Ricky couldn't tell what he was looking at. Others showed the warden posing with the patients, but they made him look less like a doctor at work than like a hunter posing with his prized trophies.

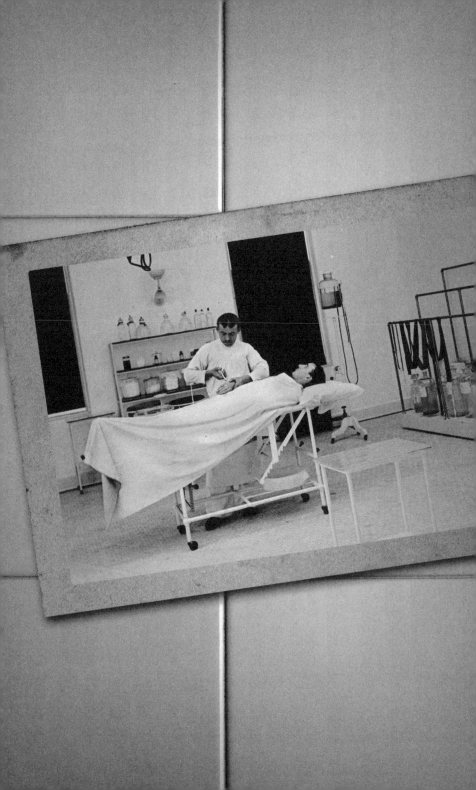

"There's no need to stall," the warden added, opening the door, keeping it held for Ricky. "We're just going for a little stroll."

"Where are we going?" Ricky asked. The steps leading down were unnervingly familiar. He remembered them from his dream of wandering the building. He gulped a nervous breath as the warden swept by him and walked ahead, descending.

Ricky's curiosity about what was really down below might be strong, but it was the locked door behind him that actually forced him forward. He had experienced déjà vu before, but not like this. Curiosity mixed with dread. At the bottom of the stairs, the warden stood looking for his keys, but if he squinted Ricky could see what lay beyond him.

"The lower levels are reserved for our most trying cases," the warden explained. Ricky glanced down the corridor, but there were no nurses and no orderlies there, no other doctors. He was alone with the warden, and he could feel the man's impatience tugging at him.

"Should . . . Should I really be down here?" he asked. Spare emergency lights glowed along the walls, revealing little.

The warden chuckled, beckoning him forward. "Ah. You feel like I'm giving you special privileges."

"Aren't you?"

"Of course. There's even a special fund-raising gala coming up—I like to show our benefactors how Brookline can improve the lives of our patients. I'm hoping to show them patients like you, patients with real potential." He smiled and continued on, again leaving Ricky to follow or stay. But he followed. Here, at least, he was starting to see an opportunity. If he played along, sucked up to this creep, he might be able to ask him for one more special privilege—a phone call home. Once his mother heard the misery in his voice she'd come racing up from Boston.

"But why?" Ricky couldn't help asking. "What's so special about me?"

"What's this? I thought you considered yourself very special indeed. Unique. Better."

He squirmed. "I just like to mess around," he said. "Talk big, that kind of thing."

"Mm. Well, let me put it this way. I told you that the patients here are individuals, and I believe that. But at the same time, I see you all equally. You are all patients. You must all be treated. The difference is only in the approach."

A long, piercing wail came from the depths of the asylum. Ricky almost missed a step from the shock of it, grabbing for the wall on his right to keep from toppling. The warden didn't seem to notice, moving briskly down the very narrow hallway with practiced ease.

"The patients down here are waiting," he said, pausing at the top of another staircase—one that wound down in a spiral and had a single railing for support. Ricky had no idea the underbelly of Brookline was so vast or so cold. "Waiting for us to find cures for what ails them. Techniques. Physicians have failed them. They cannot be helped. Not yet."

Ricky thought of the cards, of the patients who had died within these very walls. Those weren't just failures, he thought, not just a shortcoming of science. Those people were killed.

Deceased, deceased, deceased

Unknown, unknown, unknown

"They are certainly mad. They are mad just as you are, just as I am," the warden added, continuing the journey downward.

"What do you mean?" Ricky asked.

He didn't like this. He wanted to go back up. Above them, out of sight, he heard the door to the stairwell close, the sound echoing in the cavernous basement.

"No man is truly sane in his time," was the answer. "Was Galileo mad? Michelangelo? Darwin? No. Geniuses all, but their contemporaries would never admit as much. And if I must be called insane for what I wish to accomplish in *our* time, dear boy, then so be it."

CHAPTER

№ 11

The bottom level of the basement, well below his little cell in Brookline, was just how he remembered it. How could he have seen this? It had to be some psychological trick, Ricky thought, like how when you heard a word for the first time, you could swear you started seeing it everywhere. Still, he felt chilled to the bone, his thin patient's clothing about as insulating as paper.

He heard voices coming from the tall, arched doorway ahead and to the left of the stairwell. Something banged arrhythmically against a metal surface, a hollow thud that reminded him of the heartbeat, his heartbeat.

"Galileo's dream of our solar system, Michelangelo's of our inner workings, Darwin's of our origin . . . All masterful thinking. All productive uses of their lives. Their thinking endured, certainly, but their lives ended." The warden stopped just short of the archway and Ricky did, too, shooting a single, nervous glance down the corridor to see the closed doors of his dream. Here, three orderlies mingled, talking among themselves. "And that—those ended lives—is a real shame."

Ricky didn't follow. Of course they died. Everyone did eventually.

Some sooner than others, and many right here.

He rubbed futilely at his forearms, freezing. The warden studied him, interested even in his uncomfortable silence. "Why are we down here?"

"The lost cases," the warden said sadly, sighing. "The incurable ones. We keep them here. I wanted to show you what we all *can* become so that you never do. Medicine can't help them, not yet, and the waiting must be awful. It's why I do what I do, why we all do, here at Brookline. It's why we work so hard, why there are so many rules, so many guidelines we must obey."

Warden Crawford led Ricky into the ward. The metallic banging grew louder, and as they moved farther down the hall he realized it was coming from one of the rooms. Someone was ramming against the door with shattering force. *Bang! Ba-Bang!* Ricky jumped with each hit, the noise so close and loud now that it rattled his brain. The door didn't give, but the ward vibrated with the force of it.

"Isn't someone going to go in there?" Ricky asked in a tiny voice. "What if they hurt themselves?"

"Oh, they're already hurt. They'll tire themselves out eventually. That particular case just has a flare for the dramatic."

Dramatic? It sounded more like *panicked.*

The noise had distracted Ricky away from their journey. But now he realized they were nearing the end of the ward. A door led into another set of rooms beyond, but he wasn't thinking about that. They had almost reached the final door on the right. It was impossible that the girl would really be in there. But Warden Crawford had pulled out a set of keys and walked swiftly to the door. God, he was really going to open it. Ricky didn't know—didn't want to know—what he would see inside.

"What are you doing!?"

The cry came from behind them. Ricky swung around, and there was Nurse Ash, watching them from just a few feet away, her mouth still open, frozen in horror. Her heels clicked on the raw stone floor, and she reached them in a second, taking Ricky by the wrist and dragging him away from the door.

"Nurse Ash. *Jocelyn*." The warden's voice was like steel. His face was a cold, white mask again. "What do you think you are doing with my patient?"

She struggled for a moment, opening and closing her mouth around what sounded like a choked sigh. Still, she didn't let go of Ricky's wrist. He was relieved, he realized. It felt like a rescue, even if he had no idea what from.

"He . . . complained of a migraine this morning," Nurse Ash stammered out. She searched Ricky's face. "*Didn't* you?"

"Um, yeah," Ricky replied, mimicking her slow, slow nod. "A migraine."

"Our codeine replacement just came in," she hurried on. "We couldn't dose him earlier, but we shouldn't leave him in pain, Warden Crawford."

"A migraine." The warden had lost interest in Ricky for the moment, pinning the nurse with one of his razor-sharp looks. Ricky had to pity her. He could feel her hand shaking on his wrist, her skin growing clammy. What was so urgent? Did she know what was in that room and wanted to protect him? "Ricky Desmond is suffering from a migraine," he said, slowly, as if trying out the logic of the statement word by word.

"It's . . . It's so bad I haven't been sleeping well," Ricky said, elaborating the lie for her with a seed of the truth. "I should have said something. The um, the pain made me forgetful and confused."

"Well, we can help you out right away." She pulled on his wrist, yanking him away from the warden and not gently. "Come along. Come with me, Ricky. *Now*."

CHAPTER
№ 12

*H*e didn't feel free of the warden's gaze until they were all the way back in his cell, three floors and a whole world away. Nurse Ash all but tossed him into his room, leaning hard into the door as if to brace it from anyone who could follow.

She hadn't spoken a single word since pulling him out of the basement, ignoring the obvious staring of her colleagues on the way. Order and discipline. They'd not been walking calmly down the corridor, and Ricky could only imagine that he'd looked as flustered as he'd felt.

"What's going on?" he demanded, planting himself in the middle of the room. It was hard to believe, but he was actually *happy* to be back in that dumpy little cell. "Something is going on, isn't it? Why did you lie to the warden like that?"

Nurse Ash didn't respond, still leaning against the door and breathing hard. She looked at him though, intently, carefully, squinting as if she didn't quite recognize him. Then she straightened, set her jaw, and smoothed back the frizzy red hair poking out from under her nurse's cap. Part of it had come unpinned.

She approached him wildly, but Ricky didn't budge. "Do you know what's in that room? What did he want me to see in there?"

"Nothing," she said in a hoarse whisper. Her eyes were still huge. Huge and haunted. "There's nothing in that room anymore. There used to be a little girl, but not anymore. I don't . . . I don't know where he put her."

"*What?*" The blood rushed out of his face and hands, leaving him even colder than the basement. That wasn't possible. He couldn't have known that. It couldn't have been a dream.

Nurse Ash tucked her clipboard under her elbow, taking him by the wrists with both hands. "You have to promise me, Ricky—you have to promise me you won't go down there with him again."

"Where is this coming from?" he asked, shaking his head. "Isn't he your *boss*?"

"Just . . ." She glanced over her shoulder at the door, stopping to consider something. "Just promise me," she finally said, swiveling back to him. Ricky had to meet her eye to get her to speak again. Her hands were still shaking and sweating. "Promise me you won't go down there. You can't trust him."

"But he's your boss," Ricky insisted again. "What the hell is going on?"

"Do you trust me?" she asked, worrying her lip.

He hated when people answered a question with a question. She was deflecting, maybe, but he nodded. Sure. At least this way he could keep her talking and squeeze out more information.

"Yes, I think I trust you."

"That will have to be good enough," she said quickly. Her lip looked raw where she had been biting it. "This place . . . It's not quite what it looks like. It's not what it seems."

"Well, I pieced that together," Ricky muttered.

"How?" she asked. "What specifically? What have you seen? What do you know?"

So many questions. Well, he had just said he trusted her, and appealing to the order and discipline mantra of the place hadn't gotten him anywhere with her before, so he decided he might as well go for broke. "I've been seeing strange things. I think I hallucinated going into the basement and seeing a little girl, but I don't know how I could have imagined it all. I've never been down there until today. And in the storage closet I felt a presence and saw . . . I don't know what I saw. A ghost maybe. A figure. Oh, and outside the warden's office, when I tried to touch his door it was hot, like the room was on fire."

Nurse Ash was quiet, taking it all in.

"I'm sure that sounds crazy," he said. "But you're probably used to that here."

"No, Ricky, things go on here that I can't explain either," Nurse Ash said with a sigh. "And I want so badly to help you, to help everyone here."

"The warden said something similar to me."

"*No*." She turned, clutching her hat and squishing it down onto her head. Then she thought better of that impulse and fixed the hat, carefully. Her voice sounded almost tearful. "No, I'm not like him, Ricky. I actually want to do good."

"And he doesn't." It wasn't a question, and she didn't refute it.

"There are things I want to tell you but *I can't*. The warden has a way with people. I know that doesn't make sense now, and I hope for your sake it never will."

"But I—"

"Just listen. Listen and remember this, no matter what else

I say or what else I tell you tomorrow or the day after. It doesn't matter if he's my boss," she said, squeezing her eyes shut. "Whatever else he is, he's also a butcher. A *monster*."

Her eyes snapped open suddenly and she covered her mouth. The nurse looked ashen, sick, like she was about to vomit into her hands, like just saying the words had made her ill. Then she was up and running for the door, slamming it in her wake.

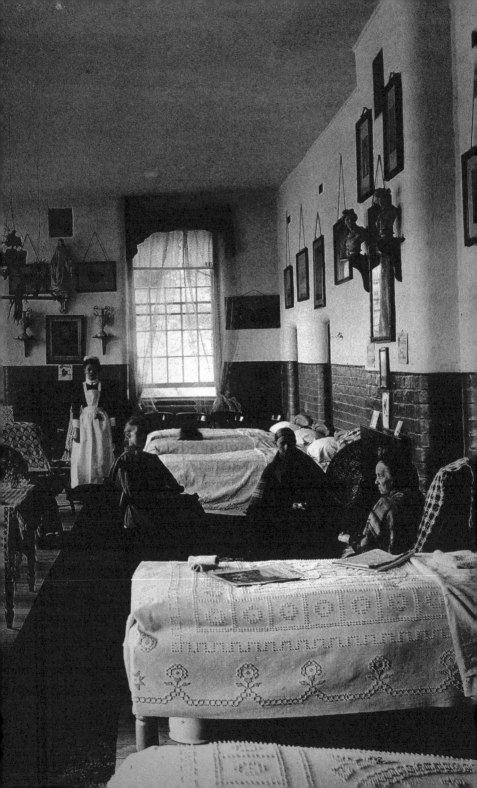

CHAPTER № 13

Journal of Ricky Desmond—June

I just have to last until September. Mom will come for me then. School will start. She won't want to answer any questions about why I'm not there. This is just for the summer, just for a few months. I just have to last until school starts.

Keep up appearances, Mom. Come for me. It's what you're good at, pretending everything is fine in the family, but that's okay. I'll forgive you for it if you just come back and take me out of this place. I don't know how you can abandon me when it was only the one time. So it was one really bad time. I know I hurt Butch and it scared you. But I would apologize. I would say anything you wanted me to if you would just be a goddamn mother and take your little boy home.

The warden is a butcher. The warden is a monster. There, Nurse Ash, I wrote it down so I can't forget it. Happy now? Next time answer my questions before you turn chicken and run away. The warden has a way with *people! I'm sure he does. This is probably some stupid game the two of you are playing. You're trying to confuse me. I'm too sure of my own sanity for your liking, and that's why you won't just leave me alone. And it's why you won't let me leave. I bet you'd get a real lecture, a real tongue-lashing, if I got out before being treated. Is that why you acted the way you did tonight? Why you saved me from the warden but won't let me call my mom? Jesus. I don't know whether to thank you or hate you. Or him.*

No, I hate both of you. I hate both of you for keeping me in this place. What the hell is going on? When aren't you coming for me, Mom? Is it easier, more convenient, to forget me?

Ricky had never folded so many cloth napkins in his entire life.

It was mind-numbing work. Repetitive. Not what he'd call an ideal way to spend an afternoon. His hands were beginning to cramp. Every single square of fabric had to be elaborately knotted and twisted and then tied with a precut piece of twine. *Just precious.* A bow, of course, with the loops slightly smaller than the tails.

The man Dennis was folding across from him at the cafeteria table; he was surprisingly deft at the whole exercise. He didn't exactly look built for fine motor skills. His hands were gigantic, with sausage fingers long and thick enough to crush Ricky's skull without breaking a sweat. He was silent now, standing very still while he did his work. The staff treated him like a jumpy Clydesdale, cooing at him and only ever touching him at arm's length. Ricky was surprised they didn't wiggle a carrot in front of his nose to get him to move from place to place.

Ricky had been at his lunch table before, but they rarely ended up on the same work hours. Today Dennis did his shift covered in bruises, his head purple and blue, a few dents and gashes running deep along his heavyset brow.

"Slip in the shower today, Dennis?" Ricky asked, tying another napkin off. "They actually hosed me down with warm water this morning. Lucky, right? I feel downright peppy."

Dennis ignored him, working twice as fast.

"Who throws a gala at an asylum anyway?" It was a question to no one, but with five days until the warden's illustrious gala, Ricky couldn't help wondering once again why this couldn't be a job for a professional staff. Angela, Sloane, Tanner, and a few other patients worked down the table from them. Ricky had begun to recognize more of his fellow inmates. Sloane was easy enough to remember, from his wild, puffy white hair to the angry scar on his neck (Ricky was pretty sure he didn't want to know how the old man had gotten it). Sloane seemed to recognize and remember him, too, and he went out of his way to keep his distance, flinching if the two of them were ever forced to enter a room together or sit at the same table. There was John-John, a boy about his age who suffered from short-term memory loss. He was here because his parents thought it was all a ruse, that he was making it up to get out of school. From what Ricky could tell, John-John had a genius's understanding of math and science, so if he was cutting class it wasn't impacting his learning much.

And there was Patty, a soft-spoken 'middle-aged woman whose cell was on Ricky's floor, and who had a tendency to speak in verse or burst into song. It was actually kind of pleasant. Sometimes it was obvious from the timing that she did it just to rankle the staff. Ricky always liked when he could hear her singing through the walls. Some nights he got entire renditions of musicals. Last night had been *Oklahoma!* It didn't help him sleep, but it did chase away some of the darker thoughts that had begun to creep in around the edges when he was alone.

He knotted and tied another napkin, sloppily, and tossed it onto the pile.

Six nurses milled near the door, pointing at different tables in the cafeteria and then to open spaces, perhaps discussing how best to arrange the room to satisfy the warden's exacting demands. Ricky was just about to daydream ways to instigate a jailbreak when Kay slipped in the doors, skirting along the wall behind the nurses before walking with purpose across the room to Ricky's table. Without missing a beat she fell in next to him, watching the way Dennis twisted and folded the napkins before doing one of her own.

"I didn't think we were on the same work slot today," Ricky said softly. He didn't really mind if Dennis heard, since the hulk of a man didn't seem prone to chattering, let alone ratting on them.

"We're not," she said. "I shouldn't be in here but I had to show you something."

"You're breaking the rules?" Ricky asked, impressed. "For me? You shouldn't have."

"This might change your mind." Her hands moved lightning fast, dropping the napkin she had just tied off and grabbing something that was hidden under her uniform top, tucked into her waistband. She slipped it into Ricky's hand and then glanced behind him. "It might be nothing. I don't know. But what you said about seeing that ghost in the closet—"

"I said I didn't know what I saw," Ricky mumbled.

"Would you just look at it?" She grabbed another unfolded napkin, copying Dennis's movements. Down the table from them, Patty began to sing one of her songs, but the nurses were too engrossed in debate to notice.

"Most of this is rubbed off," Ricky said, examining the small patient card she had found. The notes were in a long, looping hand, almost indecipherable. At the top he recognized half of a physician's name and then in the patient slot what looked like either Diamond, Dandelion, or *Desmond*.

Whoever it was, he had been sequestered for a violent episode, injuring one of the attending orderlies. He was apparently "extremely resistant to Tues. experiment therapy."

"Desmond is a common enough name," he pointed out. "*If* that's what it says."

But his hand shook a little as he read over the card. Kay didn't know the full truth about what he had done to his stepfather, but seeing his last name coupled with a penchant for violent outbursts concerned him. Frightened him.

"I know you don't care for your stepfather much," Kay said

softly. "Whatever happened to your real daddy?"

"He ran off," Ricky said. It was the only story his mother ever told about him. "He was no good for us. I was a handful even as a kid, and I guess it was just too much, so he left."

"I'm sorry," she whispered.

"I know what you're thinking."

"I'm just thinking that I'm sorry," she insisted.

"He ran off." *He ran off. He left us. Left us with Butch*. That was the truth.

Ricky clamped down on the note card harder, feeling the ugly darkness that preceded one of his incidents flaring up. No, it wasn't Kay's fault. She was just trying to help. Still, he wanted to lash out at something. He felt too full up, overcharged, and all the fear and uncertainty needed to go somewhere. But there was nothing to hit so he shoved the card into his waistband.

"Do you mind if I keep this?" he asked.

"It's already been down your pants, so yeah, it's all yours."

The need to smash something went out of him and he laughed, glancing up at her. She was smiling back, tentatively. She had broken the rules for him, and he knew how much that meant for her. "Thanks. I know you're just trying to help."

"Desmond is a common name," she said back.

"Really common," Ricky agreed. He already felt better.

Dennis jerked his head up, a napkin gripped in both hands. "*Still*," the man said, drawing out the word so slowly it sounded like he had fallen asleep mid-syllable. "So still. Like a statue, that one. Stiff. Posed. Beautiful."

"What did you say?" Ricky shared a glance with Kay. Despite

her longer stay, she seemed just as shocked as he was. "What are you talking about, Dennis?"

"Nothing. The last time I saw him. Nothing." Dennis smiled then, far away, and tied off another napkin.

CHAPTER

№ 14

The screams that woke him the next morning were not in his imagination. They jerked him awake in his bed, distant, yes, but *real*. He knew they were real because he knew who they belonged to.

Kay.

Ricky hurled himself out of bed, pacing, rumpled and exhausted. What were they doing to her? Was the shock treatment for her "problem" worse than what they'd tried on him at Hillcrest? That had been bad enough. It was humiliating. It was torture. He didn't know how anyone could do those things and call themselves a doctor. Doctors helped. Doctors cared. Just like their word "treatment," the term here was phony.

God, he felt like hell. Probably looked like it, too. He hadn't seen himself in more than ten days. At school he had never lacked for dates or attention. *Just like Burt Ward*, his mother used to coo, before she knew about his condition. She would ruffle his hair and then fix it back down. *Handsome just like Burt Ward, my little boy wonder! My very own boy wonder!*

It always sounded so stupid to him. There was only a vague resemblance, and anyway those suits they wore on *Batman* were ridiculous. *I'd put one on now and run laps in the cafeteria in front of the whole school if it got me out of this place.*

There were no mirrors around for patients to access, probably because it was assumed they'd break them for the shards. He got it now, the desperation, the need just to *get out*. The other patients seemed so calm. Acclimated. He couldn't imagine that would ever be him. He wouldn't let it be.

No matter what, it was time to come up with a better plan than sucking up to Nurse Ash or the warden and hoping for a phone call. It was clear now that a phone call was never coming. He hadn't seen much of the warden or the nurse in the past couple days anyway. So much for her trying to help.

Kay was the bigger concern now. He needed to see her. Needed to help her. He would need an ally if he was going to keep his head about him.

Nurse Ash came for him after all, but not until lunch. Another nurse had appeared to take him to breakfast, but Kay wasn't there, and the nameless nurse stayed to watch him while he ate. Ricky was ready and at the door when Nurse Ash arrived; he had heard her heels clicking in the hallway, recognizing her comparatively relaxed gait.

"Eager today, are we?" she joked, all benign smiles when she unlocked the door to find him standing there at attention.

"Eager? Are you kidding?" he snorted. "After what you said the last time I saw you, I think you owe me some answers. You ran off without really saying anything. It looked like you were going to be sick. He's a monster, remember? A butcher? What did you mean by all that? What did he do to that girl who was in the basement?"

Nurse Ash pulled back her head, lifting a single brow. "Rick . . . I have no idea what you're going on about. I'm only here to take you to lunch, then on to gardening, and then you will work in your journal for an hour."

"But you . . . No! You saved me from the basement! You told me not to trust the warden, you said . . . You made me promise not to go anywhere with him."

She frowned at him, consulting her chart. "Don't be foolish, Mr. Desmond. The warden is my superior. I would never say those things, and I would appreciate it if you kept me out of your wild delusions."

CHAPTER
№ 15

icky still hadn't adjusted to the feeling of confinement. Even now, as worried as he was about Kay, and as curious as he was to know about that Desmond patient card, he fantasized about breaking into a run, crashing through the orderly and the gate that separated him from the driveway and sprinting until he was out of sight.

Kay hadn't been at lunch, and now she wasn't outside for gardening. Looking around, Ricky didn't see a single sign that any of his fellow patients noticed or cared about this, and that was a sad thought. Kay had noticed so much about all of them.

A chill passed through him as he turned to go in at the end of the hour, like a stiff wind that became an arrow gesturing toward freedom.

"Run," a soft voice said from behind him. It was unmistakably outside his head. He twisted to follow the sound, feeling another crackle of cold against his skin.

"Ricky, come on, it's time to go inside," Nurse Ash called.

"But I heard—"

"Is it going to be that kind of day?" she asked.

Ricky heard the impatience in her voice and tried to ignore the uncomfortable drifts of cold air sliding over his skin. Subtly, he pinched his own pinkie and felt for himself how chilled his flesh had become. And here it was June.

They were only a few steps from the multipurpose room when he heard the voice again. This time closer. This time right in his ear. "Run," it said again, then, "*hide*."

He didn't expect Kay to be writing, but there she was, already sitting alone at a table in the far corner, looking so miserable that the nurses didn't even make her move to join the others. Ricky couldn't believe Kay was sitting upright at all. After only fifteen minutes or so of shock therapy at Hillcrest, Ricky had felt dizzy and confused, his memory taking an entire day to recover.

Nurse Ash lingered after handing him a few crayons and a pad of paper, following him to Kay's table and hovering over them. His skin was still cold, and his hand shook as he lowered his crayon to the page.

"You two just work quietly now," Nurse Ash said, directing this more to Ricky. "The warden is hoping to use his fund-raising gala to introduce the most improved patients to some of his donors. Wouldn't it be nice if that included you two? You might even get some of the cake at the end of the night."

"Thrilling," Ricky muttered.

"Cut the sarcasm, please," she said with a sigh.

"The warden enjoyed my observations. You should, too."

"I'm not the warden," she replied. He looked up at her at that. It was the only hint from her that she remembered their odd conversation. Was that a slip? A hint? "Focus on your journal, Ricky."

He waited until she was gone to say another word.

Tired. Kay looked so, so tired. Her head drooped on her

neck, her eyes were bloodshot, her hands trembled on the table. It seemed like further torture to make her sit there. They should have let her rest and recover properly.

Maybe she now had memory loss. Maybe she was confused. Ricky waited, but his thoughts were a jumble. His knee bounced under the table as he touched crayon to paper and left it there, trying to think of what to say. He didn't know if he should tell Kay about the voice he'd just heard. It would only make him sound like he was going off the deep end, and worse, it might make her hard day harder.

"You know," she said, doodling a spiral on her paper, "my daddy isn't a bad man. I know he isn't. Sometimes a person gets fixated on something and it's the only thing they care about. For me? I just wanted to make him happy. Not a bad thought, right? Just make him happy, any way I could, and for a while it worked."

Kay's voice was stronger than Ricky had expected. It gave him hope, that she was still her old self, at least from what he could tell.

"But my pops had a different thought in his head. He thought he should do whatever made God happy, and what makes God happy isn't what makes me happy. That's really it. Sometimes to make a person happy you'll do anything, even if it hurts like crazy on the inside."

True or not, Ricky shook his head. He peered around at the others. Sloane was there, but he didn't seem interested in his journal. He stared at Ricky, glaring. Angela and Patty worked diligently, or appeared to. Nurse Ash stood still and silent near the door with her superior, Nurse Kramer, which was fine by

Ricky. Anything was better than having the warden staring at him.

"He should've wanted to make you happy," Ricky said softly. "You should have been the thing he cared about most. You and your happiness."

Kay shrugged. "Have you been through it before?"

Ricky knew plenty about what she was going through. Or at least he assumed as much. He doubted there was much variation in the *treatment*.

He nodded.

"At Hillcrest. That place was a breeze for the most part, but they got frustrated with me toward the end. They show you pictures and give you the shocks if the wrong things get you excited," Ricky said, stumbling a little. It was impossible to phrase without sounding disgusting, but maybe that was the point. "You see a handsome guy and your little soldier goes up? Boom. Shocked. Right where it counts."

That made Kay crack a wry smile. She really was pretty, maybe even prettier than Diana Ross if she could look that angelic with her hair all matted and mangled. "Yup."

"Sometimes I couldn't get my body to cooperate even when I wasn't into their slide show. The things that happen below my belt are not a perfect science," he added, hoping to make her smile again. She did, and even giggled a little.

They were quiet for a while after that, and Ricky jotted down what he could remember of his conversation with Nurse Ash. The one they'd had before she lost her memory or whatever the hell had happened to her. *The warden has a way with people.* He wanted to know what that meant. Maybe he could brainwash her or something. It seemed far-fetched, but he didn't like believing that she was trying to trick or goad him.

The warden is a butcher. The warden is a monster. There, Nurse Ash, I wrote it down so I can't forget it. Happy now?

Kay glanced at him now and again as he wrote, but he didn't mind it. When he was finished, he waited until Nurse Ash took her eyes off him to tear out the page and stuff it in his waistband like he'd done with the patient card. Would they start searching him more thoroughly now? Or did the warden still want to give him special "privileges"?

Shuddering, he scribbled something much more mundane to leave there in the notepad.

"You all right?" Kay asked, her crayon poised in midair.

"Sure," Ricky said. "Actually, no. We're in an asylum, so obviously it's kind of relative, but I'm pretty sure I'm worse than when I got here."

She nodded, slowly, lowering her head closer to the table. It couldn't have been more obvious to the casual onlooker that she was about to whisper something secret.

"Is it the dreams?" she asked, wetting her lips, adding just as softly, "the nightmares?"

"Every night I'm wandering through Brookline. There's this sound like a drum or a heartbeat or something, and I have to follow it, just like the first time when I thought it was really happening. Now I wonder if maybe it was. It *feels* like it was. I can't really tell the difference."

"And you go to the basement," she added, her dark eyes getting bigger and bigger.

"Where there's a little girl . . ."

"In the last cell on the right." Kay sat back hard in her chair, reaching as if to chew the end of her crayon, then remembered what it was and chewed her knuckle instead. "That's one big coincidence."

"I know," Ricky said. Good, Nurse Ash wasn't watching them. Nurse Kramer had distracted her, showing her something on a clipboard. Perfect. "There's more, Kay. A lot more."

"I'm not sure I want to know," she said, wiggling a little in her chair and leaning in. "But from the look on your face I can tell you need to get it off your chest."

"I didn't get a chance to tell you yesterday, but the warden finally pulled me aside. He gave me this big talk about geniuses and how it's sad that they die. I know, don't look at me like that, it didn't make much sense when he said it either. Thing is, it felt like he was singling me out for something. Something strange. He said he doesn't *want* to change me. You know, doesn't make me want to stop liking other guys. What the hell do you think that even means?"

"That doesn't sound right. He wants to change *me*. In fact, he just tried his very best to make it happen. How is that fair?" Her eyes flared with rage, but she glanced away before Ricky could feel it directed at him. Hell, maybe she should hate him. Maybe the fact that he was a "nice" white boy from a nice white family was all it took to earn the warden's favor, but he highly doubted it. John-John seemed to be miserable in his treatment, too.

Ricky still had no idea what the warden's aim for him was.

"It wasn't like I enjoyed it," he said, a little defensive. "He took me down into the basement."

"And?" Kay pressed. "What was there?"

"It was like the dream, but not as scary, I guess. There were orderlies there and someone was banging themselves against a door. The warden was going to show me the room—the one with the girl—and then Nurse Ash showed up and pulled me out of there." God, it sounded completely insane when he said it aloud. It *was* insane. All the same, it felt good to tell someone and to have that someone nod and take him at his word. Even with the light as harsh as it was, there was a kind of angelic glow around Kay; it gave the conversation an air of holiness. Of confession. Unlike any priest Ricky had met, however, Kay's presence put him at ease.

"I swear it's all true," Ricky added softly.

"So what then?"

"She dragged me back to my room, but the warden was mad. I mean, he looked furious. She told me he was bad news, that I shouldn't listen to him or go to the basement with him again. A monster. That's what she called him. A butcher and a monster. She made me promise I wouldn't go to the basement with him again." Yeah. Insane. "Then today it was like none of it ever happened. She acted like I made the whole thing up! It's like they're doing everything they possibly can to make me feel crazy."

Kay fell silent and stayed that way for a long time. Ah. Great. He should've guessed this would happen—the story sounded bizarre even to him, and he had lived it. That momentary confession-like calm would be broken any second. She chewed over his story for a minute or two, twirling her grass-green crayon in her fingers. The fingernails were down to the quick, he could see, and cracked, as if they had been chewed off nervously, as worn as her lower lip.

"What did you stuff down your pants just now?" she asked.

"I wanted to write down everything Nurse Ash told me yesterday. It's all true, Kay, I promise. Why would I make it up?"

"I don't think you would, Ricky. But then again I don't know you all that well. Making friends in here is . . . You know, it's not always easy. Or smart. You get to know someone—like someone—then one day they're gone. They get taken away, get better, or hurt themselves so badly they can't be saved. Which one are you?"

"Taken away," he said flatly. "But because I'm already fine. Because I don't belong here. You know you and I are just different. Different isn't sick."

She let out a huge breath and teetered back toward the table, her sigh winding on and on until she was out of air completely. Then she chewed her fingernail again. She really ought to conquer that bad habit. "So what are you going to do?" she asked.

"You believe me?"

She bounced her head slowly back and forth until it eventually turned into something like a nod. He felt suddenly guilty again—here she had spent the morning in agony and he was unloading all of these heavy stories on her. And she listened. And she believed. Someone that strong was an ally you wanted.

"It's too much to be made up," she said. "Even for you."

"And I don't even take exception to that." They shared a smile, but it was brief. His heart dropped to his stomach and then to the floor: There was a commotion at the door to the multipurpose room, and when the nurses parted, Warden Crawford eased between them and smiled a slow smile. It took him just an instant to find the patient he wanted.

"You still didn't answer my question," Kay prodded.

"What am I going to do? What else would I do? I'm going to get out of here one way or another, and I'm not going alone."

CHAPTER
№ 16

"You want us to do *what*?"

Ricky trailed along behind the warden, trying not to walk too quickly and step on the man's heels. They traveled, or maybe ambled, along the corridor outside the multipurpose room, the warden with his hands tucked behind his back.

"It's a kind of therapy," the warden told him. His voice wasn't deep. It commanded a certain amount of attention, but it was also thin, like the first film of frost over a lake. Floaty and almost light one second, darker and more dangerous the next. Ricky had heard the switch when the warden lost his temper at his brother and later at Nurse Ash, and now Ricky wondered if he would hear it again. But the warden was content to wander and pause, wander and pause, stopping in front of photographs that hung in the hall.

"Some institutions do their utmost to separate patients from one another," he told Ricky. He leaned in close to one of the framed pictures, examining it before reaching over to remove the tiniest speck of dirt from the glass. "I find that approach counterproductive. A functioning member of society can interact with his fellow man. We run that test in miniature here from time to time—marking progress by allowing patients a degree of socialization and cooperation. My entire career has been about finding a kinder, gentler solution to the more barbaric practices of my predecessors."

Kinder. Gentler. That sounded fine with him, especially if it meant never undergoing shock therapy again.

"I guess the others don't seem so bad," Ricky admitted. "Angela and Patty, I mean, they have their moments, but I've never had a problem with them."

"That's very kind of you, Mr. Desmond, thank you."

It wasn't actually a compliment, but sure.

"Yeah," he said, adding the sarcastic edge only in his head. "Anytime."

"Accordingly, you should have no problem organizing a brief tableau for the gala. A skit. Nothing too elaborate. Just a small demonstration of the good work we do here, proof that our patients are stable and improving, and capable of working together."

Being put in charge of the "tableau" felt like another "privilege," and Ricky didn't like it. He didn't know how to respond, and he suspected he would be forced to comply no matter what anyway, but he was saved the trouble when something on the wall caught the warden's eye.

"This. This I love," the warden practically cooed at the photo hanging in the hall.

Ricky stared. He didn't see what there was to love. It was a patient lying down in profile, staring up at the ceiling, with what looked like a pair of scissors held over him.

"Uh . . ."

Run. Hide.

Ricky shivered. Now more than ever he wanted to take that

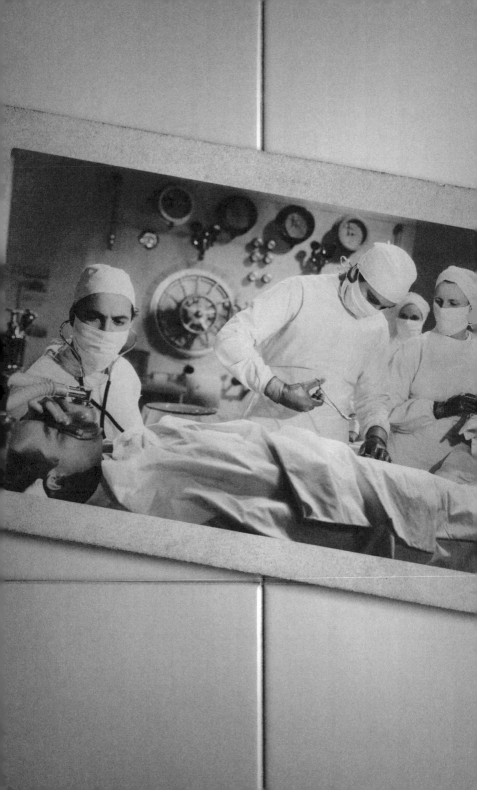

disembodied voice's advice.

"Not your fate, I would imagine," the warden said with a humorless half chuckle. "This isn't my own work, obviously. This doctor was incredibly prolific. He would do dozens of treatments in a day, dozens . . ." He sighed and it sounded almost wistful. "Those days are gone. We've replaced them with more sophisticated methods, but even I can admit there was something admirable about Freeman's enthusiasm. I still hope to meet him someday."

They lapsed into silence, and Warden Crawford didn't look like he was going to stop mooning over the pictures anytime soon. Ricky, still slightly behind him, glanced down at the ever-present clipboard tucked against the doctor's side. The man was just distracted enough . . . Slowly, Ricky shifted to the right, trying to bring himself into a decent sight line with the papers secured to the board. The warden's forearm and wrist covered most of the writing, but Ricky could make out the header above it.

He didn't plan on staying at Brookline, and he would find a way out soon, but his curiosity nagged. What did the warden really think of him? What did they *all* think of him?

It was Ricky's name and patient information in block letters. Nothing unexpected. His eyes scanned downward and he squinted, trying to make out the cramped handwriting that filled line after line. Most of it was in a shorthand he couldn't decipher, but a few bits and pieces were legible.

Smug. Arrogant. All as predicted. Move to P2 soon & 1st dose

Ricky swallowed hard, then snapped his eyes away from the clipboard and took a hasty step back, finding that the warden had, silently and without him noticing, twisted just enough to watch him. It was unsettling, eerie, the way the man's head was the only part of him facing Ricky's direction, as if he were a doll with its head wrenched too far to the side.

Well, if he was so *smug* and *arrogant* then they wouldn't miss him when he hightailed it out of there.

"About this play." Ricky spoke just a little too loudly, hoping the warden hadn't been observing him for too long. He had no idea how to interpret what he had read, but none of it sounded particularly encouraging. Leaving was the only option, and he wanted out *now*. He had to get that phone call home somehow, before P2 and the first dose, whatever that was, happened.

"So . . . Did, um, did you want me to write it myself?"

The warden pulled himself back from the photo distractedly and resolved the odd position of his head, continuing down the hall, a far-off smile on his face. "No, Nurse Ash will give you something to use. I'm confident you'll put on an impressive show."

✗ ✗ ✗ ✗ ✗ ✗

The script was as self-serving and boring as Ricky expected. The only upside was that it gave him an excuse to spend time with Kay, even if it was closely supervised.

"You have four days until the gala," Nurse Ash had said, handing him a stack of small pamphlets. They were the scripts, hand-typed. He noticed a few typos even on the title page.

"Who *wrote* this?" he asked, disgusted. He and the other patients expected to participate had been corralled in the recreation room. Angela and Patty were busy digging through the provided prop and costume boxes.

"The warden," she said with a thin smile. Then softly she winked and added, "I don't think he should quit his day job."

Ricky cracked a smile at that. His company would consist of himself, Kay, Angela, Patty, Dennis, and Tanner. He was relieved Sloane wouldn't be involved—the old man gave him the creeps, and after he'd avoided Ricky for so long, his new staring and grimacing was that much creepier. They congregated around the prop and costume boxes while Ricky looked over the script. It was worse than he'd expected, especially when it came to the dialogue. The characters sounded like talking ads for a psych ward.

"We have to say this stuff in front of actual people?" Kay murmured, frowning down at one of the scripts. "Give me a small part. I don't care if they're strangers watching us. This is just embarrassing."

"You can be Girl Two," Ricky said with a snort. "Such creativity."

"This is ridiculous," Tanner agreed. He had shut his script pamphlet, glaring at the doors to the multipurpose room. Nurse Ash was there, placidly observing them. She didn't notice or else didn't acknowledge the tall silhouette behind her—the warden. Watching. Even from this distance, Ricky could feel the man's gaze on him.

Better not waste time then. He clapped his hands, mimicking the weird theater arts teacher from his high school. Miss Calloway was constantly the butt of jokes, with her huge, dated hairstyle and cat-eye glasses. She looked more like an insect buzzing down the hallways than a theater director. It was the one after-school activity he had tried out for and promptly quit, tired of Butch calling it a "fairy freak show" whenever he returned from rehearsal.

"Joke's on you, Butch, it's fairy freak showtime and you put me here," he said to himself. Which gave him an idea. They were being watched, sure, but he could add a bit of excitement to the skit if he was careful. He leaned in close to Kay, watching Angela and Patty pull on oversized doctors' coats and laugh at each other over it. "Up for breaking the rules one more time?" he asked.

"What did you have in mind?"

"I saw something on the warden's clipboard," he said. "Something about me. I know I said we would get out of here, and I know we have to do it soon, Kay. But I need to get a better look at what they were writing about me, and I'll need your help to do it."

"Why not just leave?" she asked.

"We will." It had the deliberateness of a promise. But he couldn't avoid the sense that the warden was toying with him. Why be so nice and permissive if he really thought Ricky was a smug, arrogant brat? Something was off about that man, about Brookline, and he needed to know just how he figured into it before he left it forever.

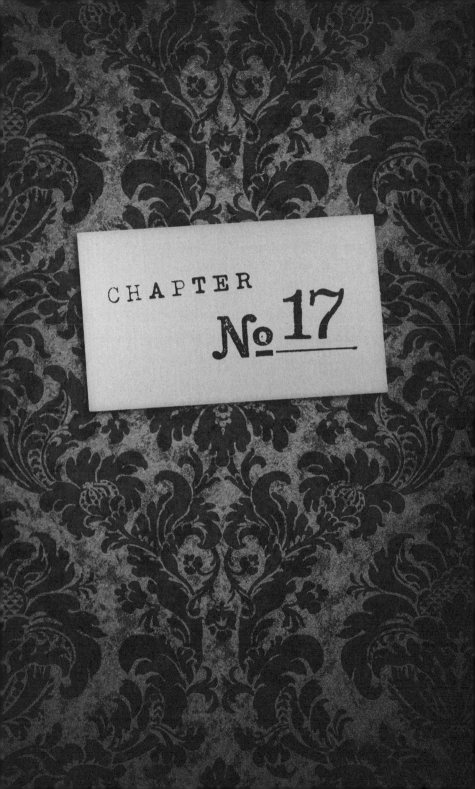

CHAPTER
№ 17

"Is this what you were looking for?"

Nurse Ash paused in the doorway in front of him, reluctant to go in. Ricky didn't blame her—the room was pitch-black.

The last couple days had gone by with surprising swiftness for Ricky. Directing the skit had kept him busy and even amused him. He really had liked those drama classes before Butch, he remembered now. And it was nice to have an activity where they weren't just allowed but encouraged to talk, even if the words they were saying weren't their own, but the warden's.

It had also given him more leeway with the staff. He still didn't have a concrete plan—more like a lot of little ideas, one of which might work—but he wasn't giving up quite yet on his phone call home. With the gala looming, he hoped the flurry of activity and the relaxed scrutiny on him would afford him a good opportunity, and he wanted to be ready for whatever the opportunity might be.

In the meantime, he made his way through rehearsals, meals, and cold nights, always with a jittery feeling in the back of his head. When would P2 come? What was the warden planning to dose him with?

"Hard to tell without any light," Ricky said, and Nurse Ash

hurried ahead and reached for a string that hung from the ceiling. Even with that light on, it was a dark, cavernous expanse, one he hadn't known existed. Attached to the all-purpose room by a damp hallway, it looked more like a shadowy cave than a storage room. Nurse Ash turned on another light farther in, and it flickered, coming gradually to life. He could see now the extra tables and chairs, banquet services, lamps, all veiled in shadows. A few medical practice dummies rose up on stands, lining the only cluttered path through the room. One dummy leaned precariously forward, its head tilted in a way that reminded him of the warden.

Always watched. Always observed.

He shivered and picked his way through the junk littering the floor.

"Do you see anything in here that might work?" the nurse asked. "I know you said you wanted more costumes, but the skit doesn't need to be overly elaborate."

"I thought the warden wanted us to impress," Ricky countered. He was surprised she had allowed him the chance to look through this old storage area. Maybe it was time to reassess his chances of winning her over.

"I'm trying my best here," he added, and he meant it. "You told me to keep my head down and follow the rules. That's exactly what I'm doing. Nurse's orders."

"You're right," Nurse Ash replied. "And I think it's a good sign that you're taking this responsibility so seriously. You have a tendency to be, well . . ."

"Smug?" he ventured, testing. "Arrogant?"

"Hm, those aren't the words I was going to use."

Maybe she hadn't seen the warden's notes then, or they hadn't stuck with her the way they'd stuck with him. "Why don't we say, 'brash'?"

Nurse Ash trailed behind him, her heels clicking softly as she navigated the debris-ridden floor. "I think there could be some old wigs and coats toward the back there. Nurse Kramer told me the staff used to put on a Christmas pageant for the patients in past years."

"Why did they stop?" Ricky asked, dodging under one of the listing medical dummies. It had been labeled and divided into sections, and it reminded him of the way a butcher would carve up an animal.

"One incident or another, I'm sure," she said. "I never did get the whole story."

"Bingo! Here we go." He spied a row of boxes about knee-high, a dark wig visible just below the edge of one. One of his ideas, the one that had led him here, was to cobble together a costume from the available junk that could pass for an orderly's uniform in a pinch. He could use it to slip outside during the gala and run (difficult) or at least get to the reception area to use the phone (still difficult, but not impossible). The appealing bonus in that second option was that he could also track down the warden's notes about him—and hopefully more information about this other Desmond.

(If it looked like neither of those options was going to work, his next idea was to sidle up to the most sympathetic-looking rube at the gala and give his sob story. He really was just a good, misunderstood boy, and would they have a heart and get in touch with Mrs. Desmond on Boylston Street and let her know how dearly her loving boy wanted to come home?)

His stomach turned as he thought of Kay's chances in any of those ideas. How would he manage to get her out of Brookline? He kept telling himself that if he could get out, then he would have the time, resources, and freedom to engineer a more daring escape plan for her.

For now, he was looking for anything resembling the crisp, white uniform shirts the male orderlies wore. A wig would help, too, if he wanted to dash out the door and down the driveway unmolested.

The lightbulb behind him sputtered, crackling as it gave another surge and managed to stay on. Nurse Ash tripped on something and swore under her breath. He could hear footsteps through the ceiling above him, slow, shuffling, like someone was wandering back and forth, a muffled staccato that penetrated the thick walls and even thicker dance of dust motes in the storage area. He wondered how many places like this there were in Brookline, darker, dirtier rooms that belied the sanitized white exterior.

He climbed over a closed cardboard box, nearing the little tuft of hair visible a few yards away. It was darker here, beyond the reach of the dying light. That scratchy, choking feeling of dust clogging his throat set in, reminding him of the almost unbreathable air in the file closet. But he was near his goal and he went to it quickly, eager to get back to the light with whatever he found.

Ricky rounded the corner of boxes and ground to a stop, feeling the blood in his veins run short and cold. A man? A corpse? No, a man, pale and fragile and bone-thin, sat in the little hollow space made by the boxes. His hands were wrapped around his knees, pulling them tight to his chest, and he heard Ricky at once. The untidy mop of dark hair on his head ruffled and then his head snapped up and he gawked, mouth hanging open, at Ricky. His eyes were huge, black, leaking murky tears.

"I'm so sorry, don't put me in the basement again," the man hissed, his cheeks lined with welts, tracks where fingernails had scored the flesh. His hand trembled as he held up a scalpel, blood running thick down his fingers. "I've been so good. I've done everything you asked! I've done everything you asked, just don't make me do this. I can't! I'm sorry, so sorry . . ."

"Ricky! Ricky?"

Someone was holding him by the arm and shaking him. He suddenly couldn't tell if he was staring down at the skeletal man or if he was down there on the floor with him, collapsed. Yes, he was definitely on the floor. He could feel the freezing cement under his palm and the coating of dust that floated over his knuckles. How had he fallen down? Nurse Ash was still shaking him, then thrusting her hand against his forehead to feel for a fever.

The man was gone.

"I saw . . ." *No, don't tell them. They're not your friends. They can't know.* "I just felt so dizzy all of a sudden," he lied.

"You're ice-cold," Nurse Ash whispered. "No fever. Did you eat at breakfast?"

"No," he lied again. "I . . . wasn't hungry. I guess I got a bit faint or something."

"I'll say. You dropped like a sack of bricks. What were you saying?" she asked, helping him gradually to his feet.

"Saying?" Ricky flapped his mouth for a few seconds, staring at the blank spot on the ground where the man had been nestled against the boxes. He could swear there was a depression there in the thick film of dust. "I don't think I said anything."

"You shouted something before you collapsed," she said fretfully, holding tight to both his arms as she steered him away from the boxes. There was no wig, he saw now. There never had been one. "It sounded so afraid, Ricky. It sounded like: *Help*."

CHAPTER № 18

*T*he cafeteria was lit warmly for a change, the air heavy with savory, herbaceous sauces, and roasting meat. Hors d'oeuvres, glistening with butter, shimmered on the banquet tables lining the outer perimeter of the cafeteria-turned-ballroom.

The smell, the kind that would normally make his mouth water, left him feeling pit-stomached and sick. He really hadn't eaten much at all today. Or the day before. His feet felt leaden in the heavy shoes provided for the patients for tonight and tonight only. He stood, numb and nervous, with his back to the wall.

"Shameless," Kay said at his side. She and the other patients allowed into the warden's gala were dressed in simple white shirts and slacks for the men, the same shirts and black, modest skirts for the women. Kay shifted in her trousers, looking miserable. It was a palpable insult from the warden, but Ricky had made sure to emerge from his fog of nerves to tell her she still looked pretty, even without the skirt. All the patients waited anxiously, watching the guests mingle and cram their faces with food. He'd been keeping an eye out for a sympathetic-looking guest, but so far he hadn't spotted a single one. Kay seemed to agree. "They're all so oblivious. I don't think we're even people to them. Do you think these clowns ever lose sleep over this kind of thing?"

"No. They go home and sleep soundly on their beds made of money and get up again without a care in the world. Anyway, look at the banner." He pointed to a giant, paper banner that was painted festively and hanging over the doors to the common area.

SAVE OUR SICK—BETTER FOOD AND BEDS FOR BROOKLINE

"They think they're doing us a favor," Ricky said. "Not that I would complain about better food . . ."

"Yeah, well, I think they're miserable. They just don't know it."

Ricky managed a grin at that. "Always looking on the bright side."

"When do we get this play over with?" she asked. Their meager props were hidden in a cloth laundry bag on Ricky's other side. His players looked to him anxiously for direction. He didn't know what to do until the play, and avoided their eyes.

"Soon, hopefully," he said. Having failed to cobble together a convincing disguise, he was desperately scanning the room, hoping for a sign that the orderlies were letting their guard down—that he could make it out of here unnoticed. "Are you still in?"

"Sure, but I'm losing my nerve by the minute over here," Kay said softly. "It would be a shame to impress everybody and then ruin all the goodwill if your scheming doesn't work."

"If my scheming doesn't work, I think we'll both have a lot more to worry about, Kay. It's starting to feel like now or never."

He hadn't told her about seeing the ghost or whatever it was in the storage closet. The fear that was gnawing at him, almost as much as whatever the warden had written on that clipboard of his, was that the longer he stayed in here, the more he *needed* to be in here. Brookline was driving him insane.

"If I . . . if I don't make a break for it, I don't want that to stop you from running," she murmured, looking at the floor.

"Kay. You know I would never just leave you in here. There has to be a way for us both to escape. You can give me a list of your relatives, the good ones, and maybe they can check you out." It was thin, and they both knew it. It was unlikely that anybody but her father would have the authority to pull her out of Brookline.

The warden entered from the doors to their left, effectively silencing their conversation. And not just theirs. The guests began to notice, a whisper of interest snaking through the crowd. Ricky couldn't believe how many people had come. Most were older, but he spied a few young men and women, too. One woman practically sprinted up to the warden as he arrived. She was short and curvaceous, with dark hair and a heavy jumble of necklaces hanging over her blouse. If he guessed correctly, she couldn't have been older than college-aged.

By design, surely, the guests wore only black and white, but here and there Ricky noticed splashes of red hidden on a lapel or lady's neckline. They were little red pins, but not everyone wore them.

The warden eschewed the drink and food, at once plunging into conversation with the dark-haired young woman who had intercepted him.

Ricky wasn't much interested in what they had to say to each other. He turned his attention instead to the doors. There was no music, but the hushed conversations around the room provided a soft soundtrack as he weighed his options. A single orderly stood at the doors, watchful, but not too concerned with his post, judging from the way his gaze strayed to the dark-haired woman draped over the warden.

Nurses milled among the guests, most of them wearing cracking smiles as they put up with the strain of playing waitress for the evening.

It wasn't lax supervision, especially not with Nurse Ash stationed close to them, though he did feel like a lot of nurses and orderlies *weren't* here. Maybe after the skit he'd have more luck charming a guest; so far none of them had strayed close to the patients. Ricky and his players were being observed and whispered about from a safe distance. Sure, these were the "tame" patients, but they were patients in an asylum all the same.

Most of the nurses and orderlies were probably spread out among the rooms elsewhere, keeping patients quiet and subdued so as not to disturb the guests. Order and discipline. That was the Brookline way.

If the smallest thing went wrong, Ricky knew the warden would snap his team into speedy action. After all this work and preparation, nothing would be allowed to go wrong.

"I'll make sure they save you all some cake for your hard work," Nurse Ash said, leaning toward them and giving an encouraging smile. "I can't wait to see how the skit came together."

"Are we going to begin soon?" Patty asked. She stood next to Kay, looking increasingly anxious. Her white shirt didn't fit very well, and on her short, squat frame, the long skirt that should have been ankle-length brushed the floor. Her big, blue eyes were a little crossed, as if she needed glasses to correct her vision but wasn't allowed them in the asylum. "The play . . . How long will they make us wait like this? I'm starving . . ."

"I'm sure it won't be long," Tanner said next to her. He stared straight ahead, his eyes narrowed and focused, as if he was trying his absolute best to shut out the chatter and smells.

Across the room, the dark-haired woman threw back her head and laughed riotously at something the warden was saying. She had a gap in her teeth so noticeable, Ricky could see it from here. He watched her disappear out the doors, where the last guests were trickling in. A moment later she returned, carrying a small gong and a drumstick with a soft, rounded end. She held up the gong and struck it twice, beaming at the room.

At once the guests fell silent, and Ricky felt like he had been left out of some kind of clubhouse.

"Formalities," the warden said, almost apologetically. "If the top-tier donors could follow me . . ."

He wore a formal black coat and white shirt with an almost nonexistent collar. A small, red pin flashed where a pocket square might go. Ricky watched a dozen or so of the guests separate themselves from the larger crowd and leave in single file. All of them, he noticed, wore those bright red pins.

"We have to wait longer?" Patty whined, fidgeting. Kay tried to put a calming hand on the woman's shoulder, but it was immediately shrugged off. "We warmed up ages ago. Maybe we should use it before we lose it. They brought us in here to put on a show, didn't they?"

Ricky couldn't tell if it was a gleam of mischief or anger in Patty's eye.

A tall, handsome man with a ready smile and reddish-brown hair strode forward ahead of the rest, extending a hand to the warden, who shook it before ushering out the rest of the Red Pins.

"Where do you suppose they're going?" Kay murmured.

"To count their money? Who knows? This might be the distraction I wanted," he said.

Nurse Ash made eye contact with him and smiled, then gestured toward the middle of the room, signaling for him to start the play.

He rushed over to her, half choking on the cloud of flowery perfume sitting over the guests. "The warden isn't even here," Ricky whispered. "Shouldn't we wait?"

"He'll be back soon, I'm sure. Things are running a bit behind schedule, so why don't you get started?"

Ricky nodded. He didn't want to care if the warden missed out on their stupid little show, but it irked him that the man would ask him to manage the whole thing and then completely miss it.

He turned to his cast, all of them looking completely uninterested but for Patty, who squirmed in anticipation of beginning.

"Here goes nothing," he mouthed to them.

"If I could have your attention," Nurse Ash was saying, waving her hand above the crowd to try to quiet them. "Warden Crawford has asked some of his most improved patients to put on a brief play for you all. I'm sure they would appreciate it if you gave them your full attention."

Ricky recognized the looks staring back at him—the expectant, mildly annoyed stare of parents forced to watch their rambunctious kids sing in the annual Christmas concert or orchestra performance. Almost all their heads cocked condescendingly to the side, lips pursed, the words "Well, aren't you just too adorable" projected silently at them.

He cleared his throat and took his place in the empty area they had cleared for the patients. Holding a piece of cardboard that simulated a clipboard, he tucked his fist thoughtfully under his chin, delivering his first line. "A physician's work is never done. Heal the ailing. Tend to the injured and downtrodden. But to tend to the ill of mind?" He made an exaggerated A-HA! and nodded. "The mysteries of the soul and mind are the greatest mysteries of all."

Polite, soft applause chased around the room. He turned to his right, to the back of the room, seeking out Kay so he could give her the line cue. "My first patient of the day!" he cried, hating every dumb word that came out of his mouth. "How exciting! The first mystery to be examined!"

But Kay wasn't listening or even preparing for her entrance. She was too busy trying to pull Patty back to the wall with the rest of them. Apparently the songstress had grown tired of waiting. With the nurses busy with their trays and the orderlies in other rooms, Patty broke away and into the thick of the crowd.

The guests billowed back, giving her a wide berth. A few giggled and pointed, and Ricky distinctly heard a man say to his wife, "Oh, fun! Look, they're starting their little show!"

Patty lifted her arms, half singing and half reciting a speech, her voice booming with Shakespearean clarity off the vaulted ceiling. Nurse Ash ran for her, and the other nurses scrambled to put down their trays without spilling and assist.

"How delightful are the pleasures of the imagination! In those delectable moments, the whole world is ours; not a single creature resists us," Patty bellowed, her cheeks red with the excitement of it all. The attention. "We devastate the world, we repopulate it with new objects which, in turn, we immolate. The means to every crime is ours, and we employ them all, we multiply the horror a hundredfold."

As she reached her crescendo, two nurses corralled her, no doubt trying their best to talk her down and keep from injecting her into silence while so many eyes watched.

"What do we do?" Kay gasped, covering her mouth.

"We let her keep going," Ricky said, seeing his chance. Nobody was left standing near the doors. "And we thank her later for the showstopping performance."

Kay shook her head once, quickly, sadly. It stung a little, but he didn't have time to hesitate. If he didn't go now, he might never escape.

CHAPTER

№ 19

*R*icky skirted the edge of the commotion, leaving Kay behind with the other patients. He couldn't blame her for not coming along—the chance of being seen or caught was high, and it only got higher if they went together. As he neared the doors, he glanced back at her, watching as she tried to comfort Dennis, who had become agitated from the noise and turned, facing the wall and leaning his forehead against it.

Patty was not going down quietly. She fought off the nurses who tried to subdue her smack in the middle of the room. He thought maybe she glanced at him and smiled, but by then he was out the doors and in the hall, breathing a sigh of relief to find it completely empty.

Moving quickly, he followed the corridor as it hooked around toward the lobby. Here he was more careful. The entrance to the lobby, a single tall door with a metal mesh window and heavy lock, was never left unattended. The door was closed, certainly, and locked, but the lobby beyond was low-lit and quiet now that all the guests were inside. As far as he could tell, nobody manned the station.

He took advantage of his good luck, rubbing his sweaty palms on his borrowed trousers and passing by the lobby door. It wasn't difficult to find the offices from here. The hall only went one way, despite plenty of doors on either side, before ending at the heavy door that led to the reception area and then down to the basement level. Ricky felt a prickle of cold at the back of his neck and slowed, remembering the voice that seemed to be following him around the asylum. It always came with that unearthly chill. Now it visited him again and he let it pass through him, determined, ignoring the goose bumps rising along his arms as he stopped outside the warden's office.

It was dark inside. Dark, but the door was unlocked. He didn't know if that was a mistake on the staff's part or an arrogant assumption that the gala would go off without a hitch. Whatever the case, Ricky didn't think twice about going inside. He had come this far, and he doubted the punishment would be much different for sneaking into a specific office than it would be for having snuck out at all. And he *wouldn't* get caught, he reminded himself.

He rushed to the tidy desk, clicking on the light and locating the warden's clock. He allowed himself three minutes. Even that felt like a risk. But whatever he unearthed would have to be put back again. If he didn't make it out tonight, the warden couldn't know he had been snooping around. So he worked feverishly, opening drawers at random, searching for the clipboard, a notepad, anything he could riffle through.

The bottom drawer of the desk on the right-hand side held a file organizer with about fifty brown folders. Tabs at the top displayed last names that filed back alphabetically. He found "DESMOND, R" and yanked it out of the drawer. This was it, and he had at least two minutes left to put everything back in order and leave. He tapped the folder open and—

Empty.

Ricky stared at the place where dozens and dozens of helpful notes should have been but there was nothing. Panicking, he picked out another folder at random. That one, of course, was practically overflowing with charts, records, handwritten observations . . .

He felt that odd, cold miasma envelop him again and froze. Either he was imagining it or there were footsteps coming from down the hall. Luckily he had closed the door behind him. He clicked off the desk lamp and stood in the darkness, listening, breathing raggedly. The footsteps were coming closer.

Run, the disembodied voice whispered hoarsely in his ear again. *Hide*.

CHAPTER
№ 20

*R*icky shut the desk drawer as quietly as he dared and ducked down under the desk, wedging himself against the corner. It was the kind of desk with the flat front and a big, hollowed out space on the other side for your legs and feet. He hid in that space, knees to his chest, clutching the two folders.

For a moment he thought maybe the footsteps had simply been in his head, but no, the door opened, a soft creak giving it away. He held his breath, shivering, helpless, waiting to be discovered.

Three separate pairs of footsteps entered, and he felt the room fill up with bodies. One pair of feet was wearing heels, he could tell, from the exaggerated clicking. All three of them congregated in front of the desk, just a few inches of wood barrier separating them from his head.

"Bit lax on the security, Crawford. You don't even lock your door these days?" a man asked. He had a deep voice, a little snide and haggard, as if maybe he smoked regularly.

"Don't be ridiculous, Roger, nothing happens here that I don't see." It was the warden.

"Can we get to the goods? There are a few canapés and cute nurses back there with my name on 'em."

Ricky heard the warden sigh and move closer to the desk. He

held his breath tighter, listening as the man leaned his weight onto the desk, half sitting on it. The wood groaned, deafening to him as he tried not to make a sound, as he tried to disappear into the desk itself.

"Phase Two will begin soon, Roger, I assure you," the warden said, sounding put-upon.

"Soon? Why not tomorrow? What's the hesitation? Do you know how many palms I had to grease to get those facilities to cough up a name? I had to mail those Brookline pamphlets to the kid's parents six times. *Six*. And now every day wasted is another day I'm paying for the electricity in this place. This whole thing is becoming too costly."

"Warden Crawford knows what he's doing," the woman said, mirroring the warden's irritation. "What's that saying? You can't rush perfection?"

"Well, he certainly rushed with you," Roger sniped back.

"That's enough," the warden cut in. "Carie, I appreciate your support, but I can speak for myself in this matter. Phase Two has been postponed because the subject is unusually cooperative and docile this time. It's a good sign, naturally, a willing Patient Zero is the goal. My previous attempts were by necessity less ambitious; they were the groundwork, not the complete project. I simply want ample time to observe him before moving forward with the treatment. These are human beings we're talking about, Roger, not lab mice. They are complex. Complicated. What is becoming too costly is the further acquisition of suitable specimens."

"I'll be dean soon," Roger told him, equally exasperated. "You can have your pick then. I *will* be dean soon, won't I?"

"The warden is stacking the committee but these things take time," the woman, Carie, answered. "You can't just snap your fingers and get that kind of power."

"Not now, at least," Roger added with a rasping chuckle. "Do you always let her talk to you like this?"

"I appreciate her unfiltered input."

"That makes one of us. Fine. Fine. Just hurry this along, all right? Phase Two needs to start sooner rather than later," Roger barked. "I don't want any surprises down the line. I want this technique of yours absolutely perfected. This kind of money pays for perfect, Crawford, not sloppiness."

Food and beds for Brookline my ass, Ricky thought bitterly. He wondered if all the guests knew what their funds were really raising or just the "top donors."

Ricky heard footsteps clap toward the door.

"Now if you'll excuse me," Roger said, "I'll be seeing about those canapés."

The door opened and closed. Ricky relaxed a little, forgetting that there were still two people in the room, one of whom was perched directly above him.

"Jerk," he heard the woman mutter.

"Yes," Warden Crawford agreed. "But a useful one. How are you feeling? Headaches? Nosebleeds?"

"I'm fine," she assured him. "Now tell me more about this new subject. Can I meet him?"

"In good time, Carie. In good time. There will be plenty of time for you to see him after his transformation begins."

The door flying open sounded like a gunshot. Ricky started, hoping against hope that the warden didn't hear or feel him jump under the desk.

"Nurse Ash? What is it?" the warden demanded. His weight eased off the desk, and the next moment he was stomping across the office.

"You had . . . It's . . . Sir, you had better come and see."

The office emptied as quickly as it had filled and Ricky finally released his breath. He squeezed his eyes shut for a moment, barely believing his own luck. Then he crawled out from his hiding spot and carefully replaced the folders, making sure to find the correct place in alphabetical order. He padded silently to the door, which had been left open, and glanced into the hall. It sounded like the commotion from the cafeteria was beginning to spill into the rest of the asylum.

He slipped out into the corridor and ran back down toward the lobby, trying to push past the guests who were pouring out, scandalized. They streamed around him, ignoring him, and finally Ricky sidled against the wall of the cafeteria, watching the chaos unfold as the warden tried to take control of the situation. Dennis had begun banging his fists on the wall, roaring in outrage when three orderlies tried to muzzle him and drag him to the ground. He very nearly fought them all off, throwing his huge arms around, pounding one of the orderlies so hard in the head the man crumpled to the floor. Patty had finally been sedated and silenced, but now Angela was in hysterics over her friend being tackled.

His eyes scanned for Kay, but it was Nurse Ash who found him first. He felt rather than saw her, a ferocious little hand clamping around his wrist.

"Where were you?" she demanded.

Two last guests thundered past them, the woman sobbing into her husband's handkerchief.

"What are you talking about?" Ricky scrambled to think up a good story.

"Where were you?" Nurse Ash said again. He had never seen her so angry. "And this time, don't lie."

CHAPTER

№ 21

"What is Phase Two?"

Nurse Ash had only just finished pushing him into his room. She froze as she reached to close the door. Her head lowered a little, her shoulders hunched, like an animal catching wind of a distant, alarming scent.

Finally, she said, "I have to go back to see if the warden needs assistance isolating the other patients."

"Just tell me, I can handle it," Ricky said, still standing. Out in the hall, he could hear the chaos of the evening dwindling, the warden's voice carrying as he tried to reassure and calm the last lingering guests. "What is Phase Two? Is something going to happen to me?"

She made to leave but thought better of it, apparently, instead shutting the door to cut off the noise in the corridor. Her gaze wasn't friendly, but she didn't seem angry now, just wary.

"Okay," Nurse Ash said carefully. She straightened up, no longer the frightened animal, and crossed her arms over her nurse's coat. "Enough of this. I know you left the party tonight. Where did you go?"

Ricky shook his head. His palms were still sweaty with nerves, and he could feel a tightness building in his chest. This was what it always felt like before he lost his temper—the surge of adrenaline, the sudden urge to slam his fist into something. It couldn't be her, he wouldn't even consider attacking her, but he felt dangerous. Wired. "I'm not answering your questions if you refuse to answer mine."

"You are a *patient* here, Ricky. How many times do you need to be reminded? This is a facility. There are rules. Where did you go?" Her eyes flared but she didn't raise her voice. "What did you see?"

He knew it. She wasn't his friend. She was one more person who would sell him out in a heartbeat—one in a long line that included his dad, his parents, the boys at school. He wanted to scream. Now, he realized, getting any assistance or sympathy whatsoever was a lost cause. The warden was planning to do something to him and he still had no idea what. Phase Two. A dose of . . . *something*. And he had his buddies involved, too, somehow. That made it worse. What had the warden called him? A specimen?

He sat down hard on his crummy mattress and stared straight ahead. "It doesn't matter, does it? What I saw or heard . . . My mom isn't coming back for me this time, is she? I really screwed up."

It wasn't an act. His limbs felt shaky. Defeat or resignation, whatever it was, it felt terrible. And now he had snuck out, gotten caught, and for what? So he could hear one more person's plans for him. Plans he could neither understand nor stop.

"You attacked your stepfather," Nurse Ash said, her tone shifting. Now she sounded kind. She was bargaining. She walked toward him, stopping at the edge of his bed. She was so young. How had she come to be a nurse so young? The job was already wearing on her, he could tell, the lines at her eyes and around her mouth too deep for someone her age. What was it like, he wondered, to work at a place like this, to watch people your own age suffering or just wasting time, counting the days of their youth they would never get back?

"You hurt him," she reiterated. "It's not a joke, Ricky. You went through two treatment facilities before this one. You have a serious problem with your temper, you know, and your family is worried about you. The going out at all hours, skipping class, the . . ."

"Boys," he muttered.

"Your parents brought you here for a reason," she said. "Can't you try and understand that?"

"I do," Ricky said, and he meant it. "Yes. You're right. I have a problem with my temper. But I don't feel like I'm getting treated for that here. Something is going on. You can tell me whatever you want but I know it's true. You can't seem to decide if you're on my side or the warden's. I don't know who those friends of his are or what Phase Two is but I know when I'm being lied to. I'm not a child."

"Rick—"

Nurse Ash snapped her head sharply to the side, hearing what he did—a loud, anguished scream from the basement below them. Her cheeks turned bright red at the sound. Good. She heard it, too. It was the perfect punctuation mark.

He turned away and lay down on the mattress, lying flat on his back. "You can give me a dose of whatever, you can try to shut me up or change me. But I know the warden is hiding something. That you're *all* hiding something. I'll find a way out of here and I won't forget who helped me and who didn't."

There was still the little piece of paper he had saved with her remarks on it. Monster. Butcher. No, he wouldn't forget. Now there were other words bouncing around in his head thanks to the warden. Specimen, dose, transformation.

Ricky took a deep breath and closed his eyes. He was afraid, deeply afraid now that the anger was gone, but he couldn't let her see that. "I'd like to be alone."

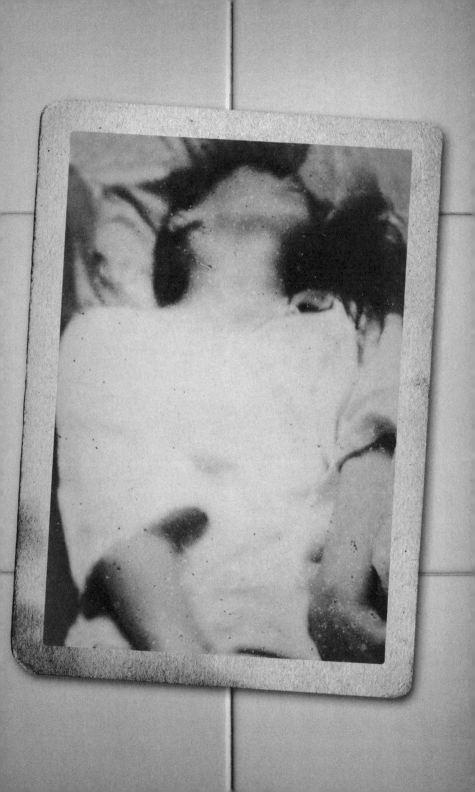

CHAPTER
№ 22

*I*n-room isolation lasted for two days. By the end of it, Ricky was almost glad to see the warden again when he opened the cell door. The man stood watching his patient for a long moment, calculating something. His spectacles shimmered in the bright light of the corridor, the glass so reflective that Ricky couldn't make out the man's eyes, just white circles.

"I think everyone has calmed down since that unfortunate outburst," the warden said coolly. He sounded like a disappointed parent. "Why don't you come with me so we can discuss your interpretation of those events."

Ricky dragged himself out of bed and shuffled to the door. He hadn't bathed in two days and his hair was rumpled and oily. His patient's trousers and shirt were new but had already begun to take on the stench of his unwashed body. Silently, his jaw locked in place, Ricky followed the warden out of his room.

"I gather that you and Keith Waterston are becoming close," the man said.

Ricky no longer mistook this for polite conversation. He'd decided he wouldn't take anything the staff said as simple chitchat. It was all intentional. It was all invasive.

"I make friends easily," Ricky said without emotion.

They snaked through the corridors leading from the

recreation room at the south end of the building down the stairs to the lobby and then left, leaving behind the relative tranquility of the waiting chairs and magazine-strewn tables to the administration hall. A group of nurses had gathered at the dispensary and fell silent as the warden walked by with Ricky in tow.

"That's certainly true. Nurse Ash is fond of you, too," the warden said.

"I don't know," Ricky said, feigning indifference with a shrug. "She seems to treat everyone the same."

"Mm. She speaks highly of you, though. Cooperative patients are a blessing. You are also not far from her age and good-looking. Young ladies notice you, Ricky. Surely you notice them, too?"

Did that mean she never ratted on Ricky for having left the gala room? He'd assumed that was the reason for his isolation, but maybe everyone had been isolated as punishment for the commotion. The warden didn't seem angry, so maybe she really hadn't mentioned any of their conversation that night to him.

"I'm not in here to find a date," Ricky said. "I have . . . issues with my temper. It makes me act out. I am here to treat those issues."

"That's very mature of you." He sounded actually impressed, like he bought it. "And you're right, of course. All we have to do is get control of your impulses to anger, and you will be good to go."

The warden ate one of his mints as he led them through his office door. He showed no sign of slowing, which meant they were going back to the basement. Was this Phase Two? Was it time for the dose? Ricky tried not to panic, but at the same time, he felt—as he had during their first interview—strangely encouraged by the warden's words. He squinted at the man's back, and he tried to make an assessment of the man based on the small handful of moments he'd spent with him. Maybe Nurse Ash was mad, too. Maybe working in this place had gotten to her like it was getting to him.

Warden Crawford didn't *seem* like a threat, but Ricky knew it was dangerous to trust any adult promising something that sounded way too good to be true, and keeping him in an asylum with no intention of addressing his "perversion," as Butch liked to call it , was way, way too good to be true. He knew it was only a half-truth, anyway—he doubted the "transformation" the warden had spoken of on the night of the gala was as minor as he was making it sound now. The crushing confusion of it all hung heavy on Ricky's shoulders.

He slowed his steps accordingly.

"Why are we going back down there?" he asked.

"You sound nervous, Mr. Desmond."

The warden's heavy footfalls already echoed on the steps. He didn't hesitate and he didn't wait for Ricky to keep up.

"Maybe I *am* nervous."

"Don't be nervous. I've stated my intentions, haven't I? A kinder, gentler future for medicine, remember? You have nothing to fear from me," he said. It was a caring voice. A fatherly sort of voice, low and filled with wisdom, plus something that resembled cheer. "I'm simply taking you to see a fellow patient."

"Who?"

Was it Kay? His mind raced. What if while he had been subjected to in-room isolation, she had been dragged down here for something even worse than shock therapy? He was jumping to conclusions, yes, and panicking, too. But he couldn't help himself.

The warden's sudden, sharp bark of laughter startled Ricky, and he stumbled a little on the steps. Automatically and quickly, the warden swiveled and caught his arm, steadying him. He continued down the stairs without a hitch. "Just full of questions today, aren't we? Where is your sense of adventure, Mr. Desmond? Your sense of *mystery*."

His sense of mystery was all he could think about lately. Ricky kept his mouth shut and followed. He began to shake from the cold, feeling acutely how long it had been since he'd enjoyed real sunlight. The way down seemed darker this time, but he knew what to expect and didn't stumble again. He wondered how the patients down here even survived. How did they get through the nights when he was freezing after five minutes?

Down they went, farther and farther. He had forgotten how long it took. It seemed faster, or at least more urgent, in his vision, always that booming heartbeat luring him forward.

When they reached the lower ward, the warden pulled one of the milling orderlies aside and pointed to the way they had come. Protection. He didn't want them to be interrupted again. Ricky doubted Nurse Ash would show up this time. He pressed his lips together, staring up at the orderly as he lumbered by. The man didn't spare him a glance, going to his post and manning it like a statue of a sentry.

They stopped outside the second door on the left. The ward was mostly silent this time, but still Ricky's glance strayed to the last door on the right. Was she in there right now, the girl from his dream? He turned his attention back to the warden, afraid to be caught staring.

The door scraped open, shrieking, so heavy even the solidly built warden had trouble with it. A minty breath gusted down toward Ricky as the man sighed with exertion, and then Ricky was peering inside, hopeless against the tide of curiosity.

"Ah, excellent," the warden drawled, motioning inside the cell. "Here is our little star. You remember Patty, of course. I thought you might like to see how she's doing after that extraordinary *performance*."

CHAPTER
№ 23

*T*he cell was not appointed the way Ricky would have expected. It was bright, for the moment, with almost blindingly white surgical lamps set up on either side of a hospital gurney.

Patty lay strapped down to the bed, her almost-crossed eyes darting in every direction. They landed on Ricky and her mouth dropped open in surprise. Their expressions matched, he assumed, because he felt like he was intruding—not just on Patty but on some kind of serious surgery. Nurse Ash stood next to the patient, looking miserable, her hands fidgeting with a full syringe. A metal table had been set up next to the bed, holding a few surgical implements scattered across a piece of clean paper.

"Patty was making steady improvement, but it was slow progress," the warden said. "With progress that slow, it becomes much easier to fall back. Sometimes, as hard as it may be, we need to help a patient make a leap forward. The gentler approaches are not always effective. You try, you fail, you come to grips with your limitations concerning certain defects of the mind."

All warmth or sense of friendliness was gone from his voice. He didn't sound like a disappointed father anymore but cold and removed, as if he'd learned how to be a human from a medical textbook. His eyes were hollow as he looked down at Patty. She struggled on the bed, but only until the warden raised his hand and gestured to the nurse, who hesitated before sliding the needle of the syringe into Patty's arm.

The door was open behind Ricky, but he could feel the solid bulk of the orderly as he moved to stand in the way, to watch. Ricky was trapped.

"What . . . What are you doing to her?" he asked. His sense of self-preservation rose swiftly, and he began to tremble. How was this the first alternative to kind and gentle? Everything the warden had said about his limitations was so unfair. Patty was the vulnerable one here. Ricky couldn't help picturing himself on that same gurney, strapped down. Patients had died in this hospital. He knew that. He had seen the patient cards for himself.

"This procedure was invented in Portugal, but refined here. It was once a much messier business, drilling actual holes into the skull and such," the warden explained nonchalantly. His voice was utterly dispassionate as he waited for the anesthesia to take effect, and he picked up a long, slender object that looked like an enormous nail.

The light caught its silver finish, a bead of white sliding down it like a tear.

"Walter Freeman perfected the procedure, honed it." The warden admired the nail implement for a moment and then drew closer to Patty, waiting until Nurse Ash took a deep breath and positioned the woman's face, tilting it up slightly. Ricky could see directly into her nose.

"Now there was a brilliant man, but never satisfied," the

warden rambled. Ricky couldn't believe what he was seeing, or that Nurse Ash could so calmly assist. Who was the monster now, he thought viciously, his fingers curling into fists. This was the secret, he thought, this dark, horrible basement and the things that went on in it.

Deceased, deceased, deceased . . .

"Never satisfied," the warden reiterated. "Rather like me!" He vented a dry laugh. "It's much simpler now. Much more humane. The transorbital lobotomy was a revolution. Some call it out-of-date, barbaric—myself included, I think there are better ways now—but it is still considered a last resort when medicine fails someone like Patty."

Ricky bolted forward. He had to stop this. Patty had been his distraction, hadn't she? And part of him wondered if she had done it intentionally to mess with the warden's big night. He respected that. He admired it. He didn't want to fail her. The orderly caught his shoulders from behind, wrestling him back.

"It will be over quickly," the warden assured him. He raised the spike without warning and Ricky flinched, closing his eyes tightly. The sounds were just as bad. He heard a sharp intake of breath, then a tap and an unmistakable crunch. There was a pause and then the same sound again. It chilled him through to the core and he shivered, his head suddenly pounding. A scream rose out from the hallway behind them, from the other cells. It sounded like rage. Like sympathy. It started with a little girl's scream, muffled by a heavy door. Other voices joined in, rising in the same horrible chorus he'd heard in his vision.

He wished he could clamp his hands over his ears but the orderly held him fast.

The minutes crawled by. He didn't dare open his eyes.

If only he could shut out the screaming, the wailing . . .

"There now. That wasn't so bad, was it? She'll be right as rain once the anesthesia wears off. I think we can expect better behavior in her future."

She had hardly behaved poorly before, Ricky thought. She might not even have been ill at all. Patty just liked to sing, and she had a beautiful voice. He would sing, too, if he had a voice like hers. He remembered how on weekends sometimes Martin would play the guitar for him in the park, and he would start to sing along, acting totally serious. He was awful, couldn't carry a tune even if he knew all the words, and they would dissolve into laughter over it every time. He wanted to hide inside that memory, fold it around himself like a warm blanket, but he could feel the palpable chill of the cell breaking through. When Ricky opened his eyes, the warden was beaming proudly from over his patient, oblivious to the muffled screams filling the basement.

Nurse Ash caught his eye, and he knew the depths of her regret. She looked as trapped, as remorseful, as he felt standing there, Patty limp and sleeping on the gurney before them.

CHAPTER
№ 24

"I don't understand," Ricky said, staring. He no longer struggled against the orderly holding him up, but sagged. If they were going to try to strap him down to that goddamn gurney, he would use every ounce of energy he had to fight back.

"Yes, you do," the warden told him gently. He set down the spike on the tray and moved to the end of the table, putting a hand on Patty's ankle. "Patty was an instigator—a threat to the health of our other patients. We don't tolerate that here."

We punish it. Ricky finished the implied threat for him. He glanced at Nurse Ash again, who looked away, her face pale. The orderly let go of him. This was not his fate. It was not his fate because Nurse Ash had kept quiet. He didn't feel grateful, exactly, but he was relieved. Why couldn't she have intervened on behalf of Patty?

"Nurse Ash, stay with the patient, please. Update me when she comes to."

"Yes, sir," she said in a tiny voice.

Ricky fought a wave of repulsion-fueled nausea. Not for the warden—whom he was now sure he disliked—but for the nurse. *This was her job*, he reminded himself. *And she protected you.*

The warden waltzed right by Ricky, humming cheerfully to

himself. The lobotomy, it seemed, had put him in a good mood. Ricky knew he was expected to follow, and when he didn't move quickly enough the orderly urged him along, then shut the door to the cell with a thud.

They were leaving behind the basement, and Ricky wouldn't complain about that, but it unsettled him the way they left it to the still-echoing noise of the screaming and wailing. It didn't appear that the warden even noticed. Maybe he didn't care.

The worst-case patients were down here, Ricky thought, but Patty hadn't been so bad. Did that mean the others were just as mistreated?

He was lost in thought as they climbed the stairs back to the first level, the chill of the basement winding up behind them, trying to escape. His posture didn't relax until they actually stepped into the sunlight streaming through to the lobby.

He said, "What I still don't understand is, why did you show me that?"

"This is the reality of my line of work," the warden explained. His good mood had vanished and now he sounded exhausted. "That procedure can be deadly. I am constantly called upon to make these judgments, to decide whether it is worth the risk to help a patient and address their abnormalities."

"She wasn't abnormal," Ricky shot back immediately. "She was just eccentric! You didn't *need* to do that and you certainly didn't need to show me! What if I tell my mom about all of this when she visits?"

IF she visits.

"I showed you because I believe in you, Mr. Desmond, and I think you have the potential to become an extraordinary young man. But I need you to understand that this is still a mental care facility. The people around you are not here on sabbatical, they are here to get better, in hopes of returning to their families, if they are fortunate. You are correct, Patty was an eccentric. Ill, too. The two are not mutually exclusive. So it is with you, only the difference is that you have the potential to be something more. Returning to your family isn't all you have to hope for." He tilted his head to the side, regarding Ricky behind his odd little spectacles. Why did he sound so sad? "Here."

Instead of directing Ricky back to his cell, he guided him and the orderly to a room on the first floor—one Ricky hadn't visited before. The warden opened the door to reveal an orderly who was mopping the floor, whistling, though there was nothing joyful about it. Ricky stared inside, his stomach twisting into a painful wreath of knots. His muscles tightened, bracing against invisible surges of agony.

He recognized the machine, its clamps and restraints. He recognized the frame that would hold a body upright. He recognized the white, pull-down screen for the slide show. The room reeked of piss, and worse, of fear.

No matter what he told himself, he couldn't make his body move. He was frozen, transported to Hillcrest, to the nasty little room at the end of the second floor's west wing. To the restraints. To the *pain*.

The warden's minty breath made his knotted guts turn, and he gasped against the urge to vomit. He'd already felt ill, but now he was sure he was going to throw up.

"This is not the room for a special program patient, for someone with potential," the warden whispered gently, soothingly,

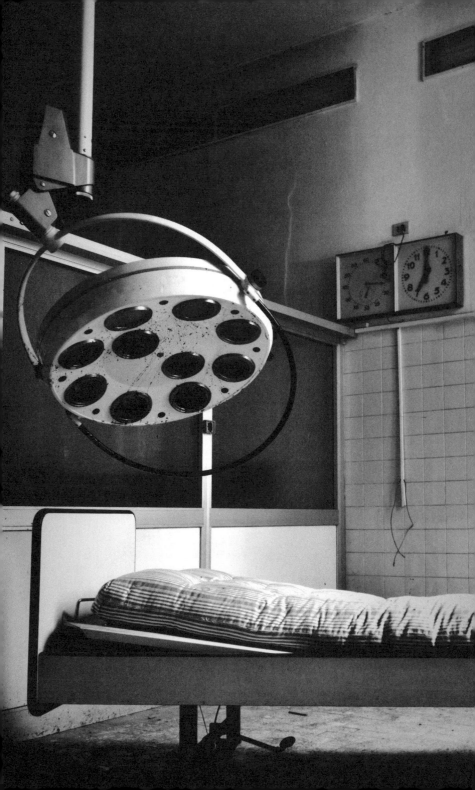

as if any kind words at all could steal away the paralyzing fear of that moment. It wasn't memory but trauma, and Ricky wanted to leap at the orderly and choke the life out of him for whistling that jaunty tune while he cleaned up the evidence of unadulterated torture. "You don't need to be in here, Ricky. You never need to be in a place like this again, and you don't need to end up like Patty. Do you understand?"

Ricky still couldn't speak. Or move. His veins felt like cold, stinging threads, lit up with the memory of being gagged and shocked.

The warden's voice was no longer kind. *"Do we understand each other?"*

"Yes," he heard himself say. It was the only thing *to* say. He didn't want to end up like Patty. He could still hear the crunch as the spike went in. "Yes."

The door closed and he sobbed, and shrank. He wondered if people would ever stop making him feel so small.

CHAPTER
№ 25

The orderly marched him back toward his room. He wasn't imagining it—this first-floor hallway really did seem dimmer. He glanced up as they walked, noticing that one of the bulbs in the overhead lamp had gone out and nobody had bothered to change it. The cracks in the facade were mounting.

They passed the lobby and Ricky pulled himself out of his fear and confusion to pay attention, listening to the raised voices as a familiar man shouted down at a nurse behind the metal grated door.

It was the warden's brother, the man from the other day with the same pale skin and sharp cheekbones, the same dark hair. Ricky saw now that this man's clothes were shabby. He vaguely remembered something about a mother's estate that needed to be settled, and he wondered if the warden had come by his own money honestly or if this was part of the reason for their fighting.

"What do you mean he won't see me? I'm his brother, for God's sake. I had an appointment! You tell him I'm not leaving. I'll wait all day and all night if I have to!"

Then Ricky lost sight of the argument as they rounded the corner and left the lobby behind. The multipurpose room was shut up, and no voices came from inside. It truly was a lockdown,

Ricky realized. The warden was punishing everyone after the gala disaster.

The orderly unlocked his door impatiently and nudged him inside just as thoughtlessly. He shut the door without another word. At least Nurse Ash would remind him how long until lunch or dinner, or tell him to try to get some rest. He wondered if this orderly even knew his name.

He felt like he had returned to death row, and now he had to await whatever fate the warden had in mind. He shut his eyes tight and tried to collect himself, but it wasn't helping.

Then he opened his eyes and gasped. He wasn't in his small white cell, but *home.* His home in Boston. The tiled floor was gone, replaced with a stretch of overlong summer grass. His heartbeat fluttered. This wasn't possible, but it was there, and he was walking up the front drive of their prim, white Colonial. Nothing looked quite like it should, though. The flower boxes, normally filled with the bouncing heads of cheerful red blossoms, hung crooked underneath the windows. Red petals wept from the plants, their bare heads drooping and dry. The front door was slightly ajar, the opening strains of his mother's favorite television show drifting out onto the lawn. Static muddled the music, breaking up the rhythm and lyrics into a random collection of notes and words.

Still, he ached to go inside. This was home, whether he got along with the family inside or not, and even if he hated his mother sometimes there was love there, wasn't there? What if he had just talked to her that day when Butch came home swinging? What if she had actually listened?

The door opened to greet him, slowly and just enough to allow

him through. Something was burning in the kitchen, filling the air with a greasy, smoky tang. His mother's laughter burst out from the living room to the right, and Ricky followed the sound. She was hoovering the carpets, but the vacuum wasn't on and she twirled the cord like a lasso.

"Mom?" he asked, standing in the doorway.

Her favorite show was on, but the television flickered so badly it was impossible to know what they were saying.

"Oh, Ricky, honey, you're back. I'm so glad you're back. Just in time for dinner, too! What a nice surprise." She sighed, swaying back and forth to the skipping television track.

Her head was canted back as she pretended to vacuum, her skin paler than usual, eyes fixed open and staring, a wide grin on her face. That smiling mouth didn't seem to move as the words came out of her.

"Are you all right, Mom?"

"Perfectly fine, honey," she said, and again her mouth remained frozen. "Why don't you go upstairs and get your father? I'm sure he'll want to eat soon."

His father. Ricky darted for the stairs. She never called Butch, his stepdad, "his father." He was always Butch. That meant his real father was upstairs. He had come back finally, the thing Ricky had always wanted but never dared to admit because it was just too cliché—it was exactly what those creeps at Victorwood wanted. The only time he'd ever said as much out loud, it had reduced his mother to furious tears. His father had left, she reminded him, he had left them alone, too selfish to stay and try to make it work.

But now his father was back. He would put the house to rights.

He would plant new flowers in the flower boxes and shake his mother out of her weird daze. The floor upstairs seemed to swim as Ricky stepped onto it, the hall tilting as if part of a fun house maze. Ricky steadied himself with a hand on the wall, stumbling down the hallway, bare feet squishing into soaked carpeting. Thick, red ooze bubbled up between his toes, staining his skin.

The radio was on in the bathroom, the only room with a light glowing beneath the door. Ricky found his way there, fighting the nauseating back and forth of the hall as it tried to throw him off balance. His feet were wet and cold, his head stuffed with cotton, too disoriented to make out the song on the radio.

The bathroom door was freezing to the touch, but he knocked. He knocked again. The song on the radio was clear now—one of his favorites. "Tears of a Clown."

"Dad?"

But don't let my glad expression

Ricky knocked harder, trying to overcome the music.

Give you the wrong impression

No matter how hard he hit the door it didn't make a sound. Ricky pounded and pounded, shouting, screaming so hard his throat began to sting. His father was in there. Why couldn't he hear him? Didn't he want to see Ricky again?

Panic set in and the music cut out abruptly.

"What's a matter, son? What's with all the knockin'?"

Ricky turned, and there was Butch down the hall, his usual huge, bulky self, but something was wrong with him, too. He was turned away from Ricky but bent back toward him, neck and head twisted at an impossible angle, so that even with his back to Ricky his face was visible. Pale. Sickly. He had the same fixed, wide smile as his mother.

"Why all the racket?" He was moving toward Ricky now, fast, taking exaggerated steps on tiptoe, unnaturally fast and scuttling, like a daddy longlegs. "Why all the knocking?"

Ricky backed up against the door, huddling. Oh God, there was no getting away, no doors to open, no rooms to hide in. He couldn't look away from that horrible grin, the one that didn't move, the one that got closer and closer until Butch was right on him.

"Don't you know he's dead? Don't you know he's dead, DEAD, DEAD? DECEASED."

Ricky hit the floor with a grunt. Reality slammed into him just as hard—it was another vision. A dream. His chest ached and he had bruised his chin. He rolled onto his back, pressing his fingertips to his breastbone and gulping down breaths until the last of the dream evaporated. The cold floor was the only thing that felt real. Solid. Even his body, shaking and weak, couldn't be trusted.

Why did the visions he had here feel so real, and when, he was desperate to know, would they *stop*?

CHAPTER
№ 26

"'m getting out of here. I have to. Nothing here is right, nothing is . . . And Patty."

Ricky punctuated the statement with a grunt, tearing a clump of weeds out of the flower bed. The lockdown was over. They had been given supervised gardening, which now felt like a gift. He and Kay weeded side by side, and a few yards away other patients did their best to prune or plant. Even on this warm day the sky was hazy, and the same, the odd fog lingered at the fringes of the yard. It made him think of a wizard's spell cast on the place to keep anyone from getting in or getting out.

"Work time is probably our best shot—times like this." He was rambling, but it helped to fill the silence. "Maybe we can get someone else to help us, you know? Cause a distraction. We could make a break over the fence, and then stay off the road. It won't be easy but we have to try. I won't let us end up like Patty."

Angela, who was usually glued to Patty's side, worked on her own. Patty was just a few yards away, obediently tending to the plants. She was quiet now, no more bursting into song.

Wiping at her forehead, Kay sat back on her heels. A little smudge of mud stayed on her skin, mingling with sweat. "You know that's not possible. You *saw* what they did to her. Do you really want to try and cause a fuss after that? They would just catch us and then what?"

"I know, Kay, I know, but that's all the more reason why we have to go," he said. Ricky dumped a handful of dandelions into a plastic bucket, shooing away a fly from his arm in irritation. "Since I'm no longer worried about sounding crazy, I'll tell you that I had a vision last night about my family. My house was falling apart and my mom and stepfather looked like monsters. They had these awful smiles." He twitched just thinking about it. "I think it was a sign."

"It's like the Scouring of the Shire," Kay said offhandedly.

"The who-what of where?"

Ricky had no idea what transgression could possibly merit someone rolling their eyes as hard as Kay did right now.

"Oh, come on, don't you read? Tolkien? *Lord of the Rings*?"

He blushed, staring at the weeds in his fist. "Does *Tiger Beat* count?"

"No, it most certainly does not." But she lightened up, leaning into his shoulder and nudging him. "Anyway, it's from a book. These little hobbit people go on a long journey away from home. At one point, the main guy has a vision of his hometown burning down, and when they get back at the end, they find everything really has gone to hell in a handbasket. I'm simplifying, but it's an allegory anyway."

"A what?"

At least she didn't roll her eyes this time. "The point is you can't ever go home, not really. There was still danger at home for the hobbits, and there's still danger at home for you. Even if you get over that fence, when your parents find out they'll just send you back, yeah?"

"Yeah," he admitted. He slumped down, sighing. "That's probably right. I don't think I'll ever be cured enough for Butch. Or for my mom, honestly."

"Well then. We need a better plan," Kay told him quietly. "And when we get out of here, we don't go home. We go anywhere else."

The thought of being out on his own was a scary one, but she had a point. And he would be eighteen next year. He'd never had the best grades, and he already hadn't been sure whether he'd go to college. He kind of liked the idea of going to New York, seeing the West Village his friends at Victorwood had told him about. "Do you think we could really make it on our own?"

"I don't know, but we could try."

Ricky nodded. It sounded wise. Grown-up. "God, my dad was in that dream, too. I stopped dreaming about him years ago when I realized he wasn't really coming back."

"Why'd he run out in the first place?" Kay asked. She wasn't doing much work, pulling out healthy flowers when Nurse Ash had her back turned and fashioning them into a flower chain. "Do you think he'd be nice to us if we managed to find him?"

Ordinarily a question like that would make Ricky's temper explode, but for some reason he didn't mind when Kay asked. Probably because he knew she didn't want to tease him about it. The kids back home were a different story. His mother must have done something wrong to make his dad run off, or so the common story went. That was just how it was. No self-respecting man up and left his family, so his dad was a bad person or his mother was a hussy.

Ricky thought of the strange photo he had found in the file

room, the one with a man that looked weirdly like Ricky. That plus the patient card Kay had found . . . It was almost easier to think of his dad going off the deep end and winding up at a sanitarium. That would mean he'd had no choice, that something was actually wrong with him, other than him being a selfish jerk.

Ricky yanked out another bundle of weeds. "My mom never settled on a good story. One day he'd always been a do-nothing bum, the next time I asked she'd say he was a dreamer who just never wanted to settle down. Butch says it's because he'd get drunk and slap her around, which was why she hated talking about it. But I don't remember ever seeing him drunk. Hell, he might take us in, but I just don't *know* him."

"Where would you start looking if you could?" she asked.

"California, probably. That's where he grew up."

"Tell you what, we get out of here together and I'll come with you," she said, laughing softly. "Know why?"

"Why?"

"Because it's as far away from here as you can get without being in China. And it's nowhere near my daddy." She finished the flower chain and plopped it on Ricky's head. "I'm sorry you had to go down into the basement. I can't even imagine what it was like seeing her get—seeing her like that."

"Thanks," he muttered. The flower chain tickled the tops of his ears but he let it stay. Nobody had ever made him a crown before. "I'm surprised he didn't just come out and say: behave or you're next."

"But you're teacher's pet, right?" Kay teased. There was an edge to her voice, and Ricky picked up on it immediately.

"I shouldn't have said anything about that. I am not his pet."

"Right. Maybe that Phase Two thing was just a misunderstanding. You might have heard them wrong."

"It doesn't matter what I am, I'm getting out of here."

"What's your next plan? Now that the gala failed."

"I don't know yet," Ricky said. "I know it sounds twisted, but maybe this thing with the warden could be a good thing for us. I could get more freedom, maybe. Tell him it helps me calm my impulses to walk outside at night."

It sounded just as stupid and thin as their last plan, but just saying he would do something made him feel better. Staying in Brookline with no direction, no plan, would be worse.

"Sure," Kay said, and she sounded as beaten down as he felt. "Just don't fly out of here without me, okay, Superman?"

"I wouldn't."

Kay made a soft grunt of agreement and began to pick more perfectly healthy flowers. For a moment they were quiet, and there was just the sound of the errant bird chirping above them in the trees or Sloane muttering to himself. Then he heard her inhale deeply. "The problem is, my daddy would pay anything to see me *normal* again. I'll never let them win, so he'll just keep paying and paying, and I'll never get out."

"Would he really do that?"

"Oh, most definitely. That's what happens when you get a little bit of money. You think you can throw cash at anything and it'll be *fixed*." Kay finished her second flower chain and crowned herself, watching Ricky while he weeded. That didn't sound too far off from the warden's friends, Ricky mused.

"How'd he make all that money? My mom inherited hers."

"Music. Morris Waterston and the Getup Seven, getting famouser by the day, and in no need of a problem child." She sighed and pulled on her work gloves, halfheartedly raking her fingers through the dirt.

"*The* Morris Waterston?" Ricky didn't know whether to tell her that he had all three of their records at home. It had never occurred to him that one of his favorite bands might be led by a person willing to lock away their kid.

"Mmhm. He got thrown in jail once for a bar fight, but he cleaned up since then. I'm not the kind of clean he wants to be. I thought one day he'd let me in the band. Trumpet. But can't have a lady trumpet player in that kind of group, and definitely not a lady trumpet player like me." She picked up a handful of dirt and searched through it, pulling out a worm and flinging it over Ricky's head toward old man Sloane. "Joke's on him, next time I see him I'm shoving my trumpet so far up his—"

"Waterston! Back to work!" Nurse Kramer had spotted them from the opposite direction, marching up to them with her cheeks red and puffy. The heat, apparently, did not agree with her lily-white complexion. "And you—" She pointed at Ricky and then leaned over, tearing the crown off his head and throwing it into the mud. "Get up. Warden Crawford wants to see you."

CHAPTER
№ 27

Journal of Ricky Desmond—Late June

I keep dreaming of my father. He comes to me every night, looking like the guy from the picture I found because I can barely remember what he looked like when he left. Sometimes he leads me out of my room, out into the lobby, and right out into the sunshine. Other times he leads me into the black, empty shadow of the basement. Maybe he really is as bad as Butch says and maybe I'm just like him. Maybe that's why I'm here, because we're both bad and bad people are supposed to disappear.

Sometimes I wonder if he was born like me, too. I wonder if he liked men and women or maybe just men and Mom found out. She wouldn't be able to take that. She always needs all the attention on her. All the love for her.

Not enough love for me, though. No love for me. It's not fair. It's not fair that she can just lock me away in here *and there's nothing I can do about it. Whoever said a mother is always right? If I can be sick and broken, then she can be, too.*

Kay is right—my dad could be out there somewhere. Then we could disappear together.

Be strong. Ricky put on a placid smile for the warden, watching with dread as he collected a few instruments into a case in his office. Had he somehow heard what he and Kay were talking about outside?

"You wanted to see me?" Ricky prompted, his skin prickly with anxiety.

"Yes. Now that the hospital is back to business as usual, it's time we began this collaboration of ours in earnest," the warden said. He was serious today. Stern. Tucking the case under his arm, he bustled around his desk and went to the door, pausing only to brush a flower petal out of Ricky's hair. "Hard at work in the garden, I see."

"It was just a bit of fun," he defended lamely.

"Palling around with Keith again?"

Kay, he corrected silently, trying to keep a lid on his rising temper. "Like I said, just a little fun. Hard to keep morale up around here, you know? After Patty . . . Well, I mean we can all tell there's something different about her. She doesn't sing anymore."

"Hm," the warden replied, as if that were completely boring and irrelevant. Right. The warden had made it clear he felt justified in sticking an ice pick in Patty's eye and scrambling her brain. Why would the feelings of his patients on the subject matter? "You won't need Keith's friendship much longer. Or Patty's. This project will demand total focus from you and from me. We're developing your potential, testing the bounds of the human spirit and mind. It's exciting, Ricky, but very taxing. Now, we should get going to your new accommodations."

"New what?" he blurted. A shadow fell across him from behind and he turned to see one of the male orderlies behind him. "W-Wait, where am I going?"

"Why, upstairs, Mr. Desmond," the warden said cheerfully, popping a mint into his mouth. "I told you, we're beginning in earnest. It's become clear to me that I was wrong about your fraternization with fellow patients. It isn't helping you to gain the appropriate perspective. Patty demonstrated that quite clearly to me—I was wrong to make you spend so much time with the others."

His tone darkened and Ricky heard the implied threat—agree to the warden's terms, or be strapped to the contraption across the hall and suffer aversion therapy for the rest of his stay. Or worse, the spike.

Ricky didn't respond, which was apparently as good as an answer in the affirmative. The orderly, he knew, was there in case he tried to change his mind.

"Nurse Ash has cleaned out your room and prepared your new place."

"Can't I say good-bye?" Ricky asked, feeling the orderly's hand close around his upper biceps. He was being manhandled out of the office. This didn't feel like favoritism, he thought, his pulse racing, it felt like *exile*. "Can I just talk to Kay before you move me?"

"Of course not, Mr. Desmond. Didn't you hear a word I just said?" The warden clucked his tongue, sweeping by with his head thrown back, a smile on his lips. "Trust me, soon Keith will be the furthest thing from your mind."

✗ ✗ ✗ ✗ ✗

Room 3808 was warmer but still spartan, furnished almost identically to his last cell except for a few more amenities. The windows were still barred, but the bed had a thicker mattress and a pillow bigger than a marshmallow. The blinds were open, the sunshine in the room almost blinding, reflecting painfully off every white surface.

Ricky shielded his eyes and then dropped his hand, noticing an odd window cut into the wall on the right side of the room, near the door. It was about a foot and a half wide and about that tall, with a white wooden frame outlining it and a single pull-down slat lowered past the bottom edge. The handle there made it look as if it could be drawn upward into the ceiling, giving one a view into . . . something.

"This will be your new room for the time being, Mr. Desmond," the warden explained, entering behind him. "Nurse Ash cleaned the place up admirably. Excellent."

His pulse hadn't slowed since they left the first floor and now it tripped over itself in a renewed panic. If Nurse Ash had cleaned out his old room, then she must have found the journal entries he'd been tearing out and keeping. The patient card for

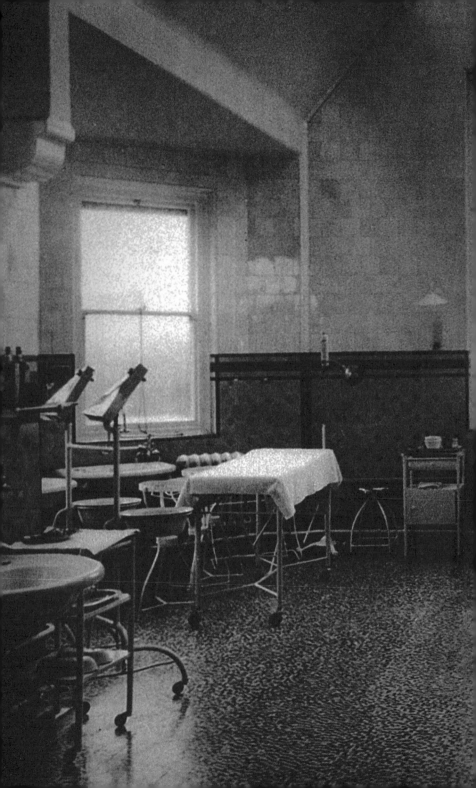

the mysterious Desmond before him. *Idiot*. He hated that she was the bearer of all his secrets. She might not have ratted him out on the night of the gala, but she was still the warden's puppet at the end of the day.

"Now then, I think it's time for your first exercise," the warden said, striding to the bed and taking a seat. He rested one ankle on the opposite knee and opened his doctor's case. It clicked open and Crawford reached inside, pulling out a bright red stone on a silver chain that snaked and snaked out of the case, rustling softly as it came free.

The orderly who'd accompanied them moved inside, bringing a chair. He set the chair down and waited, passive, silent. He reminded Ricky of Lurch from the Addams family. Ricky took a seat without prompting.

"What is that?" He couldn't take his eyes off the red stone in the warden's palm. It seemed to flicker with its own internal light, spidery veins of deeper red shooting out from its irregularly shaped core.

"Just one of my many methods," the warden said calmly. He cleared his throat and shifted to sit on the very edge of the bed. Then he lifted the chain, letting the stone swing at the end, a glistening heart of a pendulum. "I want you to follow the stone with your eyes, Ricky. Deep breaths. Relax. Yes, that's good. Is the chair comfortable?"

It was hard enough to look away from the stone when it was stationary, but now his gaze followed its trajectory automatically.

"Yes, it's comfortable," he said absently. The chair wasn't really even there for him. He couldn't feel it. He could feel his pulse regulating, feel with almost disturbing clarity the thumping of his heart and the warmth—the speed—of his blood flowing through his body.

He wasn't getting sleepy like those goofy hypnotists in television shows always said, but he couldn't help but focus on the stone. Back and forth. His breath began to go in and out to the pace of the swinging. The warden's face disappeared behind the pendulum. It was the stone and the voice, the deep, warm voice that kept him anchored and alert.

"Continue to watch. Continue to follow. Mesmerizing, isn't it? Almost . . . comforting. That's good. I knew you would take to it. Now, Ricky, I want you to listen to my voice and concentrate as hard as you can. My voice will keep you safe. My voice will help you."

Yes. That sounded right. Back and forth. A calm, loose sensation settled over him. It reminded him of skipping school and nipping into a stolen bottle of brandy with Martin on the pier. Butch would throw a fit when he found out the bottle was missing from his liquor cabinet, but in that moment, on the pier, with the gulls crying in the distance and the waves lapping near their feet, Ricky had felt utterly at peace.

"When Nurse Ash comes in later you will take the medicine she brings you," the warden told him gently. That sounded like good advice, too. He was in a hospital. When you were in hospital you took your medicine. A dose. The first dose. "You will swallow it. Taking the medicine will keep you safe. You're safe here, Ricky. This is where you belong. You don't want to leave, do you? Why would you ever want to leave us when you're perfectly safe."

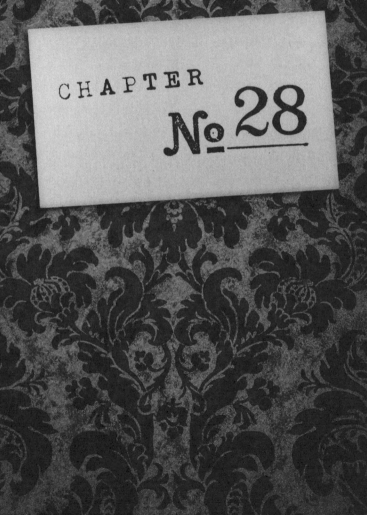

CHAPTER

№ 28

reamless sleep. Beautiful, peaceful, restful sleep . . . It was such a relief to sleep soundly, but it didn't last long. He came awake and out of his blissful stupor in a panic, feeling a strong grip around his wrists. Cuffs? When had he been cuffed? His head was so foggy. He couldn't remember anything before coming to his new room. They had moved him to room 3808, and then the warden had taken out a red stone on a chain and after that it was like someone had reached into his brain with an eraser and wiped half the board clean.

"Sh-hh!" It was a woman's voice. The room was dark but if Ricky squinted he could just make out Nurse Ash kneeling next to his cot.

"What are you doing? Why are you . . . Why are you putting me in cuffs!?"

It was too much. He had come out of darkest sleep to this shock, and his heart began to ache. Flailing, he tried to knock her away from the bed but Nurse Ash held on tight, shushing him again.

"Hush. I'm taking the cuffs *off*, Rick. I'm letting you go."

"Oh . . . Damn it. Why can't I think? And why did they tie me up?"

"I told you," she whispered, shaking her head. A few

halfhearted moonbeams broke through the blinds, striping the floor. He saw there was a tray of food on his bedside table, but he was hardly hungry. "You can't trust the warden. You can't trust me either."

"That's very obvious now! I think I figured that out when I watched the two of you shove a needle in Patty's face."

She pulled the keys away and Ricky was free. The cuffs fell to the floor with a soft jangling, and he tried to sit up, rubbing at his chaffed wrists.

"He made me help with that for a reason," she said softly, standing. "That's what he does. He doesn't want you to believe me or trust me. He doesn't want you to think I'm . . . good, and he wants to keep us complicit in his deeds. Keep us afraid of being seen. I don't care if you believe him or me. It really doesn't matter. All that matters is that you trust yourself."

"Said the crazy person to the crazy person."

"I'm not crazy and neither are you," she insisted. A blue, knit shawl had been draped over her shoulders, and without her paper cap she looked much more human. Normal. "I wish I could tell you everything . . ." She closed her eyes tightly and whimpered, a sheen of sweat glossing over her face. "Whenever I try it's like there's a hand just hovering there, waiting to slap me."

"Now you really *do* sound insane."

"This isn't how I wanted it to turn out," Nurse Ash said, kneeling again. She reached for his hand but Ricky tore it away. "I'm not myself, Ricky, and I haven't been since I started working here. He gets under your skin. *Controls* you. With medicine, with hypnotism . . . Can't you see what he's doing? He's isolating

you. Everyone is an enemy. He'd hoped that a few weeks mixed in with the other patients would have you doing anything to get away from them, but now that that backfired, he took you away from Kay and he won't let me help you anymore."

He was still struggling to catch up, his brain slowed from the drugged sleep. She looked like she meant all of this, but it just seemed insane. Why would the warden bother going to all this trouble just to get him alone when he could have ordered that from the beginning?

"Funny, you say he won't let you help me and yet here you are. Helping me."

"Not in the way he wants," she hurried to say. "I'm trying to help you fight off the meds. The influence. It's the best I can do. Here."

Nurse Ash reached into her dress pocket and pulled out a handful of pills, then dropped them onto the mattress at his side. "I'm supposed to give you these."

Ricky stared at the pills and felt his mouth flood with saliva. The next dose. What the hell was the matter with him? He *hated* taking pills. They almost always made him gag. Yet here he was, reaching for them.

"It's my medicine," he heard himself say in a weird, childlike voice. "I'm supposed to take my medicine now."

"No!" The nurse lunged forward, batting them out of his hand. They scattered quietly to the cracked tile floor. "Don't take them. From now on I'm bringing you fakes. Aspirin. He might follow me . . . He might watch. God, this would be so much easier if I could just—" She winced, grabbing her head with both hands and squeezing, her eyes screwing shut so tightly that tears leaked out the sides. "This is how he does it," she gritted out between her teeth. "Testing me. Testing you. Setting. Us. Up. Against . . . *Agh*!"

She partially collapsed against the cot, grabbing the frame for support.

"Jesus, what's wrong with you?"

"You have to listen to me," she hissed, smacking her temple with what Ricky considered way too much force to be healthy. "You have to listen before I forget."

This didn't look like the right time for the conversation, but he didn't know what else to do. She looked so desperate . . . Shaking . . .

"Okay, okay, stop hitting yourself! What are you trying to remember?"

"Jocelyn," she said. "Call me that. It helps me remember."

"What are you trying to remember, Jocelyn?"

"*Madge*." She cried out as if just saying the name twisted a knife into her back. "She killed herself, Ricky. This place drove her to it. It drove her out of her mind. The warden was giving her medicine. Dosing her, secretly. She became so strange, so different. I don't know why he did it, maybe to torment me, but he drove her to kill herself. Tanner saw it. He was there, and it broke him, just like it almost broke me. Madge wouldn't kill herself. She just wouldn't."

"He what, hypnotized her into killing herself? I don't know if I . . . If that's . . . God, I don't know if I believe you," he said, inching away from her and toward the wall. "That doesn't seem possible."

"Good." Nurse Ash let out a breath, finally letting go of her head. She blinked, collecting herself, and then stood, hunting down the scattered pills and putting them back in her pocket. When she was finished, she returned to the cot. Ricky didn't move, feeling safest wedged in the corner, away from her and away from the cuffs by the pillow.

"Be skeptical. Don't trust anything you hear in here. The warden thinks he has a tighter leash on me," Nurse Ash said. She glanced down in embarrassment. "A tighter leash on my *mind*. He thinks you're secured to the bed in here, but you won't be at night. The door won't be locked then either."

Escape.

"Officially, I'll be by twice a day, with breakfast and medicine and dinner and medicine. I can't guarantee there won't be sweeps of the floor at some point, but as far as the warden's concerned you're behind two sturdy locks."

"Why?" Ricky murmured. It was all he could think to say. "Why are you doing this?"

Nurse Ash took a few steps toward the door, tucking her frazzled red hair behind her ears. She glanced at him with a sad half smile. "Go back to the first-floor storage room. I tried to look for your files but they're missing. They're all missing. There's something the warden doesn't want me to see. I don't know if there's any way to know what it is, but you have to look."

"Why can't you do it? You're the nurse."

"Because I have to get back to my night rounds. Someone will notice."

"What am I even looking for?" he asked, exasperated. She sounded mad, not just crazy, but *mad*.

"It's something about you specifically," Jocelyn said

distractedly, shaking her head. "He's hiding you from us, hiding the files . . ."

Her heels clicked softly on the tiles. Ricky remained flat against the wall, watching as she pulled out a few folded squares of familiar paper and set them on the bed.

"Hide those better next time," she said, turning to go. "I'll be back after my rounds to lock you in. If you're still here."

CHAPTER
№ 29

*F*ree.

He felt free. Or at least, when the momentary euphoria started to wear off, freer than he had felt since arriving at this godforsaken place. When the euphoria was gone completely, he felt paralyzed, as sure as he'd been that first night that somebody was on the other side of his door, listening in.

But nobody burst into the room when he stood, and so his steps grew more confident as he went to the window and touched the bars. Then he walked a circle in the middle of the room, just to be sure. In his first cell they had left him cheap slipper-shoes to wear when he left the room, but now those were gone and his feet were freezing. Ricky let that sink in.

They didn't expect him to leave the room anymore.

Before Brookline, the concept of making a deal with the devil had always seemed like an obvious bargain to him—something for nothing—but now he understood what it meant to trade one hell for another. A deal with the devil meant the illusion of choice, not a real one. Ricky tiptoed to the strange, window-like frame in the far wall. It was opposite the bed, the closest feature to the door. He paused, reaching out for the handle of the solid cover and testing it.

If he pulled up, it would raise. It wasn't heavy, it wasn't locked.

Ricky let go of the handle. It would be just his luck for the slat to be covering a two-way mirror or maybe a window into the hall, and for the orderlies to realize he was roaming his room, untethered. He would lose the first advantage he'd had since the gala. He might not get another one at this point. Instead he tiptoed to the door, still half expecting it to shock him when he touched the knob. But nothing happened. He turned it slowly, experimentally, and it gave.

Ricky tugged hard, once, and watched the door swing inward. He couldn't believe it. This had all the hallmarks of a trick. He could just imagine the warden hiding around the corner, making a note on his clipboard—*subject waits four minutes, ten seconds before trying the door.* It all came down to whom he trusted, which was a tricky proposition when even Nurse Ash herself had said he shouldn't trust her. But she had brought back the journal pages. She had denied him the "medicine" the warden wanted him to take. (Sedatives, no doubt, something to knock Ricky out so he would be pliable and quiet until the warden needed him again. Disgusting.)

At a certain point, he had to stop trying to figure out everyone's motives and just take a risk. After all, he knew better than anyone that even his own motives could be a mystery to him.

This was his chance to escape. To *leave*. Whatever Nurse Ash had said, he wasn't going to waste it looking for files or clues. He was going to get the hell out of here. There'd be time for questions later.

The corridor outside room 3808 was empty and quiet. Somehow, it seemed quieter for the cold, the way a heavy coating of snow made even the noisiest parts of Boston fall silent in the winter. He paced down the hall as far as he dared. There didn't appear to be anyone patrolling this floor, but there was no telling how many would be stationed on the lower levels this late. The staff had to stay somewhere, and he didn't fancy the idea of accidentally knocking on Nurse Kramer's bedroom door.

He explored slowly, running back to his room at every little hint of a noise. Most of the doors in this hallway were identical to his, heavy and secure, but either the rooms were empty or else the patients inside were sedated. The sounds when they came were from above or below, not from these rooms.

Finally, Ricky made it all the way to the door to the staircase at the end of the hall, and here he could definitely hear milling about on the floor below him. He waited under the bare light of a bulb dangling from the ceiling, trying to make out words in what sounded like idle chitchat, a few nurses or orderlies maybe, followed by laughter. It would be almost comforting to know the staff was capable of laughter, if he wasn't so scared. The better part of that laughter was that it meant they almost definitely weren't expecting a breakout. The laughter grew farther away, and Ricky dared to try the door into the stairwell. He almost screamed with elation when it gave, and he found himself tumbling down the first few stairs, his excitement making him reckless.

But he drew himself up short and listened again when he reached the second floor, pressing himself flat to the wall. The giggling was farther away still, and when he chanced his head around the corner, he saw that the two nurses he had heard were now at the very opposite end of the corridor, their heads bent close together as they talked. This ward was lit with even

circles of light, and a silent orderly lingered halfway down the floor. He had his nose in a magazine, to Ricky's relief, and so Ricky dashed quickly across to the next door that would take him down yet another staircase.

He neared the first floor and the lobby now, which he knew would be the most treacherous part. He had no idea what waited for him in the lobby, or how he would get through the gated door and then out the main entrance, but he had to try. It occurred to him then that Nurse Ash—if she really was on his side against the warden—might get in serious trouble for this escape attempt once it was discovered, whether that was when he was caught or after he'd made it all the way. It gave him a momentary pang of regret, but his safety had to come first. If Jocelyn was smart, she would spend tonight getting far away from this place, too.

A door shut somewhere on the first floor and he stilled, trying to hear what might be waiting on the other side of the door that led out of the stairwell. There was a sound like distant calling and then a shout. He didn't know whether to backtrack or press forward, and, petrified, he simply froze.

Just as he resolved to try for one more push to the lobby, the door burst open, and a pale, gangly figure surprised him, sending him sprawling. Ricky gasped as the back of his head hit the tiles, his vision spinning for a moment. He smothered a groan of pain, remembering the orderly with his magazine just above.

He stared up at Sloane, who had forced his way through the door. Half dressed and wide-eyed, the old man trembled at the sight of Ricky. There was no telling where he had been off to or how he had gotten out of his cell, but now he backed away in terror, pushing the door behind him open with his shoulder, even as he held his hands out in front of him like he was fending off an attack.

The vivid scar across his throat seemed to pulse wildly.

"N–No! It's you! You died, I saw it! I won't let you finish me off, you hear me? I won't let you!"

Ricky scrambled to his feet, hearing a pair of orderlies on the first floor sprinting to catch them in the stairwell. Sloane must have lost them at some point, maybe near the lobby. He was impossible to miss now.

"Sh-hhh!" Ricky tried to hush him, looking frantically down the hall, then back up the stairwell. "They're going to find you!"

"You were like my brother! How *could* you? How could you do this to me?" Sloane burst into tears, huddling against the door to the stairs and clutching his neck. The orderlies were almost at the stairs now, Ricky could hear their heavy footsteps, and he swiveled around, sprinting away, back up the stairs to the third floor without another glance behind him.

He wasn't getting out of Brookline tonight, no way, and he already felt sick from the rush of fear and adrenaline. That was close. Too close. He'd been mere seconds from getting caught by those orderlies. Ricky carefully slid back into his room, shutting the door as quietly as he could, hoping that no one would come by to check this floor before Nursh Ash could lock it again. Hot thunder rushed in his ears as his terror died down. For the moment, he was too scared and relieved to be furious at Sloane, and he couldn't help pitying the old man, too. Ricky wondered what he'd meant with all that brother business. Maybe it was some trauma from the war or something. That would explain a bizarre outburst like that, and why he was here in the first place.

Ricky probably just resembled some soldier he had served with.

Ricky sighed and rubbed the back of his head, feeling the tender place where it had struck the floor. What a total failure. He paused on his way back to the bed, his eyes landing again on the covered opening in the wall. He was determined to answer at least one question tonight. To do something rash to remind himself he was still in charge of himself.

Ricky leaned in, fevered breaths warming his knuckles, curiosity and unease making his fingers tremble as he took hold of the handle on the slat and pulled. It stuck at first, giving him trouble, and he yanked harder, putting real muscle behind the effort.

It paid off, the slat flying up and free of his grasp, revealing a spotless pane of glass that gave him a clear view into the neighboring room. A room that was most certainly occupied. Ricky gasped, frozen in place as he'd been on the stairs, his breath fogging the glass, blurring the sight of what had been waiting for him on the other side.

A girl, a little girl staring directly into the window at him, hair and eyes, all of it dark. Those dark, dark eyes, the eyes from his visions, there on the other side of the wall and staring back.

She didn't blink. She didn't scream. She simply raised one finger to her lips and pressed it there, hushing them both.

CHAPTER
№ 30

Journal of Ricky Desmond—[Barely legible, written in blood on the back of his previous entry] Late June

So I've seen her. She's real. The girl from my nightmares is here and on the other side of the wall. I can't sleep tonight. Jesus, I don't know if I'll ever sleep again.

Ricky woke locked in the cuffs. His initial instinct was to struggle, but he fell still as soon as his head cleared and his eyes focused. As promised, Nurse Ash was there, a small cup in her palm with his medicine. And directly behind her, the warden presided, looming over them with his mouth set into a hard line.

"I need to remove his restraints or he might have difficulty swallowing. It's easier if he's sitting up," she said.

"Do it," the warden replied.

Then he took a step back, fidgeting impatiently while Nurse Ash took the key ring out of her pocket and adjusted the fit on the cuffs. When they were loose enough, Ricky slipped his hands free and groaned, sitting up. He had tossed and turned all night and his forefinger burned from where he had pricked it on the metal cuff tine to scratch a message on one of his journal pages.

Nothing seemed real or lasting in this place, and it had felt urgent to make note of seeing the little girl, to confirm that it was really happening. She might disappear the next night. Part of him hoped that she would. *Most* of him.

So this was Phase Two. Medicine and handcuffs. Hypnosis and isolation. He should have feared it more. He should have tried harder to get out when he was still being kept on the main floor. But how was he supposed to know it would become more difficult, not less?

Nurse Ash handed him the little cup of pills and water to help take them. Curiously, they looked identical to the ones that had scattered across the floor the night before. Then again it had been very dark, and it was hard to say for sure . . . But they appeared more or less the same. Had she lied? Were these really just aspirin as she'd claimed they would be?

He had no choice, not with both of them standing there. Gulping the water, he tossed back the pills and swallowed. That satisfied the warden, who nodded, made a note on his clipboard, and turned to the outside window, unlocking the cage bars over it so he could pull the blinds up. Ricky almost missed the soft scratch of paper against his palm, but no, there it was— Nurse Ash had slipped him a tiny note while the warden's back was turned, palming it to him while she took back the water.

"Now eat your breakfast, Ricky," she said sternly. Her voice didn't match her expression, and Ricky could swear she gave him a wink before bustling out of the room. "Shouldn't have your medicine on an empty stomach," she added over her shoulder.

"Quite." The warden's shoulders relaxed when she was gone. He crossed to the bed, the morning sunlight glinting off his gold watch and spectacles. "You look exhausted, Ricky. Didn't you sleep?"

Damn. He needed to lie and quickly. "It's just the new mattress," he muttered, taking a bite of his eggs so he didn't have to look the warden in the eye. "I wasn't used to it."

"The treatment should help with that," the warden said matter-of-factly. "You won't notice the new mattress or the cuffs soon, I'll see to that, my boy. You'll be strong. Invincible. Impervious to discomforts and pain." He took a step closer, leaning over to inspect Ricky's eyes and then the rest of his face. "How do you feel otherwise?"

Ricky curled his hands around each other, being sure to keep the note hidden. How had he felt the day before during treatment? That might be a good enough answer. It might just be too soon to tell whether the "medicine" was having an effect, but so far he didn't feel any different, and he didn't know whether it was safer to tell the truth or tell the warden what he thought he wanted to hear. "Calm," he said. *Play the game. Keep his trust.* "Ready to feel better."

"Such progress! And so quickly!" Then, softer: "I knew it. Born to it. I just knew it."

It's something about you specifically.

"What did you know?"

"What don't I know?" the warden said, brushing him off with the joke. Ricky smiled as brightly as he could.

"Anyway, I'm ready," he said again, taking a deep breath as the warden cracked a wide smile. "But I wanted to ask you something," he added.

That smile vanished.

"I . . . want assurances." Squirming, Ricky looked down at his hands, picking at nothing on his nails. Thinking about devil's bargains last night had given him this idea. The people who outsmarted the devil were always the ones who weren't asking for things for themselves. "Kay. Leave her alone. Please, I'll do whatever I can to help you, but just let her be."

The warden weighed the request quite visibly, shifting from foot to foot with his hands tucked behind his back. Ricky had to wonder if perhaps he had miscalculated. He'd assumed that Crawford would do anything to get Ricky's full cooperation, and Kay hardly seemed to matter to the man.

"If your progress continues," the warden said at last, "I will consider lessening her treatments. But *only* if your progress continues."

He made the outer circle of the room, looking everything over, then he returned to Ricky and gave him another brief inspection. Ricky clenched his fists tight when Crawford leaned in, took him by the wrists, and secured his cuffs again. He almost lost his grip on the note, his fingers cramping from curling so hard. The warden stepped back, dusting off his hands in an exaggerated way that irritated Ricky beyond reason.

"Well, I'll leave you to your thoughts. In a few hours we can start again, Ricky. You have no idea how happy it makes me to hear that you're *ready*, my boy. My Patient Zero."

Ricky had heard those words before. Patient Zero. He shivered. The warden had been planning this for some time. His body relaxed just a little when the door finally closed.

How the hell was he supposed to read this note from Jocelyn when he could barely move his arms? He didn't have long to grouse; Nurse Ash returned just a few moments later under the pretense of clearing his breakfast tray, though she kept looking over her shoulder like she could get in trouble even for that.

"It's going to be like this every day?" he asked, sagging against the pillow when she had released him.

Nurse Ash looked just as exhausted as he felt, the skin under her eyes dark and bluish. "I'm afraid so."

Ricky unrolled the note, smirking.

Heard the room service is terrible up there. You have got to complain to management. Me? I've been at the spa all day. —K

"A real comedian, that one," Nurse Ash said kindly. "She . . . wasn't at the spa."

"I know what it means." They were torturing her again. The shock therapy room. Ricky folded up the note and hid it under his mattress with his other contraband. Hopefully those "spa" days would be numbered now that he had made his devil's bargain with the warden. It was worth it. At least one of them would be left alone. "Thank you for smuggling that in here."

"Of course. Do you want me to tell her something for you?" He took the last little bite of his eggs before he let Nurse Ash take the tray. "I can try to get you a crayon and paper, but no promises."

"Tell her I'm writing the manager a strongly worded letter," he said, closing his eyes. "And tell her I'll find a way to check us out of this joint. Somehow. Soon. Tell her I promise."

CHAPTER № 31

"Do you know what this is all about, Ricky?"

The warden's voice smoothed over him like a parent's comforting embrace. It was like hearing a bedtime story, one that left him sleepy but unable to nod off entirely. His eyes followed the gem back and forth, and he knew total relaxation. Total emptiness. In fact, he had never felt emptier. Like a vessel. Yes, he was a vessel, and the warden's words were filling him up.

"Legacy," Ricky answered from somewhere deep in the back of his mind. "Forever. Eternity."

It felt so good to be right. He would be rewarded.

"That's right. That's very good, Ricky." That was the reward. Praise. He was doing well. The red stone went back and forth. He could feel the sunlight coming in through the window. Smell the mint on the warden's breath. Some senses sharpened as others faded completely away. "Very, very good. What else?"

"Immortality."

"Exactly. You're getting this so fast. Do you know why I chose you, Ricky? Do you know why you had to be my Patient Zero?"

He didn't know, but the stone, the rhythm, the back and forth, all of it told him that he dearly wanted to know. In fact, knowing the answer was the only important thing. The only thing, period.

"Why? Why was it me?"

"Others were clever," the warden said. "Others were brighter, more educated, more eager to please, more interested in the science of it or the philosophy. But it turned out—to my dismay, I admit—that none of that was enough. In fact, the results were so far from what I wanted to achieve, they weren't even truly part of the same experiment that you are. Then fate, the opposite of science but also its necessary partner, intervened, and the patient before you came very close, absolutely by accident. So I formed a new hypothesis. Biology. Biology was the key all along." The warden sighed as if disappointed in himself, but he soon rallied. "You . . . You are curious like he was. Curiosity has movement, Ricky. It propels you always onward. It has *momentum*."

Yes, momentum, just like the stone. Just like the stone swinging back and forth.

"Now relax, Ricky, and open your mind completely. There's so much I need to tell you, so much you must carry onward into the future . . ."

✗ ✗ ✗ ✗ ✗

He felt like his head had been sawed open and closed back up, but something had been left behind. His head ached—pounded— like his brain was too much stuffing in a small turkey. Too many words crowding the page.

Groaning, Ricky rolled back and forth on the bed, moving as much as he could with his hands restrained. This was a torture of a different kind. A vicious hangover when he hadn't swallowed a drop. He grasped for what had happened, for the blank spot right there in the middle of the day. There was waking up, then breakfast, then reading Kay's note, and then the orderlies had taken him to a room down the hall and sprayed him with icy water, giving him a hosing down that felt like it would tear his skin off. And then he was back in his room and the warden was waiting for him.

The red stone had come out of the leather case again and then . . . Nothing. There was the blank spot. But Ricky could feel that something was different, that he was somehow changed.

Ricky was no Eagle Scout, but he could tell it was now dusk. The warden had left open the blinds on his outside window, and the once bright light in the room had darkened to mellower orange.

This time of day always reminded Ricky of looking out over the water with Martin, Martin eating a shaved ice while Ricky pretend-sang whatever song came to mind. It was harder to picture now, like someone had taken scissors to his memories. He remembered he'd once sung a song by a man named Otis Redding, for example, even though now he couldn't think of a single one of the man's lyrics.

"What's happening to me?" he whispered. Maybe it was a small thing, forgetting the words to a song, but it stuck in his mind. He would never forget a musician. That wasn't him.

The door opened and he started banging his cuffed hands against the bed frame. Nurse Ash hurried in, a dinner tray balanced on her palms. Her hair was a wreck, hastily pinned under her hat but uneven on both sides, and Ricky spied the orderly he'd dubbed Lurch lingering right outside the door.

"Not much time tonight," she said, glancing over her shoulder and making certain the door was shut before she unshackled him. "I don't know if the warden is catching on. I hope not. Be careful tonight if you leave the room, all right? I'll do my best to cause a scene downstairs. Maybe I can bribe Kay to throw a tantrum."

"Try a book," he said groggily. "She likes to read."

"I'll think about it, but maybe it's better just to leave her out of it."

"Keep her safe, okay?" His wrists ached and he sat up to rub them, feeling incredibly woozy the instant he lifted his head. "Did she send another note?"

"Of course." Nurse Ash handed it to him, along with a crayon from her pocket. "I'll try to grab you some paper tomorrow."

She had brought his little cup of pills, too, and they looked the same. The warden wasn't there to watch him take the medicine in the evenings, so he felt more confident they were aspirin. He took them, grateful for any kind of pain relief.

A hardening scoop of reconstituted potatoes and mushy, overcooked peas made up dinner tonight. He ate, losing his appetite with each mouthful. Kay's note bolstered him, but only marginally. It was amazing to him that she could manage to get one to him every day—he hoped she would keep it up, because he had to hope for something.

Nothing new to report on the first floor. I think the nurse has a crush on you. She's probably reading this, too—hi, nurse! You won a popularity contest in a mental hospital. You must feel so exceptional.

He chuckled softly and tucked the scrap of paper under his mattress to join the others. Running his spoon through the

potatoes, he glanced at Nurse Ash, who seemed suddenly fasci-
nated by the cracks in the tiles.

"Why are you helping us so much?" he asked. "Why help *me*?"

"Honestly?"

He nodded. Her cheeks turned a dark shade of magenta and
she rubbed at an invisible stain on her dress. It didn't bother
him that she avoided eye contact. Whatever her reasons for
helping, he doubted they were good. Maybe she had woken up to
some kind of truth about the warden after he killed her friend.

Or maybe she was just a good person. One of the few.

"From the first day that I arrived here, I knew the warden was
a rotten egg," she said sadly. "But I got . . . I don't know. Swept
up. He gave me all these grand talks about how far I could go,
you know? He said I could be a doctor, not just a nurse. That I
could actually advance. It felt like he was on my side. I'd run up
against a lot of old-fashioned ideas in nursing school, and I was
naive enough to think he was different. It's too late to help that
girl now, but it's not too late to help you and Kay."

"Grand talks," Ricky repeated. "That does sound like him."

"You can't take anything he says in here seriously," she has-
tened on, lowering her voice with a glance over her shoulder,
as if she'd suddenly remembered about Lurch. She whispered,
"It's all just hot air. Lies. He thinks he can live forever. It's total
insanity."

He almost made a joke about the irony of that statement but
saved it, feeling the potatoes stick to his throat. "And can he?"

Nurse Ash looked up at him, her eyes wide with confusion.
"Can he what?"

"Live forever. He seems to think it's possible and he's willing to go to all this trouble. Isn't that what he's doing with me? I'm his specimen or whatever. His Patient Zero. What if he's right?"

"It's not possible, Rick. You can't listen to him, all right? You can't fall for it."

"I'm losing parts of myself," he said after a moment, and he saw her freeze out of the corner of his eye. "I can't remember my last birthday. Or the words to my favorite songs. I can hardly remember anything that happened since I've been at Brookline. It's like it's all there, but behind glass. I can't touch it and it's getting farther away."

Nurse Ash wouldn't look at him again, gathering up the tray and medicine cup, nearly dropping both. The plate rattled noisily on the tray from her shaking hands. "You're just tired. Maybe you shouldn't go exploring tonight, just rest before I have to come back and put you in the cuffs."

Right. Go back to bed. Forget everything. Get some sleep. He would be lucky if any of those things were possible again. But he said nothing, nodding and yawning, playing a part, as if he was in a play about being a patient, good night, sweet prince.

CHAPTER
№ 32

The hall was empty by the time full darkness fell. Nurse Ash had done her part, and Ricky found the hall of his floor quiet as always, so quiet he could hear the muttered conversations going on beneath his feet. It was impossible to make out words, but he would hear a laugh here or a louder-than-average comment there . . .

He tiptoed down the hall, cringing as he passed the room immediately next to his. Creepy. It was just too creepy to think about that little girl waiting inside. The temptation to reopen the window in the wall and see if she was still there had been strong but he resisted, choosing to ignore it even as the thought scratched at the back of his mind. She was real and right there.

At least, he thought bleakly, in real life she had a face.

The room at the opposite end of the floor loomed large in his thoughts. While waiting for the floor to clear, he had obsessed over what might be inside. Old brooms and mops were the likely answer, but a tiny shred of curiosity kept his hope alive. Ricky shivered at that. Curiosity. Wasn't that why the warden had picked him to be his Patient Zero in the first place?

Or wait, what had he said? Biology? Ricky felt his breath grow shorter. The photo he found . . . The patient card Kay stole . . . It seemed outrageous, but he had to wonder if his father had once been a Brookline patient. Insane to contemplate, but casting his father as a jerk who ran out on his mother was exactly the kind of lie she would tell. Appearances. That was all she cared about. She didn't want a son who kissed other boys and she didn't want a husband who'd ended up in a lunatic asylum.

If he had ended up there.

To be fair, his father might really have been selfish and cruel, prone to the same violent impulses as Ricky, it sounded like. That wasn't a fantasy, that was the truth. Biology could mean anything, Ricky reminded himself, blood type, gender, mental disposition . . .

Ricky paused outside the door, testing the knob again to see if the staff had wised up and locked it. His luck held. The door opened with a tiny squeak, and he groped quickly for the light-bulb string, pulling it and shutting the door behind him. He leapt back, certain he had seen the flash of a face as the light came on. Black eyes. A gaping mouth. A hushed whisper.

"Hold it together," he chided softly, leaning against the wall to catch his breath. He shouldn't have looked through that window. The image of the little girl was haunting more than his dreams now.

Straightening, he examined this new room. Boxes upon boxes were heaped in sloppy rows. Most were labeled with white rectangles, the contents described in fading marker. Budgets, invoices, expenses . . . None of it interested him. Nobody had dusted the room in ages. As expected, a mop had been shoved into the corner but an industrious spider had webbed it to the wall. Dead flies and gnats gathered in the corners. A nasty pair of old shoes toppled off the one shelf in the middle of the storage room, and he stepped over what looked like a used condom.

Maybe the staff used this closet for their trysts; it certainly wasn't being used for much else.

Frustrated but still determined, Ricky waded into the boxes. He shifted a few of the lids aside, double-checking that the labels matched the contents. Nothing extraordinary. Receipts and lists. His head was beginning to ache with fatigue. He carefully picked up a box and set it on top of one to his left, sorting through the bottom row of storage. A cloud of dust choked him as he did so, but he was rewarded right away—the box underneath had no label at all. What had Warden Crawford said about science and fate?

Ricky wedged himself against the stacked boxes, keeping them balanced with his side and hip while he tore the lid off the bottom box. Leaning down, he grabbed the top sheet of paper, which proved to be a scribbled-over index card.

DISCARD IMMEDIATELY

"Someone slacked on the job," he mused, putting the card aside and digging into whatever was supposed to be destroyed but clearly hadn't been. Inside lay a bounty of folders, some succumbing to the ravages of mold. He opened one after another, finding more patient cards like the ones on the first floor. These were yellowed with moisture and neglect, but he could still read the writing on them. Names. Dates. Symptoms. His heart dropped as he thumbed through them, ignoring the nauseating smell of the dust and mold filling the storage room.

None of the lines describing the patients' ultimate fate demonstrated improvement. Just like the others. He hit a run of eleven patients in a row, all of them deceased within six months of admittance. No improvement. Worsening symptoms.

Increased paranoia. Delusional behavior. Insomnia.

Death.

God. That was quite the bad streak. It went way beyond coincidence, he thought. Some of the blank lines on the back had brief descriptions of treatments or procedures. Others had cryptic notes like "Close" or "Closer still." He flipped more quickly through the cards, faster, faster, *death, death, death.* Then he stopped. His heart plummeted. *No.* It wasn't possible. He knew that name. He had tried to forget that name.

Your father ran away. Your father left us.

Lies. It was all lies.

Maybe he had known and just refused to accept it. Forgotten it as some kind of coping mechanism, a necessary part of feeling better. Maybe he had known the second he saw the photo in the first-floor storage closet, or maybe when he saw that pale, fragile man hiding among the costume boxes, his eyes wide and pleading. Maybe Ricky knew it when that voice kept speaking to him, trying to help him, trying to tell him to run.

Shaking. He couldn't stop shaking. The card trembled in his fingers as he lifted it closer to his face and nearer to the light. If he was mad and hallucinating this moment, it would make more sense, he decided, reading the name over and over again.

Desmond, Pierce Andrew

Self-Admitted

Insomnia, MPD, restlessness, suicidal ideation

Deceased, 1967

And on the back: *Closest.*

Desmond, Pierre Andrew

Self-Admitted

Insomnia, MPD, restlessness, suicide

Deceased, 1967

CHAPTER
№ 33

*B*rookline was consuming him, devouring him, eating him alive. The walls were coming for him, crushing in on all sides. He couldn't sleep and couldn't move to toss. Blue walls neared him on every side, shot through with white, like sheer glaciers on a collision course. He had been trembling and delirious when Nurse Ash came to put him back in the cuffs. Unmoving. She had shifted him around but he refused to speak or even make a sound.

There was no sleeping after what he had found. His father. His father had died here, not one year ago. What if he had been in this same room? And he had seen him . . . Oh God, he had seen him cowering on the floor, pits of black despair where his eyes should have been.

Ricky shook his head, trying to make sense of it all. When he shut his eyes he saw that horrible, hollow face of his father huddled on the floor, and so instead he kept his eyes wide open. Shadows moved along the floor, bouncing, the trees outside his window shaking in a nighttime gust. A shadow on the opposite wall darkened, and he fixated on it. It looked denser than the others, darker, a firm, black shape that grew larger as he watched.

Just a trick of the darkness. Just a figment of his sleeplessness. His mind was being stretched thinner and thinner, led to even bleaker places. But that didn't seem to matter to the shape across the room. It coalesced into a silhouette, fuzzy on the edges. He couldn't be imagining it. He blinked and it remained, growing, humming, breaking through the stone, forcing its way through something meant to hold it. But it shook free, moving not along the wall but toward him across the floor.

A person. A figure. She had come through the wall. It was her, the girl who was all dingy dark hair and tattered white cloth. She was coming for him now and he could do nothing but watch, secured to the bed. The girl dragged her way across the room toward him with her head drooping on her shoulders, slow, inexorable, her hair so long it almost brushed the tiles. There were black spidery cracks along her skin, that odd, unnatural halo of flickering black light surrounding her.

He screamed. Fighting the restraints did nothing but make his wrists ache. She was coming. She was close now.

"L-Leave me alone," he said, and it came out in a sob. "Please, just leave me alone. What do you want? I don't have anything. I have *nothing*. Just go away. Please go away!"

When she was close enough to touch him her head snapped up and she was grinning, a huge, horrible grin too big for any human's face.

"Dead, dead, dead," she hissed. "Just like *all of us*."

✗ ✗ ✗ ✗ ✗ ✗

Ricky could barely hold his head up to follow the swing of the pendulum. Its eerie glow didn't captivate him anymore. He looked beyond it, glaring as best he could with lowered, blood-shot eyes, at the warden.

His father's killer.

The path forward eluded him, but he could only focus on that one, deadening fact. His father had come here of his volition to try to get better. He had trusted these people to help him and instead they had killed him.

Ricky hadn't spoken a word to Nurse Ash despite all her concerned frowns and coddling. The words in the notes from Kay slipped right through his mind. What did they matter? What did she or the nurse or any of it matter when the warden had killed his dad? He would probably end up killing Ricky, too. Ricky's body didn't contain enough energy for his rage, and so instead he was quiet, boiling away inside, letting the knowledge and the secret fester until he felt ready to vomit all over the warden's expensive shoes.

"Pierce Desmond," he managed to groan.

The pendulum slowed, the warden's beady eyes focusing tightly behind his round spectacles. "I beg your pardon? Ricky, I need you to focus, please . . . You're all over the map today."

"Pierce. Desmond." Then he did have enough energy and he flew out of the chair, his cuffs still loose from breakfast, throwing himself at the warden and flailing, beating him with his fists. He heard the orderly thunder across the room while Crawford tried to hold off the assault, flinging the red stone aside and grabbing Ricky's wrists. Ricky was too weak, too tired . . . They overpowered him, but not before he got in a few solid hits.

"YOU KILLED HIM! YOU KILLED HIM, I KNOW YOU DID IT!"

"Jesus Christ, sedate him, will you? Could we get more assistance in here!?" The warden ducked out from under Ricky's body, scooping up the stone and stumbling away. He adjusted his askew spectacles, watching the orderly wrestle Ricky to the bed and force his arms behind his back, pinning him until the room filled up with people.

Ricky ignored them and ignored the pain in his wrenched arms. He spat and struggled, attention pinpointed on the warden's bewildered face. "He was here. He trusted you and you *murdered* him! He didn't want to do what you wanted and you killed him for it!"

"Sedatives, yes, thank you," the warden calmly directed his staff, ignoring the screaming boy on the bed. It only made Ricky more furious. "And have his new prescription at the ready when he wakes up! Not those, these." The warden's cool veneer shattered and he dashed for the bed, fumbling in his coat pocket for a bottle of pills that he handed off to Lurch. Nurse Ash arrived and others, and Ricky could hardly hear what they were saying over his screaming.

"Just a bad episode," Warden Crawford was saying. His spectacles blurred in front of Ricky's face. They had stuck the needle in. Everything was fading. "There now, just a bad episode, mm? This will all be sorted soon, Ricky. Trust me. *Trust me*."

✗ ✗ ✗ ✗ ✗ ✗

He couldn't remember waking up, but they must have forced him out of sleep. Was it possible to be awake and unconscious at the same time? He felt it. Limbo. Strung up between waking and sleep. Ricky couldn't move. They had secured him to some kind of strange chair, locking down his arms and legs. The red stone swung in front of him and he could do nothing but watch it go back and forth; digging, metal claws kept his eyelids peeled back. No moving. No blinking. Occasionally he felt a cooling drip in his eyes to ward off the drying.

There was no telling how many people were in the room. All was blackness except for a focal point of light directly in front of him. A lamp, maybe? And the lamp illuminated the red stone going back and forth, lulling him, beckoning him away from the pain and confusion.

He drifted. This couldn't be real. None of this could be real, so that meant he must be asleep. The warden's voice melted over him. How long had this been going on? There was no sense of time passing, his entire world condensed down to the red pendulum and the warden's soothing tone.

After a while, it was the only sound he wanted to hear.

You're safe now, Ricky, you're safe.

Follow what I say, follow my voice, it's the only way to stop this, the only way to stop the pain . . .

Yes. He wanted the pain to stop. He didn't want to be locked in a chair. He didn't want a gag in his mouth or his eyes forced open. The lamp was so, so hot, burning his skin, sweat pouring down his face and soaking his pajamas.

You're so special. To be the first, to be Patient Zero, it's a privilege, Ricky, don't you like being special? I don't think you need fixing, Ricky.

That sounded true. He didn't need fixing. Finally, someone was listening to what he had been saying all along.

You're perfect as you are. But you need to listen. You need to obey. Perfect boys obey. You want to be perfect just as you are, don't you?

I am, he thought, a cough of pain lodged behind the gag, *aren't I?*

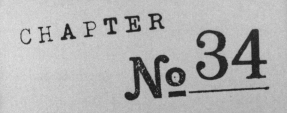

CHAPTER
№ 34

Journal of Ricky Desmond—July

Ain't too much sadder than the tears of a clown when there's no one around . . . That's it. That's all I can remember. It's all going. I live at 335 Hammond Street, my mother is Kathy Anne. My father is . . . My father is. I don't know. I remember Butch. I remember Mom. Where did it go? These aren't things you forget. Nurse Ash told me not to forget. She told me not to trust. But I just can't remember everything, it takes too much energy and when I try it puffs into smoke.

I just want to sleep. I wish he would let me sleep.

When the warden visited next, Ricky felt like he was peering out through a stranger's eyes.

They sat facing each other, Ricky on the bed this time, the warden in a chair across from him. An orderly hovered by the door, but Ricky didn't have the energy to speak, much less fight.

They had fed him gruel and water for so many days now that he couldn't count them. His stomach hurt constantly, but when he asked for more or for something different he was ignored.

The medicine left a tremor in his hands and a sour, chalky film in his mouth. He knew it wasn't just aspirin anymore. It had only been a few days, hadn't it? He couldn't stand this much longer.

"I can tell you're coming around, Ricky," the warden said softly. He pursed his lips, leaning forward to place a hand on Ricky's knee. "Punishing you is a punishment for me. It hurts me to treat you this way, but I should have known. Perfection is never easy. It demands sacrifices. Your father was like this, too, sometimes. Worse, even. He resisted because he didn't want to be part of history. Part of science. That's very selfish, don't you think?"

Ricky didn't think it was selfish at all. His lips tightened into a grimace as soon as the warden mentioned his father. His father was . . . gone. For some reason that didn't seem real.

"Things will be easier now," the warden assured him. His face had new lines on it, the masklike surface cracking. "I just need to know you're with us. With me." Leaning to the right, he grabbed his leather doctor's case and set it on his lap, clicking open the latches and reaching in. Ricky watched him produce a scalpel and place it on the bed next to his hand.

He stared at the scalpel and flinched. In the warden's hands, that was an instrument of pain. Of death. Ricky thought he was doing better. Why would the warden need that now?

"Do you want to hold it?" the warden asked.

"No," Ricky replied, but it was partially a lie. He didn't have any feelings at all about the shiny little knife at his side. "I don't know."

The warden nodded and took a clipboard from his case. He unscrewed a pen and began to scribble notes, placing the doctor's suitcase back on the floor.

"Could I have something to eat?" Ricky asked. "I'm starving."

"Soon. When we're done here you can have a treat, mm? A reward." The warden continued jotting notes and then pushed his spectacles up the bridge of his nose. "You don't want to pick up the scalpel?"

"No, I want to eat."

"You don't want to attack me with it?" the warden pressed. A flame leapt in Ricky's chest. Attack him? Why would he do that? There was a reason. There must be a reason. A wall had been built around the reason. It was hiding somewhere in his head, concealed, but he couldn't access it. It had just been there. Something about . . . Something about someone . . . Why was it not important anymore? His head pounded when he tried to reach for memories.

"It's right there, Ricky, and I assure you it's extremely sharp. You don't want to take it and slash me?"

"No," he answered, working his jaw. Maybe he did, but even if that was the case, he knew it was the wrong answer. The wrong answer would put him back in the chair. "No, I don't want to touch it."

Nodding, Warden Crawford muttered something to himself and wrote down another few lines of notes. His handwriting was long and looping cursive, too stylized for Ricky to read at that angle. The only word he could make out was "Progress."

"And what happened to your father, Ricky? What happened to Pierce Desmond?"

It was like someone in the next room over shouted the answer, right away, almost before the warden had finished asking the question. Too loud. Too insistent. It felt false, but it was the first thing that came to mind so it had to be true.

"He committed suicide."

"Where?"

"Here. Here in this room."

"That's right, Ricky. You have an excellent memory." The warden grinned at him, proudly, beaming, and Ricky mimicked the expression. Yes, he did have a good memory. He was doing well. *Progress.*

"Your friend Keith has been very disappointed, you know. I had ended his aversion therapy but we had to revisit that decision after your outburst. Perhaps you will consider his comfort and fate going forward. It really is unwise to make a deal, Ricky, if you have no intention of holding up your end of it."

Keith . . . Who was Keith? No, her name was Kay. Kay was his friend. Kay was his friend and she was suffering because of him. The thought almost broke Ricky out of his stupor. Once, what happened to her had meant something to him, though even when he concentrated now he struggled to think of what mattered. No more songs in his head. No more jokes. And friendship? That seemed too distant a concept to matter at all.

"I . . . don't know," he said truthfully. He wanted to cry. Something was his fault. A Very Ugly Thing was his fault. People cried when that happened, didn't they?

"You're all right, Ricky. Don't worry about any of that now.

Focus on my voice and what I am saying to you, yes? Just give me your attention and your focus, and all will be well. Listen: I want you to pick up the scalpel."

His hand reached for it before he could think it over. "Why?" he asked, almost as an afterthought, because he was doing it, his body obeyed even if his mind questioned.

"Because I said so."

The knife was warmer than he expected, like the metal was alive. He grasped the slender handle and picked it up, holding it at a safe distance from his leg. There was another twinge in the back of his head. He would say a word or conjure a thought and forget it a moment later. He had already forgotten about the scalpel in his hand.

"Good, now lift it. Yes, higher. Now I'd like you to hold the blade to your throat."

This, at least, he knew was wrong. But Ricky couldn't stop his hand from obeying the commands. It was dangerous, one slip and he could kill himself, or maybe that was what the warden wanted. He didn't understand. Ricky was doing everything he said! A desperate sound broke out of his throat, a whimper and a cry. Why was he being punished even when he did what he was told?

The warden met his eye and gave him a reassuring smile. "Are you afraid, Ricky?"

"Yes."

"Are you afraid of what I might ask you to do next?"

"Y-Yes."

"Don't fear me," the warden said gently. "We have a kind of pact, don't we? You are becoming my vessel. My right hand.

I would be foolish for hurting something that's part of me, wouldn't I?"

Ricky nodded, forgetting the scalpel was there and flinching, feeling the metal kiss the column of his throat. Squeezing his eyes shut, he wished for it all to be over.

"Just one more question, all right?" The warden continued with that warm smile, but it did little to comfort Ricky. His hand trembled and so did the knife.

"Okay."

"Is Nurse Ash assisting you? Has she been sneaking you things? Telling lies about me?"

No, no, no. Tell him no! She helped you so much, you know she did . . . Don't betray her now, not when you need her more than ever! Jocelyn is your friend. She and Kay are your only friends here.

But that warning meant nothing when the warden was asking. Why couldn't he just lie? Why couldn't he just save himself?

"Yes."

The warden wasn't angry. He wasn't anything at all. He nodded solemnly and sucked in his cheeks, thinking in silence for a long moment. The knife grew slick in Ricky's hand, covered in his nervous sweat. "You can put the scalpel down now, Ricky. I think it's quite clear that we're done."

CHAPTER
№ 35

*T*he water was torture, cold and then burning hot, the pressure so high it left his skin a furious red. Behind the nozzle of the hose, Ricky could see the blank face of the orderly who controlled the temperature, tormenting him, hot and then cold, back and forth, oblivious or maybe numb to Ricky's pain.

Finally, when he was scoured from head to foot, the orderly shut off the water. Freezing, Ricky dripped against the wall, rubbing his arms and then his chest, trying to stave off the violent shivers that made his teeth rattle noisily in his head.

"Sparkling clean," the orderly said, coiling up the hose and stashing it in the corner of the room. The small, cold bathing area was just down the hall from his cell, with high, unbarred windows that were well out of anyone's reach. White tile lined the room from floor to ceiling, and it was empty except for a rusted drain in the floor and the dreaded hose in the corner.

"All ready for your Big Day," the orderly added. It wasn't Lurch this time, but a shorter, sandy-haired man in his forties or fifties. He looked like a shrunken version of the warden but without spectacles.

"Big day," Ricky repeated the words, waiting for them to take on meaning. Had he forgotten something, again? What was his Big Day? The morning had started like most others, his nightmares interrupted by a nurse coming to give him his morning medicine and meal. Only it wasn't Nurse Ash anymore and Ricky knew that the swapped-out aspirin was just a distant dream.

He didn't know what the warden was giving him in those pills, but it left him in a perpetual fog. Or maybe that was the restless nights. Or being secured to a bed for most of the day. Or submitting to the warden's frequent hypnosis sessions.

"You've got visitors, Ricky, my boy," the orderly chirped. "Aren't you lucky? The warden's favorite. *Of course* you get visitors. Had to clean you up, didn't we? Can't have you looking like a slob on your Big Day. If you do well, I bet he'll give you another chance at the next gala. Wouldn't that be special?"

Visitors? The fog over his thoughts lifted for a moment. He let the orderly force him out of the bathing room and back down the hall, where he was given a clean set of patient's shirt and trousers and expected to change while the man hovered. Nobody allowed him to do anything on his own anymore except sleep. Not even the long-haired girl came to see him anymore. He didn't miss her, but it felt like just one more abandonment.

To his surprise, the orderly did not secure him to the bed again but directed him to put on the thin, disposable shoes given to all patients. Then Ricky was marched out of the room and down the hall to the stairwell door. Ricky's concept of time was wavering at best, but he guessed it had been at least two weeks since he had been below the third floor.

Even if he hated room 3808, it felt like an anchor. Now he was being taken down the stairs to the unknown. The orderly hummed absently to himself, nudging Ricky along, down a new stairwell to the first floor. It was one of two grand staircases that flanked the lobby, as if this building had once been for a lighter, happier purpose. Maybe it would be again one day. He didn't want to guess; he only knew what Brookline was now.

They skirted the lobby and passed the dispensary. For everyone else it was just a normal day at the sanitarium. Two nurses whooshed by, their heads bowed in eager conversation. Both spared a quick glance for Ricky, saw he was with the orderly, and moved on. Laughter came from the cafeteria. The first-floor patient ward, where he had previously stayed, showed no signs of life. The patients were resting or elsewhere, outside gardening or in the recreation room.

Ricky indulged his vague curiosity. It felt like he was visiting this part of the asylum for the first time. A memory of whispering out of turn with Kay as they were brought outside to work seemed like a lifetime ago. He was no longer that person.

They had fed him much better this morning, but the richer food hurt his stomach as much as the meager scraps. His gut ached, bloated and tight, the bacon and eggs sitting in his belly like a sack of rocks.

When they reached the warden's office, Ricky hesitated. "Why are we here?"

"Talkative now, are we?" the orderly chided. "Just get inside, Desmond. No more questions. It's your Big Day, eh? Smile."

Smile. The door opened and he was unceremoniously shoved inside. It felt like picture day at school, when his hair would be combed strangely and his clothes too new and starched. That same kind of false, forced grin came to him then, and he stepped inside the warden's office to find two familiar heads turned away from him. Then they heard the door and looked.

Mom and Butch. Ricky froze in place, still grinning, and tried not to break down and cry.

CHAPTER
№ 36

"Oh, Ricky!" His mother stood, clutching her handbag to her chest, and broke into a relieved smile. She was wearing her nice yellow sundress with the pleats and the sunflower print. Sometimes she wore that to church, but only ever on special occasions. Butch was squat and square as ever, a football player's physique with a protective layer of meat loaf and beer.

"It's so good to see you, sweetheart!" She ignored the distressed grunt of the orderly and flung herself toward Ricky, gathering him into her arms and squeezing.

He didn't know what to do. What *could* he do? Over his mother's shoulder, he found the warden's line of sight. Crawford hovered behind his desk, watchful, his expression oddly vacant. Ricky's mother was here. Here! This was the last-inning miracle he had been waiting for and wanted more than anything else. Was it the end of summer already? That had to be the explanation.

Slowly, Ricky lifted one hand and put it on her back, comforting her. She trembled and hiccupped, sobbing, holding him tight to her chest. It was like being stoppered up. He wanted to feel relief, to explode in every direction with joy, but the warden's influence prevented him. The pills. The hypnosis. There were two Rickys now, the old one and Patient Zero, and the latter always stood guard over the former.

"Hi, Mom."

"His state is still very delicate." The warden's voice broke through their reunion, and his mother tore herself away, quickly dabbing at the tears on her cheeks with a handkerchief Butch produced. "This is probably all very overwhelming for him. His anger issues were very pronounced at the beginning, but now he is doing much, much better. One day at a time— order and discipline, routine, it's what he needed."

"Yes." His mother took a step back, bumping into the chair across from the warden before sinking into it with a sigh. "Yes, I understand. Just a mother's relief . . . You must know . . ."

"Emotion is natural," the warden said, utterly devoid of feeling. He kept Ricky's gaze and then motioned to the open space in the office near the window. "And your relief is matched with mine, I assure you. It's always so rewarding to know a patient is improving. This is a new and improved son. Not violent. Not prone to *acting out*."

The window was open. Birds chirped outside. The college adjoining the asylum was noisy with activity as people gathered for a barbecue, for Independence Day or Labor Day or whatever day they were celebrating. Freedom. It was right there. He could smell the barbecue smoke and fresh-shorn grass. Ricky looked at his mother, at her bright green eyes, the same as his, and her black hair, just like his, and never had he thought it possible to feel so alienated from someone he knew to be blood.

"He's improving?" His mother turned toward the warden, resting her hands on the edge of his desk.

"We've heard that before," Butch muttered. His hair was

buzz-cut, flat enough to land a model plane on. Teenage acne had left his face mottled and pitted. He closed one giant paw over Ricky's mother's hand and shot a glance at him. "How do we know that ain't a bunch of bullshit?"

"*Butch.*"

"What? It's true. He doesn't look any different to me. Skinnier maybe. Hey! Kid! You still a queer or did this one get through to you?"

"Really, he usually doesn't speak this way, it's just been such a difficult time for everyone in the family. It takes a toll on all of us—"

And now Butch leveled his gaze at Warden Crawford, jabbing a finger in his direction. "Because don't think for one second we can't tell if you're lying. It makes me sick, you hear? It just makes me queasy to be lied to. Those other doctors said the same damn thing! He still liked to throw a punch after Victorwood and Hillcrest!"

Butch's face, tomato red, subsided into a fleshy bulldog pout. He had sat up straight in his seat to say his piece and now he slowly eased back down, his temper fading as the seconds ticked by. Meanwhile, the warden regarded him calmly behind tented fingers.

"Tell them now how well you're doing," Warden Crawford said softly. Soft, yes, but it was a command. "Be honest, Ricky, and let them know how you feel your time at Brookline has been."

The words started pouring out of his mouth before he could stop them. It was his voice, but he didn't recognize it. "The warden has been working with me every day, Mom. You don't need to worry about me."

"Nobody was worried," Butch muttered, glaring.

Usually that smug tone of Butch's would make him want to take a swing. And maybe that was the point. Maybe Butch was trying to goad him into a fight. He wanted to take him up on it, scream, but his rage wouldn't rise. Everything inside had been walled off.

"*Yes*, we were." His mother pressed her lips together. "We were very worried. We miss you, Ricky, we just want you to come home. The . . . old you."

"I know, Mom." He gave her a thin smile, feeling a headache build behind his right eye. A vein pounded there. Something was wrong, his face, his expression, the wobbly dam holding back a sudden flood of emotion. He chose words to say but others came out, ones he wanted immediately to take back. "I'll be the old me in no time. You just have to trust Warden Crawford. He knows what he's doing, I'm not cured yet but I'm better. I'm in good hands."

Both Butch and his mother stared at him in dumbfounded silence. Then she sprang to her feet, rushing forward and collecting Ricky into her arms again. "My little boy wonder." She squeezed him, hard, and he felt one of her tears smear across his cheek. "I knew it was just a matter of time. That if we just kept trying, kept praying . . ."

"Yeah. Well. Huh." Butch frowned, his face looking even more lopsided and bulldoggish than usual. "Time will tell. You sure he's not just putting you on, doc? He's crafty like that."

The warden appeared perfectly at peace with the accusation, unfolding his hands and spreading them open, inviting inquiry. "I do the work of ten lesser men on a bad day, Mr.

Kilpatrick, and that work endures."

"I was so worried, honey," his mother said, holding him at arm's length. She looked older, as if she had aged severely in the two months since she had dropped him at Brookline. "When you didn't return my letters or my phone calls—"

"Which as I explained upfront is part of our process, of course," the warden interjected.

"Still . . . a mother worries."

"Well, Rick? Put your mother at ease. Tell her how much you've been enjoying your little journey with us."

Another command. The words didn't gush forward so easily this time. Letters? Calls? He had spent so much time convinced that his mother had stopped caring altogether. Even if her attention was slightly misplaced, anything was better than being forgotten. But she hadn't forgotten him. She had written. And called. And now she was there grasping him firmly by the wrists, her eyes glazed with joyful tears.

Take me out of here. They're torturing me. Destroying me. I don't even know who I am anymore. Ricky Desmond is disappearing. Get me out of here before he vanishes completely.

"There's nowhere else I'd rather be at the moment," Ricky heard himself say. "Just long enough for me to complete my treatment."

"Guess miracles really do happen," Butch grumbled. Then he stood, tugging Ricky's mother away by her shoulder. "See? I told you everything was fine. And it's about time, too. We're just interrupting now. The warden has everything in hand. This is what we were praying for . . ."

"I know," his mother said, her smile wavering. She cupped

Ricky's face even as Butch pulled her away. "I just . . . If he's so much better already, maybe it's time we took him back, you know? We miss having you at home, boy wonder."

It even sounded like she meant it. Butch's expression didn't back it up, but then he had never liked Ricky, even before him and Martin.

"I'm not cured yet, Mom," he repeated automatically. "But I'm in good hands."

"Of course you are," she said, but her brow rippled, a shadow of a grimace passing over her face, like she was trying to remember something. "But if you weren't so sure . . ."

"I am."

"He is," the warden said firmly, then stood. "Now, if you'll excuse us, Mr. and Mrs. Kilpatrick, Rick should really be allowed to rest. His treatment is very intense, you see, but the results speak for themselves."

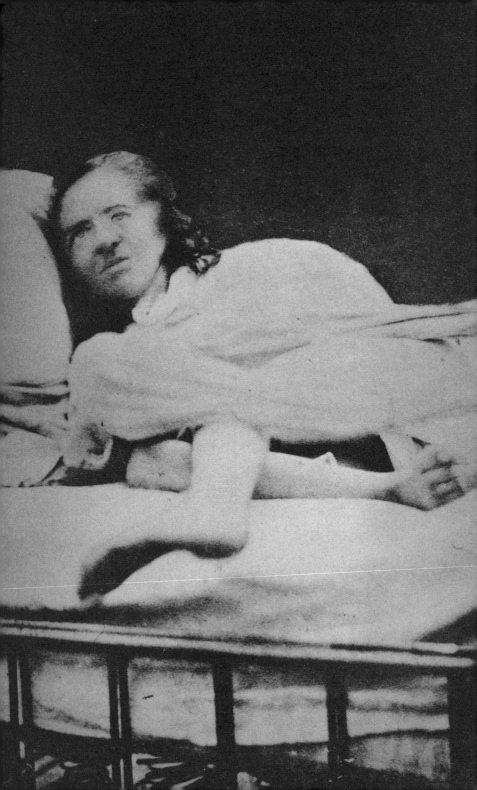

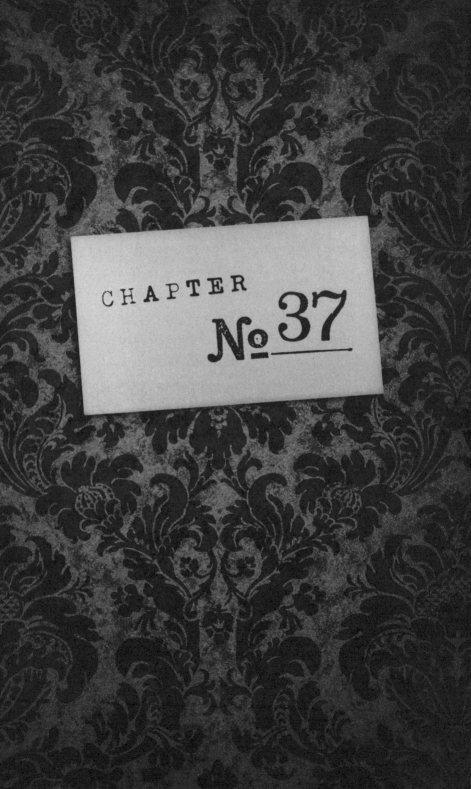

CHAPTER № 37

*T*hey no longer cuffed him to the bed in his room. He hadn't even noticed the permanent redness around his wrists until he was given a chance to examine himself. Of course, his mother wouldn't have seen the marks on him. His long-sleeved shirt hid the evidence of the warden's "results," the ones that apparently pleased her and his stepfather so much.

He stared out the window while the warden put a padlock on the slat that covered the window to the other room. That was fine. Ricky had no intention of looking again, anyway. Somehow it was easier to get by thinking he was the only one under the warden's care, and it was beginning to feel like that in earnest. He was isolated and alone, in a world of two people. Two men.

Two monsters.

Through the bars guarding the window outside, Ricky watched his mother's car driving away. He followed its trajectory down the street and over the hill, pretending to observe it long after it had faded from view. His fingers wound around the bars, absorbing the cold. His last chance for escape had just pulled away, and he had been complicit in the loss.

"I think perhaps you deserve a reward for behaving so well today," the warden told him, standing near the cutout in the wall. Ricky turned and stared at him, his fingers curling into loose fists. "Don't look like that. I know the methods are extreme, but can't you see the progress for yourself? It's marvelous. Focused, calm, all your pain and confusion forgotten. And I did that for you. No lobotomy. No electricity."

"Yes."

"Now about that reward," the warden said, chuckling. He paced for a moment, tapping his knuckle against his chin in thought. "How about something to read, mm? Wouldn't a book be nice? Something to occupy your hours while I must see to other patients."

"Tolkien," Ricky said without thinking. "*The Lord of the Rings.*"

Ricky couldn't even remember why he wanted that or how he knew the name. It must have come from somewhere deep in his mind, from beyond the wall the warden had constructed in his thoughts. Maybe his brain hadn't been wiped clean after all. Maybe it was just dormant.

The warden didn't seem the least bit surprised by that, and gave a short nod. "I think that can be arranged. Yes, I can do that for you, Ricky. After all, you have done so very much for me."

✗ ✗ ✗ ✗ ✗ ✗

Ricky didn't bother starting at page one. He would, eventually, but for the moment he was interested only in what he could remember. It wasn't much, but when he scanned the table of contents he felt certain he would find what he was looking for. And he did. Someone had told him about this.

The Scouring of the Shire

He recognized that. The rest of what he read mattered less

than the fact that he knew it was somehow connected to a memory hiding in the locked vault of his personality. If only it could be turned from a vague inkling into a key. Ricky read the last pages of the story over and over again, hungry for clues. Terror turning to relief. Loss to victory. But he wanted more.

Lying on his bed, he turned back to the beginning of the trilogy compendium, reading every word from the copyright to the first chapter and onward. Clues. He needed clues. For some reason this particular title had sprung to mind, but why? He turned from chapter four to five and stopped, watching as an index card slid down the paper and onto his pillow.

Odd. Had someone left a bookmark behind? He turned down the page corner to keep his place and then flipped over the index card, finding a note written on it in frantic, uneven penmanship. Almost illegible. Ricky held up the card, squinting, piecing together the jagged letters.

Under the jacket. Don't forget, we haven't forgotten you—

The jacket? Under whose jacket? And that last instruction . . . Ricky had to laugh. Unfortunately for the note-sender he'd been doing nothing *but* forgetting lately. The jacket. Maybe they got it wrong and meant something else entirely. It didn't hurt to check. He grabbed the pillow and swept a hand underneath it. Nothing. The pillowcase held nothing unusual. He slid off the bed and pulled up the mattress, but that too held nothing of interest.

Ricky sat down heavily on the bed, stymied. His gaze drifted back to the book and the note and he rolled his eyes. *You idiot.* Jacket. Book jacket. He slid the dense, papery covering off the novel and flipped it around, finding a card roughly the size of the mysterious note taped inside.

It was a patient card. A searing pain sliced through his head, practically cleaving his head in two. He hissed, pressing his palm between his eyes, trying to alleviate the agonizing pressure. Spots bled across his vision, then they lengthened into thick stripes. Was this what remembering felt like? Was this what it would take to slip out of the warden's grip?

He blinked through the pain, though a scattering of minuscule white dots stayed with him. It felt a little better when he opened his mouth wide, as if to yawn, so he worked at his jaw, trying to ignore the pounding in his skull.

Desmond, Pierce Andrew

Self-Admitted

Insomnia, MPD, restlessness, suicidal ideation

Deceased, 1967

Ricky read it over a dozen times, and each time the pain spiked again. Then he flipped over the card and found a mad jumble of words scribbled in a hand that seemed to deteriorate the longer the ranting went on.

Close. So close! The closest. Yet failure. Again, failure. But I must try again—perhaps this time the blood is the key. Some patients take to the therapy better, I see it now, and the only link I have not tested is the bloodline. With the next I will not fail, with the next I will achieve my legacy. I will achieve it through the blood.

Slivers of memory came to him. Fragments. He could remember the moldy stench in the storage closet, the light-bulb swinging overhead, a haze of dust around him . . . Pierce Andrew Desmond. Pierce Desmond. A face returned to him—a man with his same prominent nose and thick brows. The same big, almost goofy smile. Dad. His *dad*. Then the face changed, growing thin and gaunt, the eyes sunk in, the goofy smile opening in horror.

He closed his eyes again, involuntarily, the pain so strong now he felt certain for a panicked moment that he was going blind. Why here? Why would his father be here? Wouldn't his mother have known? It couldn't be an accident that both father and son wound up at the same sanitarium just a year apart.

More returned, and with it? Rage. Kay . . . Nurse Ash . . . The note didn't look anything like Kay's handwriting. It had to be Nurse Ash. But there was that "we." *We haven't forgotten you.* They were working together on this. Was that possible? The details became more and more vivid, like a photograph developing in front of his eyes. Jocelyn must have found the journal scraps and the patient card when she cleaned his room. Yes. She had warned him to remember, always remember, and to never trust the warden. This was her way of reminding him, of bringing him back before he was too far gone.

He hid the note and patient card under the book jacket, making sure they were secured by the tape. It was risky, he knew, to keep them like that, but what if he forgot again? He would need something to keep being Ricky Desmond, joker and crab-lover, school skipper, rule breaker, kisser of guys and gals . . . The Real Ricky.

And music! God, he had forgotten . . . Melodies flooded his head, the joy and shock of it as intense as if he were hearing them for the first time. He lay back on the bed, humming, tears filling his eyes. "Tears of a Clown," that was one of his favorites. He wondered if his dad would have liked that one. Probably. He had gotten Ricky onto the Beatles, the Stones, Ella Fitzgerald, Coltrane . . .

His father. His father had died here because of the warden's sick experiments. This time Ricky couldn't forget. He might not have everything back but he had enough. Enough to survive. Enough to fight.

Enough to fight, *after* his mother had come, after she was right there and he could have told her everything. Tears burned down his cheeks. He had been so close, so damn close, and now he was stuck. He had told his mother with his own words—no, the warden's words—to leave him at Brookline. And worst of all, she believed him.

CHAPTER

№ 38

*H*e woke to small, cold hands on his face, shaking him.

The little girl stood over his bed, nudging him awake, still pale and fragile, but with eyes and a nose and a mouth. As soon as he tried to cry out in surprise she shushed him. A horrible, vivid scar could be seen just through the filthy fringe of hair over her face. She beckoned silently, gliding across the floor with unnatural speed.

Ricky followed, watching her effortlessly open the padlocked door and turn the corner. Now he had to hurry to keep up, jogging, finding just the ends of her hair as they whipped down into the staircase. Voices drifted like clouds through the atmosphere, jumbled and nonsensical, dark mumblings that seeped from every wall and door.

Down they went, past the first-floor lobby, past the offices, down into the basement. Ricky hesitated, but she was moving so fast . . . If he didn't keep up, he would lose her. He plunged into the cold, wondering if he was mad, wondering if he had a choice. This strange little child had haunted him for weeks now, why did he insist on giving her this power?

But he went, determined, keeping pace now. Whenever he got near she sped off, unreachable.

Shadows with sharp, toothy grins slid across the walls, there in the fringes of his sight and gone when he turned to look. He focused again on the girl, giving chase, and soon they were in the lower ward. The girl flew by every patient cell, ignoring them, going instead to the tall, metal door at the very end of the hall. Through it she went, deeper, deeper into the asylum than Ricky had ever ventured.

The darkened corridor stretched on and on, endless, exhausting, until at last they reached a final door that opened onto an amphitheater-like space. An operating theater. Somebody lay prone on a gurney, skeletal scaffoldings for lights and trays set up around them like silent metal sentinels. The girl had vanished, but Ricky knew that he was still moving forward, compelled to look, compelled to know . . .

The body on the table was covered with a sheet, a strange deformity jutting out from where the head would be. Trembling, Ricky took the edge of the sheet and pulled. His stomach tumbled, and he didn't want to see anymore but it was too late . . .

It looked so like him, but older. Bigger. Dad. The corpse was almost blue with cold, the mouth open slightly, frozen in a surprised cry. A spike had been sunk deep into the left eye socket, jammed halfway in.

Ricky covered his mouth with both hands and tried not to scream. His stomach tightened again and he was going to be sick.

The head fell toward him with a thud, the spike sliding out slowly, inexorably, hitting the tiles and spinning, jangling . . . The one good eye blinked. "Don't forget," he whispered with cracked, purple lips. "Don't forget, Ricky. Don't run, don't hide. *Fight*."

CHAPTER

№ 39

*A*ll smiles, the warden whistled his way into Ricky's room the next morning with Nurse Kramer behind, hustling to keep up. She delivered his breakfast and medicine, the striped red and blue pills that Ricky had dreaded since waking. Usually the nurses held his nose closed and waited until he was gasping and choking to shove the pills down his throat. Lately, with his cooperation, they had simply watched while he downed the medication.

But today Nurse Kramer distractedly set down his tray of eggs and bacon. There were no sharp implements allowed, so he ate instead with a spoon, breaking up the strips of bacon as best he could with the blunted edge. She whirled to face the warden at once, ignoring Ricky as he tucked into his food.

"We need more staff, sir," she was saying in a heated whisper. "Yesterday Mosely broke a wrist trying to unload one of those trucks. And now with Nurse—with the *other* loss of staff, we're all spread so thin. It's simply not feasible to—"

Ricky picked up on that little self-interruption. Nurse Ash. Something had happened to her. Hiding that note in his book might have been her last act of rebellion. Oh God, and Kay had helped. Were they okay? He pretended not to listen, eating despite his lack of appetite.

"Now is not the time or the place for this discussion," the warden replied sternly.

"But you said everything was progressing—"

"Time. Place. Inappropriate." He sighed, pinching the bridge of his nose, his mood taking a sudden plunge. "We can approach this problem this afternoon in my office, Nurse Kramer."

Inspired, Ricky picked up the little cup of pills and rattled it noisily, making a big show of gulping them down while the warden bickered with Nurse Kramer. He palmed the pills before they could get to his mouth, sliding them smoothly under his pillow and into the opening of the case.

He finished miming the process, taking a huge swallow of water.

Don't run, don't hide. Fight.

"This is truly disappointing," the warden was saying, gesturing toward the door. "Today is a big day for Ricky. For us. For this institution. His graduation, if you will, and you've already tarnished it with your constant, insipid complaints. Mosely's wrist will heal, and as to your other grievance, the temporary solution must suffice until a permanent one presents itself."

"Yes, sir. Of course, sir. I'm sorry, sir."

His voice had risen loudly enough to echo, and both Ricky and Nurse Kramer shrank from the warden when he crested the bellowing crescendo of his speech. Then the nurse scuttled back to Ricky, taking his breakfast tray—he wasn't yet finished— and his medicine cup and leaving.

"I apologize for her making a scene," the warden said when the door closed. He opened his hands invitingly to Ricky. "If only our work was my one and only duty. Alas."

"Yes," Ricky parroted as mindlessly as possible. The prick. "Alas."

He still felt a little foggy that morning, and he knew the medication was probably still affecting him in one way or another, but he was already feeling better, either from the food or from his returning memory. From his father. Fire simmered inside him.

But he had more immediate problems. Whatever "graduation" meant couldn't be good for him. Wasn't lying to his parents' faces enough? God, his mother had been in *tears*, overjoyed that her son had been turned into an emotionless shell-person, because even that was better than who he was before, and it was up to them to say what "healthy" looked like in their child. The rage inside him surged, and for once he didn't want to cool it back down.

Not again. Shell-person, Patient Zero, would be banished. When the warden took a few big steps toward him and his courage wavered, he pictured his father's patient card in front of his eyes. He pictured Kay in that dark and horrible little aversion therapy room. He pictured Nurse Ash dashing off a note to him, doing whatever she could to assist.

"I need to show you something, my subject. It's not something I'm proud of, but it's important that you see it. Come with me."

Ricky stood and followed, glancing at the pillow to make sure none of the pills had trickled out of the fabric case.

The warden's good cheer had returned, and he whistled a song Ricky didn't recognize, leading him to the door and out of it. Ricky expected another trip to the office, but instead they went right and just a few feet, to the room directly next door.

With his memories returning and his body bouncing back from the medicine, he had to control his face before it gave him away.

Why would he have to go inside *that* room?

He steeled himself, forcing a nervous fidget out of his leg while the warden unlocked the cell and held the door for him. A few orderlies down the hall, including Lurch, noticed the commotion and looked on curiously. They weren't invited inside.

He thinks I'm completely under his control. He thinks I'm declawed.

Ricky couldn't have prepared himself for seeing the little girl or her room. It was spotlessly clean, but also sad. Almost empty. Her bed was much smaller than his and looked less comfortable. One threadbare sheet lay rumpled on the end of the mattress. She was small and fragile, like he remembered, with a simple white nightdress that ended below her knees. Her long, long hair hung in front of her face, almost brushing the floor.

She didn't seem to notice them, standing very still in the middle of the room.

Warden Crawford took a few confident steps into the room, unconcerned by the heartbreaking bleakness of it all. How could he keep a girl in this state? What could a child that small even do? Her legs barely looked thick enough to hold her upright. He stopped five scant inches from her and leaned down, speaking in a slow, overly loud voice, as if he were addressing a simpleton.

"Hello, Lucy, I'd like you to meet a very special young man. His name is Ricky, why don't you tell him 'hello'?"

Seeing the girl from his visions now, in the flesh, filled him less with fear and more with pity. She was so tremendously thin, a frail husk of a child, malnourishment making her skinny body and big head into doll-like proportions. A vivid scar crossed almost the entire width of her forehead.

Besides the bed and the girl herself, there was nothing else in the cell except for a tiny music box near the door. It was tipped on its side, and the warden went to collect it, still whistling that absentminded tune as he scooped it up and wound up the key, the loud *hrash-hrash* of the geared mechanism cutting through his whistled song.

"It usually calms her," the warden explained. A dirty porcelain ballerina pirouetted on top of the music box, the song slow and slightly broken, the refrain stumbling over itself in places. It was a miracle the thing even worked. "She's one of my failed attempts. As you might expect, the quest for science is not without casualties."

The girl's voice surprised them both, low and rasping, the ghost of a child's once sweet voice. "Can't live forever. Can't do it." Her English was heavily accented, Spanish maybe, so much so that Ricky could barely understand the words.

"Ah, I see we're feisty today," the warden chided, setting down the music box and striding back to the girl. He leaned down again, holding his hands behind his back as he spoke. "A body might not endure, little Lucy, it's true, but an idea? An idea once planted in the right soil can grow forever." The warden turned to face them both at once. "Lucy here was out of control like you, Ricky. At home, she would scream for hours and hours, until they thought she was possessed. When their priest couldn't help them, her parents brought her here. They gave her to me and then forgot all about her, just like your parents did with you."

"Weeds," she whispered, stirring. "Rot."

Ricky wasn't sure how much longer he could stand it in the room. A strong protective instinct flared in him at the sight of her, so small and alone; what had she done to deserve this fate? Probably as little as he had. Or Patty.

Or my dad.

"A pleasant visit with you as always, Lucy, I'm glad you could make one last friend," he drawled. Then he straightened and beckoned Ricky over, smiling so coolly and calmly that Ricky dreaded every forward step. He'd known "graduation" would be something terrible, and now that instinct flooded his body with adrenaline. "Now that you have seen one of my mistakes," the warden said, fishing something out of his coat pocket, "I want you to correct it. She might be like you in some ways, but you're far superior, Ricky, which is why she won't be much of a loss."

Lucy only moved enough to look up at them both, but even with her hair in the way Ricky knew she was fixated on the warden, who held up something that flashed in the meager light creeping in through the blinds.

A knife. The scalpel.

"Correct the mistake, Ricky," the warden said resolutely, holding out the knife to him. Lucy froze. "You're free of mind and body. Your loss of ego and id complete. This shouldn't be any trouble for you at all. Take the knife. Yes, good, your father held it just the same way."

His father again. Ricky hesitated. Had the warden made his father do this exact thing? He thought of that sad, huddled man hiding among the costume boxes, his bloody hands, and the scalpel tucked inside them.

Ricky would do it—he *had* to. Deep in his subconscious he

could feel the warden's influence tugging him back in the wrong direction. Obeying was simple. Defiance only brought pain. He couldn't go back in the chair again, he just couldn't . . .

Ricky took the scalpel, making sure his hand didn't quake and give him away. The still sadness of the room no longer registered. His mind had blanked in the face of so much unbearable pressure. A little girl. She was just a little girl.

Look around. Does she seem okay? You'd be doing her a favor . . .

The warden beamed down at him, proud as a father on his son's first day of school. He nodded, once, giving permission. Giving encouragement.

"Correct the mistake, Ricky, we can tolerate only perfection."

The scalpel, tiny, light, felt suddenly leaden in his grasp. He raised the knife and saw the girl's eyes flash toward him, huge and dark. Afraid. Those big eyes shut tight as his hand lashed out, drawing blood.

Don't run, don't hide. Fight.

CHAPTER
№ 40

*H*e would never forget the warden's scream—first of agony, then of surprise, and finally of betrayal.

Lucy gasped and took one step back, her hands flying to her face, covering the sounds of her sudden delighted giggling. But the warden wasn't laughing. He reeled back, roaring in outrage, the scalpel still sticking out of his bicep. Blood seeped through his white doctor's coat, spilling down to his elbow as he grabbed for the blade.

"No!" He kept screaming it, over and over again, and in a moment's time the door was bursting open. "Wasted! How could it all be *wasted*? Just like your father, a waste! I was so sure this time, so sure. *Another failure at the moment of triumph.*"

Ricky had cast his lot and now he saw clearly what it would cost him. The orderlies tackled him even though he hadn't tried to move or escape. The warden bellowed as he yanked the scalpel out of his arm—it was the last thing Ricky saw before the orderly sitting on his shoulder clocked him, his vision spinning rapidly into oblivion.

"You're dead!" the warden said between gasps. Lucy laughed and laughed, clapping, giggling, pounding her little feet on the floor. "Dead! Do you understand me? Dead, and I'll finish you myself!"

"You've done it now, genius."

Ricky groaned. He could swear he was dreaming. He had been in a little girl's empty cell. The warden had gone straight off the deep end, trying to force Ricky to kill the child because she was some kind of mistake. Too bizarre to be reality. But then he blinked and lifted his aching head, finding he was lying on his side in what felt like a dungeon.

The stone ground was unbelievably hard, digging into his ribs, but his head was on something soft. He blinked again. It was Kay's leg.

"Where am I?" he whispered, his throat and mouth bone-dry.

"Oh, the Ritz-Carlton, didn't you hear? The good old warden had a change of heart and felt bad for all the trouble, so he set us up in a palace," she said, patting his head. He winced, tender from the orderly's blows. "Sorry. You're in the basement with the rest of us. You really don't remember?"

"I . . . I was with the warden, and he was trying to make me murder someone."

"Yeah, and instead you went ahead and stabbed him in the arm. We'd throw you a parade but the only confetti we have is some dead flies." She chuckled mirthlessly.

Ricky could see her better now. She was thinner than he remembered, and her hair had grown out, a dark, soft halo around her head as she leaned back against the wall. In spite of the darkness, her voice was lighter than he'd ever heard it, like maybe she'd finally decided she had nothing left to lose. Her fingers sifted lightly through Ricky's hair and it just about put him back to sleep.

"I couldn't kill a little kid."

"Ordinarily that would go without saying, but I hear he was really doing a number on you."

"Who told you that?" he asked. "It was only a few days, I don't know how it could go so wrong so fast."

Kay gaped at him. "A few days? Try a month. We thought you were *dead*. Nurse Ash was keeping me in the loop for a while, but then someone ratted her out and . . . Things haven't been going well for her since then." Kay bit her lower lip, eyes straying somewhere over his head. "He dumped us all down here after you tried the shish kebab method on him."

"I'm sorry," he whispered, desperate for water. He closed his eyes again, thinking maybe it would all just go away if he wished hard enough. "This is all my fault."

"Uh-huh. I don't think so. Did you go and brainwash anybody?"

"Not that I can recall, no."

"Chain them up?"

"No . . ."

"Starve them? Electrocute them?"

Ricky snorted. "Nope. It's just . . . It feels like my fault."

"You get exactly ten minutes of moping and making this about you, but then you gotta move because my leg is all pins and needles," she said, easing her shoulders in a circle. He heard a soft pop as her spine adjusted. "I thought you were dead, Ricky."

"I thought I was, too."

"Never say never," she chuckled. "There's no way he's done with any of us."

"There's so much to tell you, I don't even know where to begin," Ricky said. The fog in his brain was quite obviously from the blow to his head, much more manageable than the disconnecting numbness of his treatment. At least he could chalk one up in the positive column.

"Does it look like there's a rush? I don't have to be anywhere."

"Even if I *am* a dead man, I'm glad I get to see you again. It was so lonely. For a while . . . For a while I couldn't even remember you. It was like being in someone else's body. Someone with no past, no memory, no future." The idea of moving from that spot was almost unthinkable. Her leg was so comfortable, even if the floor was hard and he was so, so thirsty.

"I like you in this body just fine."

"Enjoy it while you can," he muttered. "I have a strong suspicion it'll be that sicko's science project soon."

Kay brushed her hand through his hair again, *tsk*ing quietly. "What was the alternative? You said you were supposed to kill somebody, right? You did the right thing."

"Maybe. But then why does it feel so bad?" Ricky asked.

The pain gradually lifted and he became more aware of his surroundings. Their cell was no bigger than the one he had been in when the warden made him watch Patty's lobotomy. At the slightest movement, bugs scattered to the corners of the room. Persistent drips fell from unseen sources, falling unevenly like the last remnants of a rainstorm.

"This is bad, you know," Kay said seriously.

"I know."

"Tossing you in here with me . . . It can't be for long."

"I know that, too." Stirring, he tilted his head to see her more clearly. She looked gaunt, but still pretty, her full apple cheeks the surviving evidence of a healthier diet. "What do we do besides wait? Nurse Ash is probably in a ditch somewhere. We have no friends, no help, nobody on the outside to get us out of here."

A wry smile brightened her face. "That's not *entirely* true."

"What do you mean?"

"Wait for nightfall," she said with a wink. "And you'll see."

CHAPTER

№ 41

Ricky didn't have long to wait. He had been blacked out for most of the day, but now his head wound was just an occasional throb at the base of his skull. When he touched the area it was tender, but most of him hurt, so he hardly noticed it. The orderlies had bruised him all down his back and shoulders, and just flinching from one pain made another sting.

But the pain was forgotten when night fell and slowly, one by one, the doors of the lower ward opened. He heard the others scraping open first, the huge, metal hinges sounding like the inner workings of a steamboat. When their own door opened, he simply stared at it, certain he was either imagining things or this was some kind of trick.

"What the hell," he muttered, sitting up quickly and scooting back to where Kay sat against the wall. "What's going on?"

"It happens every night now. He just lets us out." Kay shrugged. She hadn't moved. "The ward is still locked up tight. No way out."

"But the others?"

"Oh, they roam around down here. Talk. Scream at one another. Whatever they want. I'm starting to think he's hoping we'll all kill one another and save him the trouble of a cover-up." She sighed and stood, helping Ricky to his feet. Out in the hall, he could hear voices and a shape passed right by their open door. "Let's go see what all the commotion is about."

"Aren't they dangerous?" he asked, trailing behind.

"Says the guy who stabbed the warden."

"That's different," Ricky defended softly. "You would've done the same thing."

"No way, I would've gone for the throat."

Fair point. Still, he didn't know what they would find out there. Kay seemed less nervous, padding out into the corridor. A few lamps behind cages hung from the ceiling, striped patterns of light making the stone floor glow yellow. Ricky stopped short the moment he left the cell. He hadn't expected to recognize so many of the people in the hall.

Tanner was there, leaning against the wall, his eyes hardened with frost as he glared at Nurse Ash. And she looked completely different now, shrunken, cuts and bruises on every visible skin surface, her red hair a fiery bramble around her head. She stood next to the little girl, Lucy, who had been transferred from the upper floors to the basement. Her eyes lit up when she saw Ricky and she beckoned him over.

He could hardly believe it. In his dreams she had seemed like an unholy terror, and now he was walking right toward her, his fear giving way to curiosity.

Glancing up at Nurse Ash, the girl tugged on Jocelyn's sleeve and pointed. The nurse—former nurse—leaned down and listened while the girl cupped her hand around her ear and whispered something.

"She's proud of you," Nurse Ash said, still bent over. "And she wants me to thank you for making the right decision."

"That makes one of you," Tanner muttered. His eyes never strayed far from Nurse Ash.

She ignored him, giving Ricky a shrug and a "what can you do?" smile. "For a while there I didn't know if I'd be seeing you again. He tried to make you hurt Lucy?"

"That was graduation," Ricky said, finding his voice. "But I found your note in the book and the card, too. I managed to dodge the medicine this morning. Everything started coming back. I remembered all of you, and my house, and my dad . . . The warden killed him. He was a specimen to experiment on just like me."

"Everything?" Tanner asked, finally tearing his eyes away from the nurse.

"Yes, well, I think so anyway. It's hard to know what's real anymore."

"If his memory came back, then so should yours." He turned back to Nurse Ash. Even after being kept in the basement he still had a bigger, more intimidating build than the others. And he wasn't shy about using it now, taking a menacing step toward the nurse. "You helped him with all of this even after Madge died. How can we ever trust you?"

"She tried to make up for it, okay? She's been helping me." Ricky hadn't meant to intervene, but he did, darting forward and holding out a hand toward Tanner. "This whole time she's been risking her own safety to help me and now she's no better off than the rest of us. You have to let it go."

Tanner's icy gaze only hardened. "I don't have to do anything."

"We all do messed-up things to survive," Kay said, joining

Ricky and putting a hand on his shoulder. "You heard what he said, she's been helping him out upstairs. She must have pissed off the warden pretty bad to end up down here, and that makes her fine in my book."

"He's toyed with all of our heads," Ricky added, using her momentum. "The warden did a lot of things, and he has *a lot* of influence. I almost cut my own throat because he asked me to. I know that doesn't forgive everything, but whatever Nurse Ash did or didn't do, she's working against him now. He probably brainwashed the entire staff. Jocelyn is the only one who actually managed to fight through it. That's remarkable, not something you should yell at her about."

Tanner turned his scowl to Ricky.

"Tanner was an orderly here," Jocelyn explained gently. "He . . . didn't cope well with Madge's death. It was hard on all of us, but he was close to her. I understand why he blames me. I blame all of us. We *both* should have tried harder to protect Madge from that monster."

At that, Tanner glanced at the nurse, then to Ricky, and finally backed down. He leaned against the wall, working his jaw. "It doesn't matter anyway. We're stuck down here until he decides what to do with us."

Ricky took in each one of them in turn. A tall silhouette lumbered up behind Lucy, and he almost cried out to warn her. But the man stepped into the light and simply stood, watching, his dark, balding hair mussed and powdered with dandruff as big as snowflakes. He looked vacant, almost like a mannequin come to life. One that had been left out in the rain to decay.

Dennis.

He recognized Patty and Angela lurking in the shadows around him. Seeing them all under the lamps, he had to laugh. It was like getting spooked by a shadow in the dark, only to turn on the light to see a hat stand and a pair of mittens. Maybe they were dangerous, but right now they only looked bedraggled. They were the broken heart of the asylum.

"There *is* a way out," Nurse Ash spoke up, tentatively, her eyes darting from face to face. "Only . . . It's not easy. One of us would have to die."

CHAPTER

№ 42

*T*here was a loud, clanking sound from down the hall and past the locked ward door. Everyone scattered. Ricky did, too, yanked by Kay back to their cell.

"What are we hiding from?" he whispered. She had pressed him into the corner.

"You never know down here. Does it matter?"

"No," Ricky admitted. "I guess it doesn't." There were no more sounds from outside the ward, but he didn't move. It wasn't exactly unpleasant to be crammed into a corner with a pretty girl. He hadn't had safe human contact in so long; just standing in close proximity to someone he didn't despise felt like a revelation. "We don't have to do this, you know."

"Do what?" she asked, craning her neck back to see him.

"Whatever Jocelyn is suggesting. We could just ignore it, stick to ourselves."

"And wait here to die?" Kay shook her head and then rested it back against the wall. Her hands settled on Ricky's shoulders and squeezed. "There's a target on your back now, Ricky. The warden isn't just gonna let this go."

"There's one on you, too . . . Thanks to me."

"Please. I'm the only black girl in this place. Maybe in this entire state. You don't think I had a target on me the second they threw me in here? Down here we're not in trouble, Rick, we're *discarded*." She gestured to the door behind him. "Trash, get it? Forgotten. Nobody knows we're here and nobody cares. Unless that nurse is some kind of James Bond superspy we're not getting out of here. Maybe if your parents come, but then—"

He winced. "I saw them."

"*What?*"

"I was so brain-dead . . . Just not myself. The warden had me tell them a bunch of lies and they ate it up. Look, I've been thinking about what you said. About the Scouring of the Shire, and going home. Even if we do get out of here, I don't want to go back. They liked what they saw. They would rather get a different person back or no person at all. They don't want me," he said, taking in a shaky breath, "and I don't want them. My real dad died here. There's nothing for me with my family."

"Ricky . . . Jesus."

"Yeah." He didn't know what else to say. "The warden wanted me here because of my father. He thinks there's some kind of biological link in whatever he's trying to accomplish. I guess he got really close to brainwashing my dad, but when it didn't work out, he found a way to get me here and try again. I heard him talking about it with his rich friends the night of the gala."

"Then we're really stuck here," Kay murmured. There was another large bang and they jumped apart, scattering, hiding together behind the cot that didn't do much to conceal them. He heard the cell doors shutting, slamming, and they were plunged into overwhelming silence.

✗ ✗ ✗ ✗ ✗

They shared that single rickety cot. The next morning, food arrived through a slot in the door. No utensils. Barely enough for one person, let alone two. Like they were animals. Dogs. Kay was right. They were forgotten down here, given only what someone would spare if they bothered to remember the patients at all.

He still wouldn't trade it for his relatively nicer accommodations up on the third floor. And he hadn't dreamed of anything at all. It wasn't freedom, certainly, but he felt more like himself, at least a little unburdened. Faking a stomachache, he let Kay have most of their porridge.

"What do we do all day down here?" he asked.

"Sometimes we can talk to one another through the walls, but you have to shout and that makes the orderlies mad. They'll come sedate you if you get too rowdy. I say we just sing to ourselves or think about stories. Books. Keeps me from losing it." She pushed the empty porridge bowl back toward the door slot. "It'll be easier now. We can at least talk to each other."

"It's so nice not to be alone," he said softly. "Isolation was hell."

The breakfast plates were collected without a word and Ricky watched the hand shoot in and out before the slot slammed shut. "Does the warden come down here much?"

"It's only been a few days for me so I couldn't say. My guess is he was too busy messing with you, but now? Unless he's found a new favorite we might be in trouble."

"*Gah.*" He shook his head, hunching his shoulders and turning away from her. "This *is* all my fault. I should've just . . . I don't know . . ."

"Killed that little girl?" she asked.

"I could have tricked him for a little longer," Ricky said, but he knew that line of reasoning would lead him nowhere.

"And then what? If we get out of here, it's despite his best efforts not because of them," Kay said, standing and pacing. "That nurse helped you out. She helped me out. If anybody knows a way out of here, it's her."

"Don't you worry about the 'and then whats'?" Ricky asked. "We even get up to the first floor, and then what? We make it outside, and then what? We make it out of Camford, and then what?"

"Would you rather not try?" she asked, sounding defensive.

"No . . . Obviously we have to, I just . . . I don't know. Don't listen to me."

She stopped pacing and joined him, sitting facing him and leaning forward with a sigh. They all looked so rough, so abused. He wondered what it would be like to see everyone in the basement cleaned up and happy. Treated well for a change. "The college," she said. "Maybe we could go to the administration. It's right there, you know."

"Or they would think we were crazy runaways. And anyway I think the warden has influence with them, he's trying to make his buddy the dean."

"Scratch that, then," she murmured. "Does it make you feel better if I say: we'll think of something?"

"Sure," Ricky replied dryly. He remembered what his father had said to him, or his vision of his father, though he was now starting to believe it really was him. Fight. That seemed so impossible now, but they had survived this far and stayed together. His mother said she had been writing and calling, so maybe she did still care, and even if he was angry with his parents, they might at least provide a way out and that was better than nothing. He could decide if he still wanted her love and support later, when they were safely away from the warden.

"We will," he told her confidently. "I know we'll think of something."

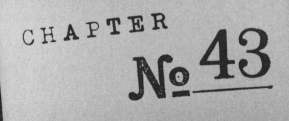

CHAPTER № 43

*T*hey gathered in the cell Nurse Ash shared with Lucy. There weren't enough rooms for everyone to be housed individually, but even if there were, Ricky had a feeling they'd be packed in together. This freedom wasn't a gift, he knew, it was a statement of their powerlessness.

Scheme together, plot together, kill one another . . . It doesn't matter.

He tried not to entertain thoughts of helplessness but they kept creeping back.

"We don't have to actually die," Nurse Ash was explaining, addressing them from the corner of the room. The rest of them were fanned out in a semicircle, their backs to the door. Dennis stood at the very back, towering over the rest of them. "I don't know if one of us could fake it well enough, but if someone even seems incredibly ill and *close* to dying, they'll have to be treated."

"What makes you think that?" Tanner asked. His attitude toward the nurse wasn't improving by much, but at least he was standing with them. "What makes you think he cares at all what happens down here?"

She centered herself with a long inhale, folding her hands together tightly at her waist. "When Madge died—my friend, *our* friend—Tanner and I were there. We saw it. He could have killed us, too, to cover it up but he didn't. We're a liability. We know things. If more and more bodies start piling up here someone will notice, and attention is the last thing he wants."

"The warden was furious about what happened at the gala and that wasn't even such a big deal," Kay said reasonably. "Things look pretty good if you don't see what goes on down here."

Nodding, Nurse Ash went on, speaking more excitedly now. "Exactly. He tried to use his techniques on Tanner and me to solve the problem. If he could control us, then he could control the situation and Madge's death was one instead of three. I know some of us don't have much family, maybe nobody is looking for us, but there has to be a way to get some outside attention." She paused, pursing her lips, apparently steeling herself for what she wanted to say next. "I have people in Chicago who care about me. They'll start to wonder if I don't check in soon. If I disappear for good, my family will start asking questions."

"This is all about you," Tanner said with a snort. "You want to get carried out of here and taken to a hospital. And what, we should just take your word that once you're out you'll get us help? What if nobody believes you?"

"It's not just that," she shot back just as irritably. "I know the schedule. Intakes and visits don't happen every single day. There's a pattern to things. The warden scheduled a second fund-raiser after the first one ended so miserably. He's going to try again. That's our opportunity. Even if we can't get out, we can at least make enough commotion to startle whoever is waiting in the lobby. It doesn't exactly look like we're being fed, cleaned, and clothed properly."

"That's thin," Tanner said. Even if the guy was being extremely combative, Ricky had to agree with him. The plan revolved around too many Ifs and Maybes. They could give it a shot, of course, but he doubted it would cause so much as a ripple. "They'll sedate you right away; if the warden is so worried about his reputation he won't risk that kind of trouble."

"True, but they're low on staff. I'm gone and Mosely is out with an injury."

"She's right," Ricky rejoined. "I heard Nurse Kramer complaining about it."

"So if more than one of us needs immediate medical attention, we might be able to overpower whoever takes us upstairs," Nurse Ash finished.

"It won't work," Tanner said firmly. "Say it goes exactly to plan, then what? Do you really think a bunch of ranting and raving in the lobby will get your point across? That's exactly what the warden's rich friends on the outside looking in would *expect*."

Whatever small flicker of hope had been kindled was abruptly snuffed out. Ricky groaned. He was right. Even Ricky was surprised they were having this calm of a conversation—them, the worst of the worst housed in Brookline. It didn't matter if *he* knew they deserved a second chance at a normal life. No one else would.

"Do you have a better idea?" Nurse Ash asked, placing her hands on her hips.

"No," Tanner admitted with a shrug. "But I never promised one."

"It's worth trying," Kay said. She had been gazing at the wall with her brow furrowed, and for a while Ricky had assumed she had just tuned out the conversation entirely. "Worst-case scenario is that nothing happens at all."

Or the warden tries to shut us up for good.

"Who else would have to get sick?" Ricky asked, fearing the answer.

"Well . . . You, right? Your parents think you're improving. It would shatter the illusion if they heard you were having episodes."

I knew it.

"I'll do it," Ricky said. "But we need to be organized."

"Yes. Real. It must be real." Dennis, who still had unhealed cuts from his outburst at the gala, had finally spoken up.

"Thanks for joining us," Kay muttered under her breath.

"Yes, Dennis." Although Nurse Ash addressed him politely enough, she avoided looking in his direction. "It needs to be very realistic. We won't get pulled out of here for anything less than a life-or-death situation."

He felt Kay's hand wrap around his wrist, her whisper taking him by surprise. "You don't have to do this, you know."

"Funny, that's what I said," he replied with a half smile.

"Yeah, well, I didn't know *this* was her big idea."

"I do have to do this. Targets on our backs, remember?"

"I like you already, no need to be a hero," she murmured, tightening her grip around his wrist.

"But it wouldn't hurt."

"Seriously, Ricky, don't risk this. We can think of something else."

It was tempting to back down. He had, after all, thought he could survive Brookline by doing nothing, making it into a game, the way he'd done at Hillcrest and Victorwood. But that chance had passed, and he saw now that the inaction of others, hundreds of others, from the nurses to the janitors to the orderlies to the doctors, had allowed the warden to run amok unchecked.

"No, we're getting out of here," Ricky said finally. "No matter how many times it takes, we have to try."

CHAPTER
№ 44

*E*veryone was asleep and the ward was silent when the warden came to visit.

Ricky knew it was him just from the tread of his footsteps. He heard soft whistling, a merry, winding tune, and he shuddered, sitting up slowly so as not to disturb Kay. On she slept, curled on her side away from him. The footsteps grew louder, coming nearer, the song coming with the light rhythm of his feet.

It was not a dream, he was sure of that, but he pinched his arm anyway just to be sure. Soon the warden would be at their door. He slid off the cot and crossed to the opposite side of the cell, flattening himself against the wall. Parallel to the door, only Kay could be seen if anyone looked inside through the observation slot.

Just as he predicted, the footsteps halted and the observation window eased open, so slowly and softly it was almost imperceptible. He breathed through his mouth, deeply but soundlessly, straining his ears to hear through the drips of the damp cell and the creaking of the pipes overhead. Kay looked so vulnerable on the cot, alone, an empty space where he should be lying next to her.

"Don't be shy, Mr. Desmond," the warden cooed. His voice was low, thin as a knife's blade and just as sharp. They were back

to Mr. Desmond. It figured, of course, since Ricky was no longer his chosen one. That was his hope, anyway. He wondered if going off the medication was enough. According to Kay he had been up on the third floor for weeks. He had lost track of how many days he had spent in that chair, strapped down and subject to the warden's constant hypnosis.

"I thought I would check on you personally and see how these new arrangements agree with you."

He kept up a conversational tone, as if Ricky were standing right there in front of him.

"How long do you think you'll survive down here?" he asked, chuckling. "Nurse Ash is dangerous. She's one of us, but you know that already. Dennis is unpredictable. A gentle giant one moment, and the next he might have his hands wrapped around your neck. Tanner is broken. Watching his friend die destroyed him. Patty is docile as a clam. Can you even trust your cellmate? Are you sure I haven't gotten to him? These misfits aren't your friends, Mr. Desmond. I am your only friend in this place."

Ricky shook his head but kept quiet. Just the sound of the warden's voice pricked at something buried deep in his mind. So he wasn't totally free. He had suspected as much, but the confirmation terrified him. Cold sweat beaded on his forehead, his breaths coming in more rapidly now. Part of him wanted to cry out for help, to respond to that voice inside that insisted he could trust the warden.

Under the jacket. Don't forget, we haven't forgotten you—

The warden lingered but got no reply.

"I'm excited to see how long you last, Mr. Desmond. It's only a matter of time before you come crawling back. I'll be seeing you real soon, won't I? I know you. I accept you. I wanted you. You know, I went to a lot of trouble to get you here. We were sending information about Brookline to your parents for months, and nothing. I thought I might have to drag you here myself, but your mother did the work for me. She took the bait. I found your father, I found your mother, and I found you, too. *You* did the rest. *You* attacked your stepfather. This was the natural place for you after that. The perfect place, in fact, because I wanted you here. And isn't that what you wanted all along? To be wanted for who you were?"

And then he was gone. His footsteps retreated, unhurriedly, his whistled tune even happier as he left. Ricky slumped to the floor, pressing both palms to his face. He wanted to be wanted, but not by a snake, not by a *monster*.

x x x x x

"You didn't sleep."

Ricky had been—almost—dozing on his feet while Nurse Ash and Tanner debated the ins and outs of their grand plan. The more they talked, the more Ricky saw holes appearing in the scheme, but he let his concerns go unvoiced. Exhaustion was leaving him inarticulate at best.

"The warden was down here," he confessed. "He wanted to talk to me. I didn't say anything back, but *God*, I wanted to. He set it all up. He made sure I wound up here so he could experiment on me like he did to my father. And I wanted to *scream* at him. Does that ever go away, nurse?"

"Joss," she corrected him. "I'm not a nurse anymore." Her

hair had been tamed down a bit but she still looked frazzled, the spaces below her eyes just as dark as his. Sometimes he heard Lucy crying out in the night. Maybe that's what was keeping Jocelyn up. "And to answer your question, I don't think it does go away. I know that's not exactly a morale-booster, but it's the truth."

"He did it to you, too? And Tanner?" he asked. They wandered slightly from the group. Lucy played patty-cake with Angela, and Dennis stood still as a statue in the corner, watchful.

"Yes, and he did it to Madge, too," Jocelyn replied. She rolled up the sleeves of her simple patient's dress and shrugged. "I knew something was off about this place when I started work, but nothing could have prepared me for this. I wanted to make a difference here. I tried to protect Lucy but failed at that, too. Then Madge started to behave so strangely, like she was in a daze all the time. At first I just thought it was the stress of working here, but it was more than that. The warden tried to brainwash me into thinking *I* had killed her. For a long time I even believed him. I go over that night every time I lie awake in bed. Every single night. Even when I'm sure I didn't hurt her, there's always that shred of doubt. It was his leverage over me, and it worked."

Ricky picked at his thumbnail, at a loss. It all sounded so similar to how he felt. Most of the days spent in that torture chair were completely gone. Fragments came back to him and dissolved before he could make sense of them. "I believe you, Nurse Ash."

"Joss."

"Joss." He gave her a wan smile. "I might have killed Lucy if

I hadn't started coming to my senses. It was just his thoughts, his commands in my head. But that's what scares me about this plan. He might be able to just snap his fingers and control us again."

"Try to think of a touchstone. Something that should always bring you back to yourself. Mine is seeing you in the basement with him, about to go into Lucy's room. It's so vivid. Among all my other memories of this place, it's the most real. He didn't want to mess with my brain but I still need something to keep my hope alive in here."

"It's my dad's patient card," Ricky said. "Thank you for getting it back to me."

"Of course. I came to this place to help people and wound up making things worse. Now all I can do is try my best to tear down the warden's plans," she told him softly. "I'm afraid I don't really know what those plans are yet. Not the scope. Not the danger."

"We're all time bombs." He hated saying it, but in his heart he knew it was absolutely true. Even after all that had happened, even after the warden had tried to make him a murderer, hearing the man's voice the night before had almost triggered a relapse. None of them were free of his influence. "He could set us off at any moment."

"I think you're right. Gosh, I hate it. But I really do think you're right."

"You two figured out how to save the world yet?" Kay joined them, resting her head automatically on Ricky's shoulder. It did look a little funny, her being the taller of the two of them.

"Mostly commiserating," he told her. Lucy erupted into giggles, apparently having finished her game of patty-cake. Then she came and stood next to Jocelyn, tugging on her sleeve as she always did when she wanted to say something.

Kay kicked him lightly in the shin. "Sounds productive." Her eyes wandered to Dennis in the corner. He still hadn't moved, his arms straight and stiff at his sides. "I'm worried about him. I never know whether he's going to take a nap or start swinging his fists."

"The stress is hard on everyone," Jocelyn replied in a whisper. "He was never my patient. Madge handled Dennis when she was still alive. Sometimes . . ." She lowered her voice even more. "Sometimes he really frightened her. He's never threatened one of us, and most of what he says doesn't make sense. Something about the White Mountains. About posing people."

"An artist, maybe?" Kay suggested.

Dennis is unpredictable. A gentle giant one moment, and the next he might have his hands wrapped around your neck.

No, that wasn't fair. Nothing the warden said was true, anyway, and Dennis barely seemed interested in them. Ricky glanced his way and noticed that he was watching him back.

"I really don't know," Jocelyn was saying. "But he deserves to be free of this place, too. If he's ill, he should be helped, not abandoned."

Dennis seemed to perk up at that, his body completely still and only his mouth moving. A brighter, livelier light entered his eyes. "No hope, only survival. Only survival."

"Sure thing, big guy. So when do we fly the coop?" Kay pressed.

Jocelyn put her hand on Lucy's head, playing with the girl's hair absently while she chewed over the question. "If I've been keeping track of the days accurately, it should be Thursday. The warden scheduled this second fund-raiser for Friday. I'd never forget because he and Nurse Kramer wouldn't shut up about it, and he was determined to show Ricky off to everyone like a trained monkey."

"I might still get to make an appearance," he said with a dry laugh. "But that's tomorrow night." Too soon, Ricky thought. But was that possible? Why give the warden more time to come for him if they could try to get through to one of the scandalized guests now?

"It's quick, I know," she said, giving both he and Kay an apologetic glance. "It may be one attempt of many, and we can't afford to lose even one."

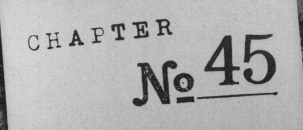

CHAPTER № 45

On Friday morning the staff took Tanner out of his cell, hauling him to the first floor kicking and screaming. When they were gone, his shouts still ringing in the ward, Ricky heard pounding on the door across from there's. It was Jocelyn, desperately trying to get his attention.

The commotion had disturbed Dennis, who banged against his cell door with his head or his foot, almost drowning out her voice as she tried to call to Ricky.

"Rick . . . Are we still going through with this?"

"We have to," he called back, wincing. Of course the warden was starting to separate them. He had to have guessed that Ricky wouldn't simply wait down in the basement quietly. "If they hypnotize him, if he's questioned . . ."

"I know!" He heard her swear. "Dennis! Could you keep it down, please!?"

The banging went on and on, then grew louder.

"Stick to the plan," Ricky told her sternly, sinking against the door. "Our first real shot, right? We have to take it."

And so they waited. He sat with Kay quietly on the bed until the agreed upon time. They were quiet for most of it, because he could read on her face the dread, the anxiety . . . She had kept up a constant stream of jokes the day before, but now they had run out of words. Dennis crashed against his door ceaselessly, robbing them all of sleep.

"If you don't get us out of here soon, I'm gonna kill that creep myself," she muttered, rubbing her temples.

"Listen, if they take us away and leave you down here . . ."

"I'll be fine, all right?" She took his hand and placed it on her knee, then leaned over and brushed a kiss across his cheek.

"Thanks," he said, strangely shy. He had gone further with other people, but this felt special somehow. "The hero always needs a smooch before his suicide mission." He forced a laugh. Neither of them smiled for very long. "This isn't like a big last speech or anything, but I wanted to tell you that I really love your dad's band. I've been a fan for years. No, let me finish. He's a selfish idiot, I get that, and you'd be a better band leader anyway. You should start your own group when you get out of here."

"If," she corrected.

"When," he double corrected. "Even if we screw this up, he'll come to his senses eventually. Nobody is that mean."

"You don't know that, Ricky, and I'm not sure how you can say that. You've seen what the warden will do, plenty of people are that mean."

Ricky shook his head. "I wasted a lot of time thinking I was so smart and so hip. Now I just want to be good, and to do that I have to believe other people are good, too."

"You *are* good. I know you tried to help me when you were upstairs," Kay murmured. "They eased off the shock therapy for a while. That was you, wasn't it?"

"I was up above you, right? Had to be a guardian angel."

She rolled her eyes, but he saw a blush creep up her neck, too. "Corny."

"Probably."

"I'll keep trying even if you mess this up completely," Kay promised. "That's as good as I can do."

"And it's plenty." Ricky leaned into her, feeling a knot in his stomach tighten by the minute. "If we can survive in here, we can do anything."

"Focus on the gala tonight," Kay told him with a wry smile. "First things first, right? We have to make it out of here before we can dream big."

It would be time soon, time to playact the tantrum of his life. He would need energy and all he felt was exhausted. Sometimes he wondered if he could just sink into the misery of the place, give up and let hope die off for good inside, just live in a fantasy of being on the outside, of running away somewhere with Kay.

But it was no good. She was there, warm and alive; dying, even just in his mind, couldn't be an option.

The time to start came too soon. The loss of Tanner weighed heavily on his mind. The warden was persuasive, if they really pressed him they might have found out what the plan was; they might ignore anything that went on in the basement. But he had to believe that Tanner wanted them to get out just as much as the rest of them did. His friend had died here, and they all would follow her—sooner or later—and Brookline was not an appealing grave. He wouldn't die there like his father had, he had to *fight*.

And the thought of those glamorous so-and-so's mingling above them made him sick. Furious. His temper wasn't a good thing, he knew that, and in an ideal world, he might really have gotten treatment for it. But just for tonight, his temper could be something useful. They probably weren't giving two thoughts to the patients stuck in Brookline. They probably thought they were *helping* science. The warden had them brainwashed in a different way, blinded to what was really happening behind the white, clean veneer of the hospital. Brookline was rotten to the core, he just had to force those people to take one worm-ridden bite.

He heard the signal through Dennis's pounding on the door. Three quick taps, a pause and then three more.

"This is Phase Three," he said to himself, to the warden, softly. "The one where we expose you for the fraud you are."

Ricky went first.

He had never hollered so hard or so much in his life. If Dennis's racket hadn't brought anyone running, then Ricky would have to outperform him by a mile. He threw himself on the floor and screamed at the top of his lungs, inhaling as deeply as he could before giving another long, piercing wail. Kay joined in, but she started calling frantically for help.

"He's having a seizure!" she cried. "Oh God! Oh God, help us! Help him, something's not right!"

It took five straight minutes of theatrics before he heard the door to the ward open down the hall. His heart pounded hard and fast in his chest. It was working. This was just part one, and they weren't even close to being out of the woods. He threw himself back into the screams, writhing on the floor, letting his jaw go slack.

Kay kicked his shoulder gently, letting him know they were

opening the door. Now was the crucial moment. As soon as the bolt scraped in the hinges, Jocelyn began her performance. They were probably accustomed to hearing Lucy throw fits, but not her.

"Something's wrong," Kay bellowed as the orderlies finally filed into their cell. With his eyes screwed shut in mock-pain, Ricky couldn't see much of what was going on, but he felt them kneel and take his pulse. "There've been bugs all over this damn place for days now. I think he got bit by something. He's been acting funny, the girl, too."

"Shit, I told the warden we should hose this place down more often," one of the orderlies was muttering. "God, this just had to be tonight, didn't it? He's going to kill me."

"Shut up and concentrate. He feels feverish," the other one said. The two of them knelt on either side of Ricky, one trying to steady him as he flailed. "Don't give him that," he said suddenly. "We don't know what's wrong, we can't just shove a needle in him while he's having a seizure."

Across the hall, Jocelyn wailed louder. *No sedatives.* "We should get the warden," the one taking Ricky's pulse said. "Where the hell is he, anyway?"

"Meeting with his guests, of course," his partner replied. "God, that *noise*. Would someone check on Heimline? They're all having bad reactions to something!"

He heard footsteps scurrying in the corridor, and soon Dennis was no longer pounding on the door but pounding on something else. Ricky's eyes flew open as he heard the first orderly scream in shock and pain.

"Who let him loose!? The ward isn't secured!" This came

from down the hall. It sounded like Nurse Kramer, her voice rising in shrill panic. "Oh my God, get him back in his cell and—"

Her scream was cut short by a loud, gasping crunch that made the hairs on Ricky's arms stand on end. The orderly left with him dropped Ricky where he lay, fleeing into the corridor.

"Ricky, get up." Kay was kneeling over him, shaking him. He was already trembling. Her eyes were wide with fear when he collected himself, climbing to his knees and then stumbling to his feet. "Dennis is . . ." There was another scream as something was slammed into the wall outside their door. He heard a gurgle and a whimper, only loud enough for him to make out over Jocelyn's tantrum. But she sounded different now, genuinely afraid.

"We have to get out of here," Ricky said, turning and sprinting for the door. Kay followed fast on his heels, but they both skidded to a stop as a huge shape darkened the way. Someone was on his back outside the door. One of the orderlies. He wasn't moving and his neck was bent the wrong way, a bluish mark already spreading across his throat.

"You have to calm down." Ricky stared up at Dennis, who had finished throttling every staff member in sight. His thin hair was plastered across his forehead with sweat, that same forehead bright red and bruised from slamming into his door repeatedly.

"Ricky, we have to go! We have to run for it, now!" Jocelyn stumbled out into the corridor, her eyes brimming with tears. He could tell she was doing everything she could not to look at the carnage all around them. A trembling hand closed over

Ricky's shoulder and tugged.

"Close the door," Kay whispered. "Close it now. For God's sake, close it."

He did, grabbing the handle and slamming the door shut without another thought. They were locked inside, cut off, their chance for escape to the upper levels gone. And worse, he could hear Jocelyn shouting his name, and then it turned to a whimper. He heard her feet on the stone outside as she tried to make a run for the outer ward door.

Then there was a grunt and a *thump*, the sound of a skull hitting the floor.

"No! Dennis! Dennis, stop! You know me! You know me!"

Ricky couldn't stop him. The door had locked them in. He pounded as hard as he could, trying to draw the man's attention. Lucy was screaming now, too, but it did no good. At his side, Kay banged on the door, too, yelling, pleading . . .

"You know me!" Jocelyn managed to cry out one last time.

"I know you," came Dennis's low, monotone voice. "I know you would look so perfect posed, posed and still in the White Mountains."

Ricky huddled against the door and covered his ears. He couldn't listen to it. He couldn't listen to the sound of his friend die.

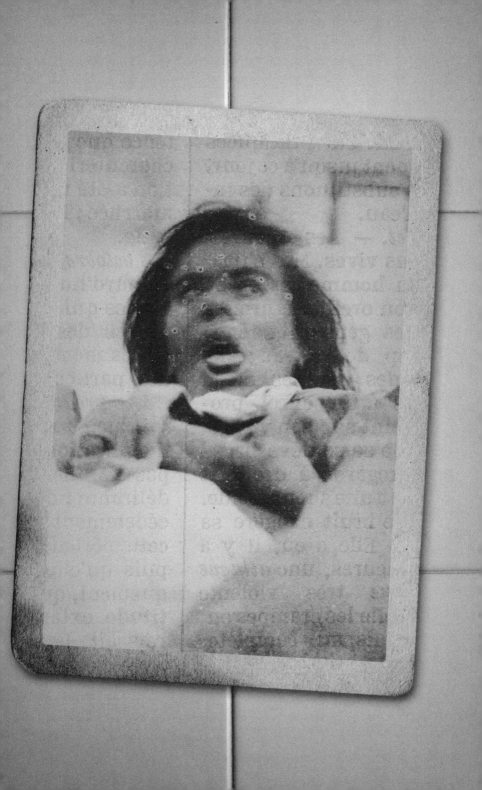

CHAPTER
№ 46

They were moved back to the first floor and into clean, separate rooms—fragrant with fresh paint—two days before the government inspection occurred.

It should have felt like a victory, but Ricky was numb. Only a select number of patients were interviewed to make sure they were being treated correctly. Ricky and Kay were not among them for obvious reasons. That morning, Ricky suspected his breakfast had been heavily drugged. He slept through the entirety of the inspection, waking up with what felt like a massive hangover.

Any movement outside his room was strictly policed. He had no idea which room Kay had been put in, or where they had stashed Lucy. No doubt Dennis was either dead or chained up somewhere. He had to wonder how they explained his murders.

He moved through the days riddled with guilt, crippled by it, full of questions. It could have been different. The plan was messy and ill-conceived anyway, and it had gotten Jocelyn killed. He no longer had nightmares of Lucy, but of that last cry from Joss, just before Dennis took her life. And what had changed? They weren't in the basement anymore, sure, but now he was alone again and they had succeeded at precisely nothing.

The warden came to him finally, a week after Jocelyn had

been killed. Ricky hardly cared. It felt useless to fight now. Whatever the warden had planned for him he'd have to suffer alone, all hope of escape lost now that they had been separated and broken. The only shock was that the warden seemed cold, removed. He expected gloating. He expected smugness.

"Of all the outcomes I foresaw," the warden began, standing close to the door and a good distance from Ricky. "This was not one of them."

"Just go away," he muttered, turning toward the window and staring out at the lawn. Sometimes a car passed by and he would feel a flare of hope in his chest. Then that little spark would die as quickly as it had come. "I'm done talking to you. I'm done playing your stupid games. Do you even care that Jocelyn is dead?"

"I'm afraid I can't leave you alone," the warden said. He was speaking between his teeth, as if every word were a chore to squeeze out.

Ricky deflated, readying himself for whatever came next. The chair, probably, maybe another attempt to "treat" him into submission. That was fine. He felt defeated anyway.

"No, you will be the one going away."

Ricky froze. He played the words over again. When they began to make sense, he twisted to glare at the man. "Getting rid of me. How? Feeling brave now that the inspection is over. You can clean up all you want, but they'll come back and next time they'll find something. You can't hide what this place is for forever."

"Oh, I wish that was what I meant," the warden replied coldly. "You're leaving. Your mother has returned for you and I cannot hold you against her will."

"You're lying." He didn't want to say it but he had to. It just couldn't be true. This was another lie. It was always another lie with the warden. *But he didn't lie about Dennis, did he? He was dangerous. He was a killer and you didn't listen and now Jocelyn is dead.*

"Get up." The warden stepped to the side as the door opened and a nurse bustled inside. Most of the staff had been replaced in the aftermath of Dennis's mayhem. He hardly recognized anyone anymore. None of them were friendly, none of them wanted to help like Joss did.

Still in a daze, Ricky stood, letting the nurse undress him. He finally began to help, going through the stupefying motions of putting on his real clothes, clothes he had arrived in. They hung on him now comically, as if they were sewn for a teenager twice his size.

The nurse left without a word to either of them. He cringed whenever he saw one of their paper hats go by. It only reminded him of Jocelyn, how he used to perk up with hope whenever she entered his cell. The warden gestured to the corridor and waited, and Ricky marched to the door. He didn't hold his head high. He didn't so much as glance at the man as he passed by. There was still a chance, a good one, that this was all a deception.

"Don't count this as a victory, Mr. Desmond," he hissed as Ricky passed. "You might be gone, but you are not forgotten. I've been inside your head. There's no freedom in this. There is no escaping your own mind. Ah, there they are."

Ricky almost ran into the two people coming down the hall toward them. It was the tall, sandy-haired man that resembled the warden. His brother. He had a boy with him, younger than Ricky, and the boy had the same sandy hair, though his was curly and he had a frank, open face that fought the severe cheekbones that seemed to run in the family.

"Good to see you again, nephew," the warden was saying, kneeling to greet the young boy. "You've grown so tall since the last time I saw you, Daniel."

The boy glanced up at his father, the warden's brother, and frowned, shying away from the doctor.

"We have the same name, you see," the warden added. "So we will be fast friends."

"Are you sure about this?" his brother was asking. Ricky drifted down the hall, catching a few last words before losing track of their conversation. A chill ran hard down his spine, and he didn't know whether to run or dash back and warn that poor little kid.

"He'll be in good hands here," the warden said with a light chuckle. "After all, he's my blood."

CHAPTER
№ 47

*B*utch wasn't there to collect him.

His mother waited in the lobby, wringing her purse out like a sponge. She had worn the same sunflower dress again, the one she only put on for special occasions. On the long walk down the hall, Ricky had swept the place with his eyes, frantically searching for signs of Kay. He couldn't leave without her. There was no future for him outside of Brookline unless she came, too.

"Oh, my boy wonder!" She didn't wait for him to get through the lobby door. This time when she hugged him it felt real, and good. Her tears dampened his face again and he held her back.

"Have you been eating?" she implored, pulling back to search his face. "Rick, honey, you look so thin."

"Just a side effect of his medications," Nurse Cruz, Nurse Kramer's apparent replacement, interjected smoothly. She had been the one to complete Ricky's final paperwork. "I will have Nurse Edmonds arrange the proper prescription for you."

"Yes," his mother said, but she only glanced at Cruz. This nurse was much younger than Kramer, and softer spoken, with the kind of gentle demeanor Ricky could see the warden walking all over. "Yes, thank you. Thank you for all you've done, but it's time my son came home."

"It is at your discretion, of course, Mrs. Kilpatrick, though I would advise against removing him from our care at this time."

"Well, I'm sorry you feel that way but I heard about the inspections on the news. It's . . . It's troubling to hear that kind of thing. I'd feel much better knowing Ricky was home with us. I'm sure you understand."

Nurse Cruz dipped her head, sighing. "Yes, well . . . I understand."

"The warden spoke so confidently about his improvement when we were last here, it really does seem like the right time to bring him back. This way he has time to prepare for the school year," she replied steadily, though her voice wavered. Ricky kept quiet; he had no intention of telling her that he was done with school and done with her. He would be leaving, and soon, but first he needed her to get him out.

"I'm sure he's excited to be back in school. Rick has a bright future if he can just concentrate. We're getting him an algebra tutor."

"That sounds good, Mom," Ricky said convincingly. "But I can't go, not without my friend."

She frowned, glancing between him and the nurse. "Your friend?"

"She's not sick, Mom, she doesn't belong in here and neither do I."

The nurse made a soft, fake *tsking* sound in the back of her throat. "I'm afraid nobody but his parent or specified guardian can check him out of Brookline. Don't worry, Mr. Waterston will be safe and sound with us."

Ricky fumed, his energy returning all at once as he whirled

on the nurse. He calmed himself at the last second, remembering that he was supposed to look improved. All better. His voice
dropped at the last second. "I'm coming back for her," he whispered. "You had better keep her *safe*, because she's getting out of
here and I'll be the one to do it."

"I'm sure," Cruz said, calmly, staring through him.

"We were leaving," Ricky added, taking his mother by the arm
and leading her toward the doors. "Please, Mom, can we just go
now? I'll explain this on the way back."

"All right, honey," she said. Then she paused and turned,
putting out her hand to shake the nurse's, but she was gone.
Flustered, his mom kept her eyes over her shoulder, trying
to find her as Ricky pulled her through the lobby and out of
Brookline.

"Thanks for springing me," he said, feeling the sunshine on
his face for the first time in weeks. He breathed deep, feeling
it hitch, saying a silent promise to Kay that he would return.
"You heard about it on the news, huh? I'm glad. It wasn't great
in there, Mom. They didn't treat us very well."

"Oh, honey, that's . . . I know. I shouldn't have let you go, but
there was that night with you and Butch, and it just seemed like
you were so out of control. I didn't know if I could even help
you anymore."

The birds were silent as they walked down the drive. A few
college students picnicked in the open grassy area down the
block from the hospital. He wondered if they had any inkling at
all of what madness went on just next door.

"It wasn't just the news, sweetheart. It was something you kept
saying," his mother murmured, frowning. She was patting his

wrist, walking arm in arm with him. They hadn't done that in years. "That you were in good hands. I just kept thinking, that may be so, but you should be in my hands. I should be the one taking care of you."

"It's okay," he told her, feeling another surge of hope flood him as their family car came into view in the drive. "I mean, I'm glad, but I think I've learned to take care of myself. There's a lot I need to tell you. About what happened in there, about me. About this special girl I met. About Dad. About where I'm going next."

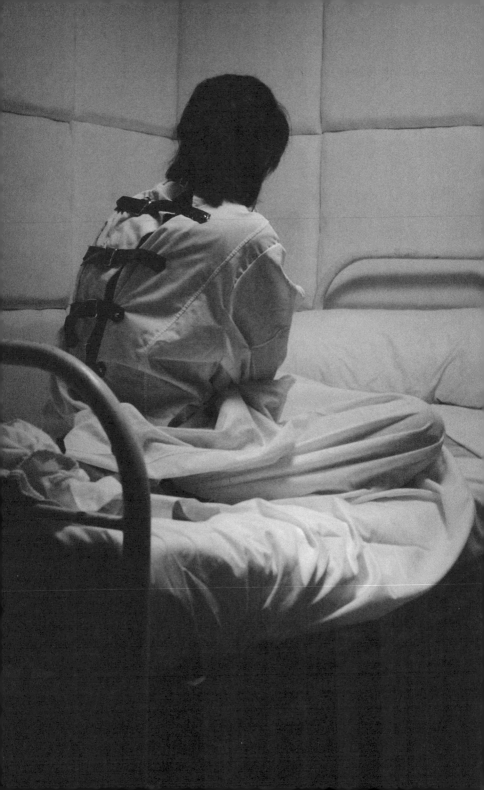

EPILOGUE

New York, One Year Later

He had walked through Central Park to get there. That wasn't necessary, of course, but he had left his apartment early. Very early. He didn't want to admit just how nervous he really was. What if she didn't show? What if things had changed too much?

The letter in his hand was wet with nervous sweat. It had been read and reread and folded and refolded until the words on it looked more like muddy hieroglyphics than English. That didn't matter—he knew the whole thing by heart.

The birds sang loudly overhead, the smell of popcorn and hot dogs thick on the air, almost like the park was a carnival and not a snippet of green relief in the midst of a sprawling city. Sometimes he missed Boston's parks, but New York's had their own funny charm. He whistled a little as he walked, trying to remember all the records he had to show her as soon as they got back to his tiny walk-up in Queens. There was a stack almost as tall as he was in the living room, the musical gems she had missed while still locked away.

What would he start with? Three Dog Night? No, probably too predictable. Not the Archies, either, that was too saccharine and mainstream. Johnny Cash would be the first record, he decided. You could never go wrong with Johnny.

The pathway dumped him out onto Fifty-Ninth and he paused, jittery, unfurling the mangled letter like a treasure map and checking the directions for the sixteenth time that morning. A curl of fog wound through the grass behind him, the last cool breath of morning before the summer sun baked the park. He took a right and made it to the end of the block, then stopped, finding the little metal sign marking the bus stop. This was it. Now all he had to do was wait.

He scrubbed at a stain on his sleeve and sighed. Most of his clothes were dirty or torn now, since every penny of his money went to rent and records. His mother would fuss if she ever saw him looking that ragged, but he didn't think she would be seeing him for a long, long time.

It was just a shirt. The grease mark on the wrist was like a battle wound—he had gotten that while bussing tables the night before at the only jazz club in the neighborhood that would hire him. If he was lucky, whoever played that night would let him help pack up their instruments and speakers at the end of the set. There was nothing like feeling part of something cool and good, even if for a moment.

He looked up at the sky—even there, even with the whole city spread out in front of him—he still felt the warden encroaching every now and then. There would always be a few remnants left inside him, he knew; dangerous, stifling walls he would have to continue knocking down and flattening for the rest of his life.

A sudden screech drew his attention from the airplane flying overhead. He smiled and shifted nervously, shoving the letter deep into his jeans pocket and shielding his eyes to watch as the bus came to a squealing stop, the front right tire rolling up slightly onto the curb.

The doors opened with a hiss and he watched the passengers file out. No, no, no, not that person . . . He was starting to get nervous. What if she didn't come? What if she had changed?

Truth was, she had changed. She looked better than he remembered. Her hair had grown out and she smiled at him the second she stepped off the bus. A little bit of dark magenta glowed on her cheeks and lips. Makeup. She had put on makeup for him.

"Hey," she said, joining him on the curb. She had a single carpet bag, torn at the edges, and she wore a summery yellow dress with dragonflies skipping across it in turquoise.

"You really showed up," Ricky said, taking her bag.

"So did you."

"We, um, have to walk a ways to the subway stop. I don't have a car or anything like that," Ricky said shyly. "I wanted a better welcome, sorry."

Kay smiled, blushing, and leaned in, taking him by the arm. "You got a place for me to sleep?"

"Uh-huh."

"A bite or two? Maybe a Coke?"

"Got that, too," Ricky said, leading her down the block and back to the big, beautiful green expanse of the park.

"Records?"

"Don't insult me," Ricky teased. "Of *course* I have records."

Kay nodded, and it seemed like she was saying yes to it all—the city, him, this new freedom. "Mmhm. Then this will do just fine. *We'll* do just fine."

ACKNOWLEDGMENTS

*T*his book was a challenge for many reasons, and without a doubt, the first acknowledgment goes to Andrew Harwell, who was so unbelievably patient and understanding during this process. Working on this series with him has been beyond what I could have imagined, and none of it would have been possible without him. His loyalty, generosity, and vision have been the driving force behind the Asylum series, and he deserves more praise than I can eke out in this little paragraph. Basically, he's the best, okay? Kate McKean has been in my corner during this process, too, ever supportive, knowledgeable, and energetic. When I am just about at my wit's end with a project she's the upbeat voice keeping me on track. The team at HarperCollins has believed so firmly in this series that they also must be recognized—the editors, artists, and publicity mavens have turned out beautiful product after beautiful product. It's a joy seeing what they come up with next.

The NPR story on Howard Dully and his experience with lobotomies was a major point of influence and inspiration for this story. There are also many callbacks and nods to Doug Wright's amazing play *Quills*, which I would be remiss in not citing as an inspiration.

My family and friends are always nothing short of amazing,

and that becomes crystal clear whenever a stressful deadline rolls around. They put up with an embarrassing amount of venting and griping, and bless them for still wanting to be around me at the end of the day. Mom, Pops, Nick, Tristan, Julie, Gwen, Dom—I'm eternally grateful to all of you for being inspirations in my life. To Anna, Katie, Michelle, Jess, Taylor, and Jessy—you ladies are coming with me in the apocalypse, I claim you all now, because a more badass squad of women has never existed. Thank you for dragging me out of the house or listening to my problems, thank you for putting up with my first-world problems and keeping things in perspective for me. When I was just about at my breaking point on this one, Brent Roberts reminded me that it's just a book and that I would survive it. Your family was very patient with me while I worked over Thanksgiving, and for that I'm extremely grateful. Thank you for the playlists. Thank you for listening. *Amoowa ekla teeket.*

Finally, I have to acknowledge the real-life inspirations for this story, namely the Atascadero State Hospital victims, who were treated abominably simply because they were different. I urge everyone who reads this novel to educate themselves on the atrocities committed there in our very recent past.

The images in this book are custom photo illustrations created by Faceout Studio and feature photographs from actual asylums.

—— ⚭ ——

161	Patient being held down	Wellcome Library, London / Wellcomeimages.org. L0074938
177	Surgical room	OFFFSTOCK / Shutterstock.com
182	Outside of house	1000 Words / Shutterstock.com
198	Operating room	Wellcome Library, London / Wellcomeimages.org. L0028124
204	Bed with restraints	Rikke68 / Thinkstock.com
213	Eerily dark hallway	Ingram Publishing / Thinkstock.com
231	Eerie hospital hallway	Tonkovic / Thinkstock.com
237	Patient cards	badahos / Shutterstock.com
	Old paper	worker / Shutterstock.com
	Stack of cards	Oleg Golovnev / Shutterstock.com
	Handwriting	Torrey Sharp, Faceout Studio
241	Haunted figure	Lario Tus / Shutterstock.com
264	Asylum patient	Wellcome Library, London / Wellcomeimages.org. L0074958
292	Shadowed figure walking	Anki Hoglund / Shutterstock.com
310	Blurry figure in hallway	Petr Klempa / Shutterstock.com
325	Insane patient	Wellcome Library, London / Wellcomeimages.org. L0074949
336	Restrained patient	Alvaro German Vilela / Shutterstock.com

6, 8, 15, 24, 29, 41, 50, 63, 67, 73, 80, 88, 93, 99, 107, 111, 121, 129, 136, 146, 150, 156, 162, 168, 173, 179, 186, 193, 201, 209, 217, 224, 232, 238, 245, 252, 257, 265, 272, 275, 283, 289, 296, 302, 308, 317, 326, 331, 337, 341

Floral background   Jomwaschara Komvorn / Shutterstock.com

6, 8, 15, 24, 29, 41, 50, 63, 67, 73, 80, 88, 93, 99, 107, 111, 121, 129, 136, 146, 150, 156, 162, 168, 173, 179, 186, 193, 201, 209, 217, 224, 232, 238, 245, 252, 257, 265, 272, 275, 283, 289, 296, 302, 308, 317, 326, 331, 337, 341

Vintage postcard   Karin Hildebrand Lau / Shutterstock.com

45, 46, 56, 61, 82, 83, 84, 124, 161, 325

Photo card   val lawless / Shutterstock.com

43, 45, 46, 56, 61, 83, 84, 124, 161, 325

Tiled floor   Andrea Astes / Thinkstock.com

JOIN THE Epic Reads COMMUNITY

THE ULTIMATE YA DESTINATION

◀ **DISCOVER** ▶
your next favorite read

◀ **MEET** ▶
new authors to love

◀ **WIN** ▶
free books

◀ **SHARE** ▶
infographics, playlists, quizzes, and more

◀ **WATCH** ▶
the latest videos

◀ **TUNE IN** ▶
to Tea Time with Team Epic Reads